I0733140

Whispers In The Dark

Whispers In The Dark

Whispers In The Dark

Avril Sabine

Cracked Acorn Productions
Australia

Whispers In The Dark

Published by

Cracked Acorn Productions

PO Box 1365

Gympie, Queensland 4570

Australia

978-1-925131-04-8 (Kindle)

978-1-925617-48-1 (EPUB)

978-1-925131-60-4 (Print)

978-1-925941-33-3 (Printed In Australia)

Genre: Young Adult Contemporary Paranormal

Copyright 2014 © Avril Sabine

Cover design by Caitlyn Petersen

All rights reserved

For my children, I love you because of and regardless of those things that make each of you unique.

Looking for his teenage children, Larry kidnaps Shelby, convinced she is his daughter. Kept in a dark room, told day after day she's Melissa, Shelby barely manages to remember who she is. Cameron, a voice in the dark room, helps her hold onto her identity, but they have to escape before Shelby forgets who she really is.

*

This story was written by an Australian author using Australian spelling.

Chapter One

Shelby paused at the front door, one hand on the doorknob, the other delving into her large handbag as she checked she had the essentials, including the food she planned to smuggle into the cinema.

"Why don't you do something different for a change?" Her fifteen-year-old brother, Kyle, glanced up from the television screen as he hit pause on his controller.

"Like you do?" She looked from the PlayStation to her brother, raising her eyebrows. "At least I'm getting out of the house."

"You could invite Courtney here." Kyle grinned. "I'd make her feel welcome."

"Like last time? Freak."

Kyle laughed. "That girl is hot."

"That girl," she emphasised the word, "is my best friend and too old for you. She said never to invite her over again when you're at home. You creep her out. Find a girl your own age and stop hitting on my friends. Freak."

"I like older women. Two years is the perfect age gap."

Shelby glared at him. They had the same dark brown eyes and their brown hair was dark enough to be only shades away from black. Kyle had their mother's narrow cheekbones and sharp nose, while she was stuck with their father's rounded cheeks and broader nose.

"You two aren't fighting again, are you?" Their mother, Katherine, paused in the lounge room doorway. "Well?"

Kyle's grin remained in place. "I was just asking when Courtney was visiting."

Katherine sighed. "Do you always have to stir?"

Shelby glanced at the time on the DVD player. "I'm going to be late."

"Weren't you even going to say goodbye?" Katherine asked.

Shelby opened the door and flung over her shoulder, "Bye."

"That wasn't exactly what I meant." Katherine raised her voice as Shelby started to close the door. "Take care."

"Yeah." Shelby pulled the door shut and strode towards the front gate, squinting at the glare. If it was this warm already in mid October, summer was going to be a killer. She lifted her long hair off her neck and wondered if she should have tied it up. Letting it fall back into place, she decided the bus ride wasn't that long and she'd soon be in the air-conditioned cinema.

Shelby reached the empty bus shelter and sat on the bench seat in the shade. Her phone beeped and she rummaged in her bag, grinning when she read the message from Courtney. *Horror?*

Her fingers flew across the keys. *Again?*

It was only moments before she had an answer. *Not romance?*

Well… She sent the single word then waited a second before she sent the rest of the message. *Joking. Of course horror.*

Courtney sent her a smiley face, and still grinning, Shelby returned her phone to her handbag. She leaned forward and looked down the street. Still no bus. Typical of Brisbane's public transport. When you wanted them to be late, during the week so you didn't have to spend as much time at school, they were always on time. Come Saturday when you had better things to do than sit around waiting, they were late. She leaned back, her foot tapping.

About to reach for her phone again Shelby stopped as a man entered the bus shelter and sat at the opposite end of the seat from her. She kept her head straight as she checked him from the corner of her eye. He wore faded denim jeans and jacket, had scruffy light brown hair and a matching beard. She guessed he was about her parents' ages, mid-forties.

When a beeping came from him, the man pulled out a phone and Shelby had to turn away momentarily as she hid a smile. The phone had to be ancient. The type of phone that had probably started the use of the word 'brick' when describing old phones. Her smile under control, Shelby turned back to see the man patting the pockets of his jacket.

The man swore and turned towards her, holding out his phone. "Could you read my message to me? I've left my glasses at home."

"Uhm." Shelby looked between the outstretched hand and the footpath in front of the bus shelter. There was no way she wanted to close the small distance between them. She'd rather stand in the sun.

"Here." The man placed the phone on the seat and shoved it so it slid across the metal to rest against her leg.

"Uhm. Okay." She picked up the phone and stared at the dark screen. How did something this ancient work? Just because he was old it didn't mean he had to use old technology.

"The button on the side. The right side. At the top."

Shelby pushed the button and nothing happened. "Maybe your battery's flat." She looked towards the man.

He frowned. "Actually, it might be the one at the front. Down the bottom in the middle. The large button."

Shelby slid her thumb across the face of the phone to the large button and pressed down. A fine mist sprayed into her face and she dropped the phone with a yelp, coughing and wiping at her face with the back of her hand. Rising to her feet, she turned to face the man. She started to back away, hitting her shoulder on the edge of the shelter. "I… what-" she broke off coughing.

"Everything will be all right, Melissa." The man picked up his phone then reached out towards her.

Shelby tried to take a step back, but the ground felt like it shifted under her. "I'm not… I don't…" She reached for the edge of the shelter, missing it as it swam in front of her. She would have fallen if the man hadn't put an arm around her waist.

"It's all right, I'm taking you home."

"Home?" Shelby tried to focus. The world around her shimmered and danced and her brain felt muddled. "I don't…" she didn't what? She couldn't think. A moment of clarity had her trying to pull away. "I don't know you."

"Come on. We can talk when we get home." The man guided her along the footpath, his arm keeping her at his side.

Beneath her feet the concrete buckled and twisted like they were in the middle of an earthquake. She closed her eyes and stumbled beside him. Him? Her eyes flew open and she tried to pull away again. "Who are you?"

The man opened the door of a white sedan and gently pushed her into the seat. He smiled and the skin around his green eyes crinkled. "I know I've got a perfect disguise when my own daughter doesn't recognise me." He pulled the seat belt across her, clicked it into place and closed the door before he strode towards the driver's side.

Daughter? Her father? Shelby frowned. Her father had black hair. Pitch black. Blacker than bitumen. Blacker than… what was black? She tried to remember. Something was black. The sound of a car door closing made her jump and she turned towards the man seated beside her. She frowned. "Who are you?"

"You'll feel better once the drugs wear off. Then you'll remember. Just rest. It won't be long and we'll be home. Everything will be all right." He patted her leg, then with another smile started the engine.

Home? Shelby continued to frown. She was meant to be going somewhere. Where? Horror. Something about horror. She shook her head, trying to think. Movement caught her attention and she turned to meet her own dark brown eyes. A giggle escaped as she reached out towards herself. Her fingers encountered a cold smooth surface and she giggled again as she realised it was a mirror. A hand drew hers back and she turned towards the man. His image swam before her and her stomach lurched.

"Rest. You'll feel better if you rest."

Shelby nodded and closed her eyes. Her stomach settled slightly as she listened to the hum of the engine. There was something she had to do. She fought against the lethargy that settled over her. Her eyes refused to open and her body felt like it was made of stone. The hum of the engine surrounded her, drowning out all other sensations.

Chapter Two

Shelby struggled to wake, feeling bare timber floor beneath her body and hearing only silence. She opened her eyes and everything remained black. Panic rushed in on her as she sat up, reaching into emptiness. She tried to rise, but nausea hit and she curled on the cold floor, a hand pressed to her mouth as she took shallow breaths. She struggled to focus. An argument with her brother. Walking to the bus shelter. Waiting. The heat. The man. Her thoughts stopped.

The man. She cautiously sat up. A man saying he was her father, but he wasn't. He'd been taller and more solid than her father. And there was no way her father would wear denim. He probably slept in business suits. A scream bubbled up and Shelby had no reason to keep it in.

Her hands covered her ears and she took another

breath to scream louder. She stopped abruptly when a door swung open and a path of dim light entered the room, broken by the shadow of a man. He stood in the doorway, arms at his side, a gun in one hand. Her gaze remained fixed on the gun.

"See, I told you everything would be all right. We're home, Mellie. No one can take you from me. I'll keep you safe."

She wasn't Mellie and this wasn't her home. "I want to go home. Please. I just want to go home." She felt the tears begin, but still she couldn't take her gaze from the gun.

"This is your home now." The softness disappeared from his voice. "You're not going back to that bitch. She's kept you from me long enough. She won't find you here, no one will."

"Please." The tears ran freely now. "I don't know you."

"Of course you do." The roughness was replaced with anger. "I'm your father. Daddy. Say it."

"Please." She shuffled backwards. The floor felt rough against her legs where her sundress didn't cover them.

He strode into the room and crouched beside her, the gun resting on his knee. His other hand reached out to grab her chin, tilting her head to face him. "Daddy. Say my name."

Fear trembled through her as she thought of the gun in his other hand. "D…Dad…Daddy." Her breath came faster and her mouth opened as she fought for air. Only her chest moved rapidly, her heart pounding away as the rest of her froze. "Daddy." The words were whisper soft, fear threaded through them.

The man smiled, a glimmer of white in his shadowy face. His hand lightly patted her cheek. "There. Everything's going to be all right now. When I find your brother it'll be the three of us."

"Brother?" He was going to kidnap Kyle too?

The man continued as if she hadn't spoken. "No one will ever keep us apart again. Now you have a rest and I'll come and get you in a few hours for dinner." He rose to his feet.

Shelby shook her head. "No. Please no. Don't leave me in the dark." She started to reach out to him then froze as her gaze returned to the gun.

"I have to go out for a bit. It's safer for you to stay in here. It's okay. No one will find you." He turned away and stepped out of the room, swinging the door shut behind him. Seconds later the strip of light under the door disappeared.

Shelby was left in darkness again. Taking a shuddering breath, she launched herself at the door, pounding on the timber as she screamed to be let out. When minutes passed with no reply, she slid to the floor, laying her head on the floorboards. She tried to see under the door, but there was only blackness. Suffocating, pressing darkness. She had to get out of here. It didn't matter how. She just needed to get out.

"Daddy." Desperation crawled through her. "Please, Daddy."

"You better be careful that doesn't backfire on you. It'd suck to forget who you really are." A masculine voice came from somewhere in the room with her.

She shrieked, sitting up to press herself against the door, turning her head as she tried to search the darkness. It didn't help. There was only endless, terrifying blackness. "Who's there?" Her voice was hesitant.

"That depends on who you ask. Now if you were to ask Larry, he'd tell you I'm your brother Robert. So how're you doing sis?" The lighthearted words held an edge of bitterness.

"Brother?" Nothing made sense. "Who's Larry?" She kept her back pressed against the door, sliding her fingers under the gap. She needed to get out.

"Yeah, you know, Daddy." The bitterness was stronger now.

"Who are you?"

"Cameron Morgan. And you? I'm guessing it's pretty damn likely you're not my long lost sister, Melissa."

"Shelby West." She paused. "This is all a nightmare. Or a…a-" she struggled to find the right words. "I was hit by a car while I waited for the bus. I'm in a coma, or… or…" her words trailed off. She couldn't bring herself to say the alternative.

"You're not dead. This is real. I'd offer to come over and shake your hand, but I kinda like this spot. I'm not sure I'd be able to find this exact spot again in the dark."

"You're an hallucination. Something brought on from whatever drugs Larry gave me. If Larry is his name." Shelby shuddered. "I'm talking to myself. I'm sitting in the dark and talking to myself."

"I exist. Do you want my date of birth? I turned nineteen at the start of October. My birthday finally landed on a Saturday. The sixth of October. What day is it today?"

"It's Saturday. The twentieth of October. At least I guess. How long was I…" she shied from the first word that came to mind then settled on, "asleep?"

"Several hours." Cameron swore. "My family must be frantic. Two weeks." He swore again. "No one's going to find us." His words were soft, despair evident.

Shelby felt the same despair hit her. "They have to. Don't say that. Don't you dare say that. My mum won't give up. She'll find me." Her voice rose with each word until she screamed them at him.

"That's what I thought about my dad."

Shelby took a shuddering breath, trying to hold onto hope. She pressed her hand further under the door. The wood scraped against her knuckles. Her breath came faster. There had to be a way out of here. There were two of them now. Maybe they could overpower Larry. "When he comes back, I'll distract him and you rush him."

Cameron laughed, short and sharp. "I might have been fit before I was locked up in here, but not anymore. Larry probably lifts weights. And in case you didn't notice, he has a gun. We're not exactly superheroes."

"Then what are we meant to do? Live with him forever?" Her voice rose again and she fought for control.

There was a long pause before Cameron answered. "All the windows upstairs are boarded up. The windows downstairs have bars on the outside. I threw myself against that door enough times I probably dislocated a shoulder. I'm buggered if I know how they do it in the movies."

"Then what's your idea?"

"Practice saying Daddy."

"Give up? Give up!"

"No. Just don't do anything stupid."

His tone made her pause. "What did you do?"

Bitter laughter filled the darkness. "What haven't I done?"

"Why can't he find you?"

"What?"

"Larry. He said when he found you we'd all be together." At least she hoped this was the brother he meant and he didn't plan to kidnap Kyle. "Why can't he find you?"

The silence stretched between them before Cameron answered. "Because he doesn't think I'm in this room."

"Where does he think you are?"

"He doesn't think I'm in here anymore. But he still keeps everything locked up. There's no escaping through the door."

"I can't stay here. My family will be worried. And Courtney. She'll be frantic." She froze. "My bag. My phone." She reached for the strap of her handbag. It was gone.

"As if he'd leave your phone for you to ring for help. He's insane, not stupid."

Her eyes closed. It made no difference. "I can't do this, I can't stay here." Her words were a jagged whisper. "I have to get out." She turned to press her hand against the door, her other hand still under it.

"Shh, we'll think of something. I'll help you get out of here." There was a moment of silence before Cameron said, "I promise."

"I want to go home. Right now."

"How did you end up here?"

Shelby hesitantly told him about the bus shelter and Larry's trick phone. She fell silent for a moment before she asked, "What if we never get out of here? What if Larry shoots us?"

"As long as you play the game you'll be safe."

"What game?"

"Larry's game."

When Cameron fell silent Shelby tried to think of a way to keep him talking. She didn't care what he wanted to talk about, as long as he did. His voice made the dark feel less threatening. And it wasn't as if she could do anything about trying to escape just yet. Not while she felt unsteady and like she wanted to throw up. "Cameron?"

"Yeah?"

"How did you end up here?"

"That started well before my birthday."

"Does that mean you're not going to tell me?"

"It could take awhile."

"Like I'm going anywhere." She was startled to hear herself sounding normal, like she was chatting to someone she'd met in a normal situation. Maybe at the cinemas with Courtney.

"Well, I guess you could say it started with my uncle. Or maybe my father. Actually, it kinda started with both of them."

Shelby shook her head, even though it was pitch black and he couldn't see her. "I really hope you're going to make sense soon."

"So do I." There was another long pause. "It started ages ago, but I could start the story sooner rather than later since it was all pretty much the same." He cleared his throat. "It's probably a good thing we're sitting here in the dark or I'd never be able to tell you any of this. I guess we could start with a Friday afternoon. I got home late after chilling with mates…

Chapter Three

Cameron strode into the kitchen, opening the fridge, running his fingers through his short, sun streaked, dark blond hair. "Mum. Uncle Bryce."

His mum, Emily, rose from where she was seated at the kitchen table with her brother and pushed the fridge door out of his hands, closing it. "Dinner is about half an hour away. Surely you can last that long."

Cameron looked past Emily's shoulder at Bryce, still seated. "Dad was pulling up as I came inside."

"You didn't park on the driveway, did you?" Emily kissed his cheek, standing on tiptoes to reach him.

"No. And before you mention it, yes I'll fix the oil leak. This weekend." He turned to his uncle. "I don't suppose you want to help." He grinned.

Bryce rose to his feet with a shake of his head. "Not this weekend, I've got a race. Ask one of your mates.

Who's the one that always seems to have grease under his fingernails?"

"John. And really? You notice things like that? Isn't that a cliche or something?" He swung the fridge door open again and reached for the orange juice, unscrewing the lid.

"I'm standing right here beside you." Emily pointed at the orange juice.

"I'm going to get a glass." His grin returned momentarily. "Honest."

"Right." Her tone was dry as she reached into the cupboard and handed him a glass.

"I'd better go." Bryce strode towards the back door, which opened as he approached it.

"Too late," Cameron said softly.

"Don't start." Emily's voice was just as quiet, before she walked towards her husband. "Dinner will be less than half an hour if you want to shower first."

Steven gestured towards Bryce. "He's not staying for dinner, is he?"

Emily's lips tightened. "No."

Bryce turned back to Emily. "I'll catch you another day, sis." He smiled before stepping around Steven and out the door.

Steven didn't even wait until Bryce was out of hearing. "What's that fag doing here? You know how I feel about him visiting." He glanced towards Cameron. "You're not drinking out of the bottle are you?"

Cameron pulled the bottle from his mouth and filled the glass he'd set on the bench.

"It's not contagious," Emily said. "He was born that way."

"Bullshit. Your parents ruined him by spoiling him. I bet your father wishes he hadn't treated that fag like porcelain." Steven gestured towards Cameron. "He could have turned out like that. There isn't a sport Cameron can't play. I've lost count of the trophies he has."

Cameron shifted from one foot to the other. He wanted to tell his father to get over it. There was nothing wrong with Bryce, but he knew better than to say anything. "Can't I have something to eat? Half an hour's ages away."

"Feed the boy, Emily. The last thing we want is for him to be some weakling who's not man enough to look at a girl let alone talk to one." Steven strode from the room.

Emily rested her hands on the table, her eyes closed. "There's fruit in the crisper, cake in the pantry. Take your pick."

Cameron stared at Emily's profile. "You okay, Mum?"

She turned to face him, her hands on the edge of the table as she leaned against them. "Weren't you hungry?"

Cameron stared at her a moment longer. "Why does Uncle Bryce stay so long? He could have left before Dad got home."

"He's my brother. I'm not ashamed of him and you shouldn't be either."

"I'm not ashamed of him. But, well-" he gestured in the direction his father had gone. "Wouldn't it be easier not to have to be treated like that?"

"It might be easier to hide, but it would also be harder."

Cameron winced. "This isn't going to turn into one of those lectures, is it?

Emily smiled as she reached out to rest her hand on his shoulder. "Sometimes we have to take the hard path so we can face ourselves in the mirror. Now do you still want a snack before dinner?"

He shook his head. "Nah, I'll wait. I'll give John a call and see if he'll help me with the oil leak this weekend."

* * *

"Cameron?" Shelby frowned when he fell quiet.

She wasn't certain what any of that had to do with being kidnapped, but it was better than silence.

"Shh. Did you hear that?"

She shook her head, then answered. "No."

"I think Larry's back. Be careful and don't mention me to him."

"Okay."

"And don't make him angry. If he wants you to call him daddy, call him that."

"I just want to go home." She hated the whiny, lost sound in her voice.

"I know. I wish I could too."

She heard it this time. A muffled noise that seemed to come from below. She dropped her voice to a whisper. "What if it's not him?"

"Depends on who it is. You're either saved or screwed."

She started to ask then changed her mind. "I don't want to know what you mean by that." She shifted. "How long have I been in here? Do you think he'll let me out to use the toilet?"

"There's an ensuite. When your back's to the door it's to your left."

"I-" she broke off, her need to stay by the door warring with her need to use the bathroom. "I can't. What if I get lost?"

"Keep your left hand on the wall. It's not that big a room."

"It's not the room that's big, it's the dark." And the fact that this was the way out. She didn't want to move away from the exit and lose it.

"You could always pee where you're sitting. Although the nights do get a bit cool and there's nothing in here to keep you warm. No bed, no blankets, nothing."

The thought of wetting herself brought Shelby to her feet. With her left hand on the wall she took a step forward. "Talk to me, please?"

"Shh, not so loud. You don't want him to come up here."

Shelby shuddered. "No." She kept her voice low. "But I can't stand the silence. It's suffocating me." She closed her eyes. Maybe if she pretended it was her choice the dark wouldn't be so bad. She took another couple of steps, her hand still pressed against the wall. Who was she kidding? She needed light.

"What do you look like, Shelby?"

"Uhm. I don't know. Brown eyes, long dark hair. It's such a dark brown it's almost black. Uhm, average height. Do you know how hard it is to describe yourself? Why don't you try? What do you look like,

Cameron?" She kept moving, her hand sliding along the wall.

He laughed softly. "You have no imagination. It's pitch black. You could have told me you have movie star looks."

"Oh, you wanted fantasy. And here I thought you wanted truth. In that case, I'm tall, slim and famous." She reached the corner of the room and started moving along the next wall.

"Tall, slim and famous? Ah, I understand. You're in the Guinness Book of Records for being freakishly tall. No wonder you're famous."

Shelby giggled, then pressed her free hand against her mouth in surprise, her eyes wide open. "Thank you."

"For?"

"Making me forget for a second." When the silence stretched out, pressing in on her, she felt a moment of fear. "Cameron? You still here?"

"Yeah." He paused. "Sometimes it's the remembering that's the hardest. Forgetting is the easy part."

Shelby stumbled as she reached a gap in the wall. "What is it you want to remember?"

"Everything. Every last second, every moment.

Everything that makes me who I am. Not who people expect me to be."

Shelby had no idea how to answer. After struggling for a moment she gave up. "I've found the bathroom."

"Then use it. Or were you asking permission or something?"

"No, I-" she broke off. It was stupid, she was stupid. Here they were, kidnapped and she was worried about a boy listening to her use the toilet. "Never mind." She stepped inside, keeping a hand on the wall as she closed the door.

Keeping her palm pressed against the wall she took a step into the bathroom, her other hand stretched out in front of her. There was nothingness. She stretched as far as she could without losing contact with the wall. She waved her hand in front of her. It was a bathroom. How big could it be? A single shuffling step took her away from the anchor of the wall. Where was everything?

"Are you okay in there?"

The sound of Cameron's voice made her jump. "I can't find it." There was a high note to her voice she wasn't accustomed to hearing. She closed her eyes at the sound, wishing she could take back the words.

"Everything's on your right. Sink, toilet, shower."

She took a deep breath and taking several shuffling

steps to her right stubbed her toe on something solid. She swore.

"What's happening?"

"I kicked my toe. And my sandals are missing." She frowned as she stared down at her feet she couldn't see. "Why would he take my sandals?"

"So you can't run fast if you get out of here."

She reached for the vanity, grasping the edge. The cold porcelain chilled her fingers and made her need to use the toilet more urgently. "I don't care if the place is surrounded by broken glass, having bare feet isn't going to stop me from going." Finally a tone she recognised. Determination. Running her hands along the vanity she reached down beside it, seeking the toilet. Her fingers touched the closed lid. "A guy who shuts the toilet lid? Are you sure you're not a figment of my imagination?"

Cameron laughed. "Many years of training. Mum is a fanatic about closing the lid."

Finding toilet paper on a holder attached to the vanity, Shelby quickly used the toilet. "What happens when we run out of paper? This roll's half empty."

"There's another in the cupboard under the sink."

She flushed the toilet and inched her way back to the basin, running cold water over her hands to splash on her face. Water dripping as she straightened. "Are there towels in here?" She stretched out her hand feeling a smooth coolness she guessed was a mirror. She muttered under her breath, "How do blind people manage?"

"On the wall opposite the shower. There's only one and I've used it. Sorry." There was a pause. "Shelby, he's coming up the stairs. One of them creaks."

Chapter Four

Shelby had taken a step towards the opposite wall. At Cameron's words she froze, hands outstretched as she swayed in the darkness. Water dripped off her jaw onto her dress and still she stood there, unable to move. Then finally she could. Her legs gave out and she sank to the floor, her hands covering her face. "I want to go home." Her words were a whisper. No one answered. A sob escaped and she struggled to think. What could she do? He had a gun, she didn't even have shoes.

"Melissa? Dinner's ready, honey."

Her stomach rolled. Food wasn't a possibility. Even the thought made her want to throw up.

"Melissa."

Her shoulders shook and her breath came in gasps. She continued to huddle on the floor, the cold of the tiles seeping into her skin.

"Answer me, damn it. Melissa!"

The anger in his voice made her start. The words began slow then fell out of her mouth in a tumble. "I… I'm in the bathroom."

"Hurry up. Dinner's getting cold. All that effort'll be wasted. I cooked a roast. You always loved roasts. We're celebrating tonight. You and me together again."

She couldn't answer. She couldn't move.

"Melissa." His sharp tone cut through the darkness. "Get out here now. If I have to come and get you I won't be happy."

"I'll be r…right out." Hands pressed against the tiles, she struggled to rise, but trembling limbs had her in a crumpled heap in seconds. Water continued to drip down her face and she wiped it away with the back of her hand. And still her cheeks stayed damp. After several more shuddering breaths she managed to get to her feet, pressing herself against the wall. The edge of a towel brushed her fingertips. She turned her head and buried her face in the towel, the material thin and worn. It made no difference. Her cheeks remained damp. It took her a moment to realise it was tears.

"Melissa!"

The roar of the name had her blindly stumbling to

the door. She found a blank wall. Panic flared until she realised she'd been turned around. Heading in the opposite direction she noticed the slight greyness at the bottom of the door. Her seeking hands found the knob and swung the door open. She froze, squinting at the light. He stood in the bedroom doorway, the gun in one hand, a small torch in his other, a dim pool of light on the floor. She wanted that torch. Closing her hands to keep from racing across the room and grabbing it, she tried to answer him instead. "I… I'm…" her voice trailed off. She had no idea what to say.

"Dinner. Come on." The pool of light raced across the floor as he gestured towards the hall behind him.

Each step was an effort. Her body shook as she tried to control the impulse to run screaming. Her gaze returned to the gun. Running wouldn't help.

The floor was rough against her feet and she saw places where bits of carpet clung to glue. She wondered who'd torn out the carpet and how long ago. Then asked herself why it even mattered. How to escape should be her only thought.

"Come on, Mellie. Don't take all night." He gestured towards the hallway with the torch again, stepping out of the way.

The hallway was carpeted, but it didn't help. Each

step was still an effort. The stairs even more difficult, the tremble in her legs making her fear she'd tumble.

"You're starting to annoy me," Larry growled behind her.

She spun at how close his voice was, losing her footing. Shrieking when Larry grabbed her arm, her gaze met his. Green eyes. Ordinary green eyes. Concern in the depths as he held onto her so she didn't fall backwards.

"Careful, honey. We can't risk taking you to a hospital if you get hurt. She'll find you and take you away." He tugged her forward, letting go when she regained her balance.

Shelby half turned, a hand reaching for the support of the wall as she inched the rest of the way down the stairs, constant glances towards Larry. Denial rested on the tip of her tongue. She longed to tell him she was Shelby. That she didn't know Melissa. Only the gun kept the words from spilling. The second last step creaked and then she was standing at the bottom of the stairs. Ahead was a door. A deadbolt and padlock kept it closed. A half step towards it was quickly halted.

"This way." Larry placed his hand at the small of her back and guided her towards the back of the house, passing an open doorway that led into a lounge room. They entered a kitchen. "Sit down." He gestured towards the seat on the other side of the table then turned off the torch. A single, low wattage light bulb hung above the table. Even though it only let off a dim glow, Shelby had to squint against the glare.

Shooting a quick look at Larry, Shelby hurried across the dimly lit kitchen, glad to put the table between them. She held onto the back of the wooden chair and stared at the two plates of food. Large slices of roast beef lay beside vegetables, all of it drowned in dark gravy.

"Sit down. I'm getting sick of repeating myself." Larry drew out his own chair, sitting as he placed the gun beside his plate, the torch next to it.

Gaze still on the gun, Shelby sat. "How did you…" she tried to think of a word that wouldn't upset him. "Find me?"

Larry picked up his cutlery. "You're mother's not as smart as she thinks. I heard she'd remarried. But no matter how many times she changes your names, she can't change the way you kids look, I'd know you anywhere. I watched the schools until I found you. Then I watched you. And waited. Waited until I knew you'd be alone." He pointed his fork at her plate. "Eat up. You're not going to waste good food."

"I'm not hungry."

"Don't back talk. Eat your dinner."

"I feel sick. I'll throw it up."

Larry slammed his cutlery down. "Eat. Your. Dinner."

Shelby gasped, her hands grabbing the cutlery and trying to cut up the meat. The knife scraped and clattered against the plate. A quick look showed Larry watched her. She shoved a small piece of the meat into her mouth, then another glance at Larry before she cut a piece of potato and ate it too.

"It's good, isn't it?"

She looked up to see him smile, his cutlery in his hands again. She nodded.

"Just the way you like it?"

Another nod.

"I haven't forgotten a thing." He laid his cutlery down, a smile still in place. "That's all that kept me going. Knowing that once I got out I'd get you and your brother back. They tried to tell me you were dead, but I knew it wasn't true." His smile became a grin. "And I was right, wasn't I? Here we are, together again."

She didn't know what to do, so she nodded, trying to swallow the food she couldn't taste. "Can I have a drink? Please?"

Larry stared at her for a moment, then with a nod,

he rose to his feet. He started to turn away then stopped, picking up the gun before he crossed the room to the fridge. The jug of water went on the table and was soon joined by two glasses. He returned to the table, placed the gun down and poured them each a drink. Remaining standing he watched her as she drank. "Did you miss me, Mellie? Did you think of me too?"

She stared up at him. "Yes." When he continued to stare, she added, "Daddy."

Larry's smile lit his entire face and he reached across the table to tuck a strand of hair behind her ear. "I knew it. Even when you were little and I came home from work you'd tell me how much you missed me. You'd throw yourself into my arms and demand I swing you around. And when I did you'd laugh and say you'd missed me. Even when you were getting too big to be swung around you still demanded it."

"Larry, I-"

His smile vanished and he slammed his palms against the table, jarring everything. Water sloshed out of the glasses. "Is that what she taught you? To call me by my first name? What do you call her new husband? Does she make you call him daddy?" He leaned forward, towering over her.

Shelby could only shake her head. The cutlery she

held dropped to the table, smearing gravy across the timber top.

"Does she?" He roared.

"N… no. No, Daddy." She tried to push away from the table, but her legs trembled too hard to work properly. Instead she shrank back in her seat.

"That's right. I'm your father. No one else. She can't replace me no matter who she marries. Who stayed up with you when you were sick? Who paced the floor with you when you were teething? And taught you to ride a bike. Picked you up when you scraped your knees and couldn't stop crying."

"Y… you?"

"Of course me. It wasn't that other bastard she's tried to replace me with. And who took you and Robert to the park each weekend and pushed the swings until your demands for higher became squeals of laughter?"

"You did."

He came around the table and crouched beside her. "Do you remember, Mellie? Do you, really?"

She nodded, unable to tear her gaze from his.

Chapter Five

Larry took Shelby's hand, patting it with his other hand. "What do you remember? What memory's the best?"

Her mouth dried and she frantically tried to think of a memory she could give him. A memory nearly any child could claim. "Christmas." Relief coursed through her at his smile.

He nodded then chuckled. "You were a terror on Christmas Eve. We could never get you to go to bed. You'd come out a million times. And there'd be a different excuse each time. A glass of water. Had you remembered to leave carrots out for the reindeer? The toilet. One last thing you needed to add to Santa's letter." He chuckled again. "And Christmas morning." He shook his head slowly, his smile still in place. "You'd race into our room and launch yourself onto our bed, bouncing as you screamed, 'He's been!'

No one could sleep through that racket. The neighbours halfway down the street were probably woken too."

"The tree. Presents." They seemed safe enough words to speak when he looked at her expectantly.

"Yeah. You'd run to the tree, counting presents. Then dash back to us, dragging us along. Poor Robert couldn't keep up with you either. He'd get dragged along too. You couldn't wait. You were so impatient. Always running when you were little. You didn't slow down much when you became a teenager. Our friends complained their teens were sloths. Not my Mellie. Robert was. Couldn't drag him out of bed till lunch on the weekend. But you were up at daybreak. There was always so much to do. You wanted to experience everything."

Shelby ached for Mellie who probably hadn't got to experience much. "What happened?" Her words were soft and she curled her fingers around his.

Larry's eyes narrowed. "What do you mean what happened?"

Her heart skipped a beat as she realised her mistake. She was meant to be Mellie, meant to know what happened. "Uhm, you. You and Mum." She held her breath, her body perfectly still as she waited for his reaction.

His hand tightened around hers. "We were too young, both nineteen when Robert was born. Then a year later you came along. It wasn't what we expected. I had to work long hours and Cynthia was stuck at home with you and your brother." He shook his head slowly. "Things just didn't work out. We tried. We both loved the two of you, so much. And we wanted you both. It broke my heart every Sunday I had to take you and your brother back to her. But every Friday afternoon when I picked you both up and you rushed out to me, throwing your arms around me and saying how much you missed me, it made my heart sing."

"Why can't you still share us? You could have us weekends. Mum could have us during the week."

"Because she wouldn't share." Anger filled his voice and his grip tightened.

Shelby tried to pull her hand away, fear flaring. His grip tightened even more.

"She told everyone I'd killed you and Robert. She wanted the both of you all to herself. She lied." Letting her go, he stood up, staring down at her, pointing a finger at his own chest. "I'd die for you and Robert. Do you understand? Die. You're my world. You and your brother. Her lies put me in jail while she kept you to herself. They wouldn't listen. I had to play their games. It was so hard, but I never forgot. I waited my time knowing that I'd find you as soon as I was free." He reached out and cupped her cheek.

She froze, wanting to pull away from the warmth of his hand, but she was too scared to move and risk angering him.

"How could I forget you? I loved you the moment they put you in my arms. All red and wrinkled, hair dark and thick. You looked up at me with wide eyes and wrapped your little fingers around my heart."

Silence stretched between them and Shelby fought the urge to put her arms around him and tell him everything would be all right. It wasn't. And it never would be. The police wouldn't have sent him to jail for killing his kids just because his wife said he had. Exhaustion swept through her and she fought to remain seated. She wanted to go home, to her bed, to her own family. She wanted to ring her father and tell him to leave Melbourne and come home, that they needed him more than his girlfriend did.

"Eat your dinner, honey." Larry pulled away from her.

Shelby shook her head. "I can't, I don't feel good. I still feel sick from… from before."

His eyes narrowed. "You like roast."

"I do, it's my favourite." The words tumbled out.

"Please, Daddy. I just want to sleep. I'll feel better in the morning." She had to escape the kitchen. Even the dark was better than the uncertainty.

After staring at her for a moment, he finally nodded. "I'll put it in the fridge. You can have it tomorrow." He started for the door, stopped then turned and picked up the gun.

Shelby nearly cried out in protest. She'd forgotten all about the gun. She could have grabbed it when his back was to her, made him let Cameron out, taken his car and gone.

At the doorway Larry turned back to her. "Well? Didn't you want to go to bed?"

With a nod, Shelby rose to her feet. When she reached the doorway, she paused and looked at the kitchen, the light bulb reminding her how dark the bedroom was.

"Don't worry, honey. There'll be other meals together. I should have realised you wouldn't have felt up to a large dinner. We've got the rest of our lives to dine together. And when your brother's with us we'll have even more to reminisce about."

"Reminisce." She didn't think she'd survive another night like this. What was she meant to tell him? Melissa's memories were a mystery to her.

"Yes, I've dreamt about this. Meals like we used to

have. Talking. Laughing. Sharing. We have so much to make up for, so much time was stolen from us. I want to know everything."

Shelby stared up at him, the light from the kitchen showed his expression was serious. She wanted to beg him not to put her through another night like this. Never again. How was she meant to know Melissa's memories? There were only her own. Images flicked through her mind. Pictures of important moments. Pictures! Relief pooled inside her and she smiled. "Yes, and photos. We should look at old photos too. I don't want to forget a single moment."

Larry smiled, reaching out to grasp her shoulder and pull her to him, his hands sliding to her back to hold her close. "Honey, you can't understand how much that means to me. I don't want to forget a single moment either."

She felt the gun pressed against her back. All she wanted to do was pull away, but she couldn't. She forced herself to hug him, releasing him after several long moments.

He let her go and with a hand on her shoulder dropped a kiss on her cheek.

Shelby winced and froze. His grip tightened on her shoulder. Forcing a smile she rubbed her cheek. "It scratches."

Larry laughed, his grip loosening. "You always said that. When it's only been a day you tell me I need a shave. But I can't, honey. They'd recognise me. Even you didn't realise it was me straight away. It's the perfect disguise. They'll never find us. You'll be safe here with me." His hand slid to the small of her back and he guided her towards the stairs. "Come on. Time for sleep. If you need me in the night keep banging on the floor until I hear you. My bedroom is downstairs."

When they reached the room, Shelby froze. "I can't-" she started to pull away.

"Melissa, don't be difficult. It'll keep you safe. They won't find you in here. Come on."

She stared at his shadowy face. Once again there was only the light from the torch he held. Why couldn't he have turned on the hallway light like he had the first time? She was sick of the dark. "Please. I can't go in there."

"Go on." He gestured to the room with the gun.

Unable to take her gaze from the gun, she swallowed hard and forced herself to step backwards onto the bare floorboards.

Larry reached for the door and started to shut it. He stopped, stared at her and his shoulders slumped slightly.

Chapter Six

Shelby's hand rose to press against her chest. Would he change his mind? "Daddy?"

"Night, honey." He swung the door closed.

"Daddy!" She threw herself against the door, banging fists against it as she was swallowed by darkness. "Dad!"

The carpet wasn't thick enough to completely muffle his retreating footsteps.

"No." The word was soft as she slid to the floor, her palms pressed against the door, the floor hard beneath her. She wished she'd thought to ask Larry for a mattress. Even a blanket would have been better than nothing.

"Shelby."

She turned towards the sound, even though she knew she couldn't see anything in the dark. "Cameron?"

"Yeah. Are you okay?"

She laughed, a brittle sound that hung in the darkness. "In comparison to what? I'm not missing any limbs. Does that make me okay? I'm not bleeding, is that all it takes to be okay? I want to go home." Her words were swallowed by the dark.

"If you get a chance, don't wait for me."

She frowned. "What?"

"Run. Don't stop for me. If you can escape, you run. And you tell my family. Tell them where I am."

"I don't know your family."

"Steven and Emily Morgan. I don't have to give you Uncle Bryce's address because he'll be there. He's always there when you need him." He told her an address and made her memorise it. "And John. You have to tell him too. John Nelson. He's been my best friend for as long as I can remember." Another address had to be memorised. "And Trent-"

"Wait. I can't remember the address of every single person you know."

"Not everyone. Just three addresses."

She hesitated. "Okay. But you learn my mum's address in case you're the one to get out."

"Okay."

By the time they'd learned the last two addresses

Shelby couldn't stop yawning. "I'm so tired. I want my bed. And I want to go home."

"Then go to sleep. I'll still be here when you wake."

"How can I sleep? The room's empty."

Cameron laughed softly. "That's my fault. Sorry."

"You took the furniture out?"

"No. Larry got sick of me turning everything into a weapon."

"Even a mattress?"

"Yeah. It was foam and I held it in front of me and barrelled through the door with it, knocking him over."

"Oh." She thought a moment. "Sheets and blankets?"

"I threw one over him like it was a net. Biggest damn fish I ever caught. A pity he got away."

She giggled nervously then broke off as she thought of the gun. "He could have shot you."

"There's a bullet hole almost directly across from the door, high in the wall. There's a couple in the hallway walls and one in a kitchen wall. Only one down there, the other broke the window."

"Cameron." Fear filled her exclamation. "You could've been hurt."

"I was desperate, but don't you be that stupid. You're right, and I don't want him to shoot you."

"Then how am I meant to get out of here?"

"The windows. You need to get something to lever the plywood off. Something narrow you can slide under and work the nails up. He's used thick ply and large nails so it can't be something easily broken."

She thought of the knives that had been at the dinner table. Why hadn't she taken one? "Okay."

"But don't let him catch you, don't take any chances. Right?"

"I'm not good at taking chances. I'm an idiot. I could have taken the gun tonight. He even had his back to it. I didn't even think about it until he picked it up."

"Do you know how to use a gun?"

"No, but how hard could it be?"

There was a long pause before Cameron answered. "Don't take it, Shelby. He's got a bad temper and you'll get hurt. Play along. Be Melissa." Another long pause. "But don't forget who you are. It's so easy to be someone else and lose who you are."

"When did that happen to you?"

"Too many times to count." Silence pressed around them before Cameron spoke again, his voice a whisper. "Far too many times."

Silence settled around them and Shelby remained near the door, eyes closed and arms wrapped around herself as she drifted in and out of sleep. When she finally gave up on sleep she felt exhausted and her body ached from the unforgiving floor.

"Cameron? Are you awake?"

"What's wrong?"

"I can't sleep and it's all your fault."

"How do you figure that?"

She could hear the humour in his voice and it annoyed her. "You're the idiot who got everything taken from the bedroom. And why was the carpet taken away? How could you have possibly turned that into a weapon?"

"I didn't. He probably thought it was the easiest way to get rid of the blood."

"Blood! What blood?" Her voice rose above the whispers they had spoken in. "You said the bullets were in the walls. He shot you? Are you okay? Cameron? Answer me."

Cameron chuckled. "A bit hard to answer when you won't shut up. And keep it down. You don't want to wake Larry."

"I was worried. You worried me."

"Do I sound hurt?"

"I don't know. Maybe? No?"

A chuckle cut off her hesitant words. "Shelby, don't

worry about me. Just concentrate on how to get something to lever the ply off the window. Okay?"

"Okay." They fell silent and Shelby sat with her back against the door, her legs drawn up and her arms folded across them with her head resting on her arms. "Did you get your oil leak fixed?"

"Huh?"

"Your mum, she was complaining about an oil leak."

"Yeah, John helped me. I drove over to his place since he's got a tonne of tools. Fixes anything with wheels. Even has an old Holden he's fixing up. Do you know much about cars?"

"You put petrol in them and they have wheels."

Cameron chuckled again. "Then how about we skip to the part where the oil leak is fixed and we're cleaning up?"

"I wish I had my own car. It seems kind of pointless having a licence and nothing to drive. You're lucky to have one."

"Sometimes. The rest of the time it costs me money and sucks up entire days while I try and keep it running…

Chapter Seven

Cameron threw the oily rag he'd wiped his hands on at John. "Thanks, mate."

John wiped off his own hands before he shut the bonnet of Cameron's sedan. "Those words sound awfully like, see ya later. I believe you offered to help me pick up a rolling body."

Cameron checked his watch. "Can we do it tomorrow? I promised Mum I'd drop something off to Uncle Bryce before midday and it's as good as midday now."

"If I don't pick it up today they're selling it to someone else. How about we call into your uncle's on the way? You don't need to stick around, do you?" John threw the rag on top of his tool chest, running his fingers through his brown hair and leaving a streak of grease on his forehead.

"Nope, and you've got grease on your forehead." Cameron pointed to the spot.

John grinned and shrugged. "I'm not out to impress anyone. My last girlfriend wouldn't stop bitching about how much time I spent on my ute." He nodded towards the HQ Holden one tonne ute sitting up on blocks beside the work shed, several panels missing. "You put the tools in the shed and I'll cover the old girl up." He grabbed the silver tarp that was sitting folded in the front corner of the shed.

Cameron picked up the tool chest. "Bessie."

"No, and stop suggesting names. I'm not naming her."

Cameron put the tool chest in the shed and strode to the stretch of grass in front of the ute. "Christine."

John flung the tarp over his ute. "She's not possessed."

"Easy for you to say. She didn't try and kill you."

"No name." He turned to Cameron. "Understand?"

Cameron held his hands up as if surrendering. "Sure." He waited until John was walking away. "Helga?" He laughed when John held up his middle finger for an answer.

John pulled a shirt from the clothesline, stripped off his dirty one and threw it at the laundry door. It landed near it. "Are you simple or something?" John strode towards the front of the house pulling on his shirt before he checked the pockets of his jeans for his keys.

Cameron grabbed Bryce's watch from his car as they walked past it. "Considering my choice in friends, must be." He walked around the car trailer hooked up to John's Commodore and waited until John pressed the central locking button.

John looked at him over the roof of the sedan. "Nice try. You're not getting out of helping me pick up the body." He grinned. "But I will kick your arse later for that comment." He slid in behind the steering wheel.

Cameron hopped in the car. "Martha."

"Arsehole."

"That's a seriously lame name for your car."

"I was talking about you." John glanced at the watch Cameron played with before he pulled out onto the road. "Not again."

Cameron laughed. "Yeah, you'd think Bryce would remember to put it back on by now."

"He needs a waterproof watch and then he wouldn't need to remove it when he washes his hands."

"He probably would've picked a waterproof one. He's more practical than his boyfriend." Cameron grinned. "But I wouldn't dare say that to Simon, I couldn't handle the dramas."

John slowed for a red light, his fingers tapping on the steering wheel. "You won't be long at Bryce's?"

"Nah. Why?"

"My cousin set me up again. I'm meant to be taking the girl to a movie this arve."

"Just tell her no."

John glanced towards Cameron with a quick grin. "Like you do?"

"That was different."

"Yeah." His tone was heavily laced with sarcasm.

"So what's her name?"

"Who?"

Cameron rolled his eyes. "The girl you're taking to a movie."

John shrugged. "Beats me. I'll ring my cousin later and ask."

"Sounds like true love."

"I've got a system. It works every time."

"Yeah? What is it?"

John grinned. "I talk non-stop about my Q."

Cameron laughed. "Yep, that'll send 'em to sleep."

John parked the car across from Bryce's house. "Works every time."

Cameron started to open the car door then turned back to his friend. "What'll you do if it doesn't work?"

"Thank my cousin."

Still laughing, Cameron strode over to his uncle's house. He winced when he heard something smash. It had sounded like glass. Simon's voice rang out and Cameron hesitated. It wasn't that he was a coward, and he did like Simon. Most of the time. But Simon could turn a peaceful setting into a war zone in minutes. Right now it sounded like they had passed that point and were working on end of days.

Taking a deep breath, Cameron rapped on the door. Simon continued to scream abusively at Bryce and Cameron winced when he heard the word 'watch' in amongst the stream of words.

The door swung open and a young man Cameron didn't recognise rested a hand against the door jam, the other going to his hip as he slowly smiled. "Well hello gorgeous. Some people have all the luck. Now why can't I have someone like you turning up on my doorstep?"

"Ahh, hello." Cameron's gaze dropped from the dark blue eyes to the expanse of skin showing in the vee of the half buttoned shirt then up to the smile still firmly in place.

"Who are you here to see? Bryce or the drama

queen? Apparently none of us love Simon, or anything he gives us." He reached out and wrapped his fingers around Cameron's wrist to turn his hand. The watch rested in Cameron's palm. "This is just what we need." He plucked the watch from Cameron's hand. "You coming in?"

He stared down at his wrist, still feeling the warmth of the man's fingers wrapped there. Then he quickly looked up at him as the question registered. "Ahh, no. I've got-" Cameron turned slightly and gestured towards John waiting for him.

"Your boyfriend? Why are all the good ones taken?" He sighed heavily.

"Oh. No. No, he's just a friend," Cameron said, then felt heat rise in his cheeks at the look the man shot him.

"Really?" He drew the word out. "I'm Trent." He held out his hand.

Cameron shook Trent's hand. "I'm-" a loud crash from inside caused them both to jump.

Trent sighed. "That sounds like my cue." He pulled a slim leather wallet from his trouser pocket and removed a card. "Call me sometime." Another slow smile. "Any time at all, gorgeous."

Cameron stared at the card in his hand when the door closed. He jumped when John hit the horn and, shoving the card in his pocket, dashed across the road and got in the car.

"Was he hitting on you?"

"Ahh, yeah, I think so."

John laughed. "If you can't tell when someone's hitting on you then you need to get out more."

"Like you do?"

John pulled onto the road. "I go out every weekend, with a different girl each time."

"It doesn't count. That's only because your cousin keeps setting you up with her friends. She'll run out eventually."

"Not likely. The last one was some random she met in a lingerie shop."

"Really? What was she like?"

John grinned. "I think she was there to buy the granny stuff they use to make people look skinny. I doubt it was the black lacy stuff, but you never know. I could be wrong."

"When are you going to find a date by yourself? Your cousin couldn't match make the last two people left alive even if the world was coming to an end."

"When was the last time you saw a girl at the wreckers?"

"You don't live at work." Cameron rolled his eyes. "What am I saying? Of course you live at work."

"I get first dibs on anything that comes in. If I'm not there I might miss out on the part I need for the old girl."

"Sadie."

John's answer was a punch in the arm. "No name."

Cameron rubbed his arm as he laughed. "You know you're gonna name her. You'll need the name for the marriage certificate."

"Screw you."

Cameron eyed John up and down, tanned forearms, biceps making the band of the t-shirt look tight, black jeans, worn sneakers, broad shoulders, a streak of grease still on his forehead, half hidden by messy brown hair and green eyes that glanced towards him. He almost sighed in relief. "Nah, you're not my type." He grinned when John answered him with his middle finger. "Besides, when was the last time you even brushed your hair?"

"What are you? My mother?" John ran the fingers of his left hand through his hair, his right still holding the steering wheel. "Done, Ma." He indicated and took the next corner.

Cameron's thoughts returned to Trent. It had been the strangeness of the situation, that was all. He rubbed his wrist. Only the strangeness. There was no way in hell he could even look at a guy let alone be attracted to one. He thought of his mum and the expression she got when his dad talked about Bryce.

Chapter Eight

When Cameron remained quiet, Shelby asked, "Why did your mum marry your dad? Didn't she know he hates gays?"

"She loves Dad, but she also didn't know. Uncle Bryce is thirteen years younger than Mum. He's twenty-eight and only came out six years ago."

"What happened next? You must have seen Trent again or you wouldn't have got me to memorise his address."

It took a moment before he spoke. "Why am I doing all the talking? What about you?"

"My life's not that interesting. I've haven't even been out of Queensland. My dad lives in Melbourne and I've never visited him there. I'm still at school, but I'll be at uni next year."

"What are you studying?"

"BA. And don't ask me what I'm going to do with it because I haven't got a clue. Are you at uni?"

"No, year twelve. I was small for my age so Mum waited a year to send me to school. She didn't think it'd matter since my birthday's at the end of the year." He chuckled softly. "I didn't agree with her that I was ready for school. We lived a ten minute walk away. She'd drop me off and twenty minutes later I'd be coming in the front door. School made me repeat the year since I didn't do much of it. You should have heard Dad when he found out I was being kept back." Another chuckle. "He got over it soon enough though when I outgrew my classmates and started winning trophies. He was always the tallest in his class and the best at every sport. And Dad expected me to be exactly the same. So it's a good thing I love sport."

"Why'd it take you twenty minutes to get home?"

"I had to escape first."

"My life's so ordinary compared to yours. I haven't got any stories like that."

"You're going to have plenty of stories to tell in the future."

"If we get out of here."

"You will," Cameron promised.

Shelby pushed to her feet. "I want to get out now." She wanted to pace across the room. She needed to move, run, anything. But it was dark and she had no idea how to find her way in the dark. "I want my family. I'd even put up with my brother."

"Tell me a memory about them. Your favourite memory."

"I can't think of one." She wrapped her arms around herself. "Not a single interesting memory. I haven't lived." Her voice rose. "I'm going to die and I haven't even had a chance to live."

"Tell me a memory about your family that makes you laugh."

"What?"

"The first memory that comes to mind. It doesn't have to be interesting. Just something that made you laugh."

She strained her eyes but the darkness remained the same. She wished she could see him. Taking a deep breath, she tried to focus on what he'd asked. "Laugh. A memory that makes me laugh." Her frown became a smile. "It's not interesting."

"That's okay. Tell me anyway."

"It was the first time we met Dad's snobby girlfriend. She doesn't like kids. They have dirty hands and she likes the colour white."

"White isn't a colour, it's an absence of colour."

"I know, I said the same thing when she told Kyle

her favourite colour is white. I got in trouble for being smart."

"And that's the memory that made you laugh?"

She smiled at his tone, a mix of disbelief and confusion. She laughed softly. "No, the memory that made me laugh happened ages before that. Kyle was about ten so I would've been twelve. They took us to the park and out for ice cream. Mum told them to get the ice cream after the park because all the running around in the heat, after ice cream, would make Kyle sick. They didn't listen. Apparently it made more sense to get the ice cream first so they didn't have to go out of their way when taking us home. He got that rainbow ice cream, bubblegum or something like that. And it was just as colourful coming back up and all over the bitch's white outfit."

Cameron chuckled. "You'd get along with John."

"Doesn't he love cars?"

"Yeah, but he also laughs when people get their just desserts." Cameron stressed the last word.

Shelby groaned. "That's a terrible joke." She giggled. "But she did deserve it." She paused, still standing with her arms around herself. "How did you get used to the dark?" It pressed in on her. The world felt crooked. Like her compass was broken and she had no idea how to straighten the world without it.

"You have to make it your friend, the dark's good."

"How?"

"You'll have to figure out your own way to befriend it."

"No." She shook her head automatically. "How's it good?"

"You can hide in the dark and no one can find you."

"But other things can hide in the dark too."

"You need to learn to listen for them, be more cunning than them. It's a friend, Shelby. The dark's safe. In this house it's the light you have to fear, that's when Larry comes."

She fell silent, his words repeating themselves over and over in her head. It was true. Only the light brought Larry. When it was dark she was safe. She let her arms fall to her side. She took a hesitant step. Beneath her foot she felt a ridge of glue with torn strands of carpet still clinging to them. Another step took her past the strands. Then another. One step after the other. A single hand stretched out. Her fingers brushed the opposite wall and she took a smaller step, pressing both hands against the wall. She'd crossed the room, without a single stumbling step. She started to smile. "Cameron?"

"Yeah?"

"Where are you? If you won't leave your corner, tell me where I can find you." He didn't answer. "Cameron?"

"No. Don't push me on this, Shelby. Leave me to my own space."

"Why?"

"Don't crowd me. Please, Shelby. Just let me have my space for now, okay?"

She hesitated. "Fine, but your space better not be the bathroom. I want to have a shower. And I don't care that I only have the same clothes to put back on, I'm still having one."

Cameron laughed softly. "You don't have to worry. It's not the bathroom."

She closed her eyes and focused on where she was. If she was right, she'd find the bathroom in seconds. If she was wrong, she shrugged, it wasn't like the room was big enough to get lost in. Not anymore.

* * *

Long after her shower, Shelby lay on the floor in the middle of the room. She knew it was the middle because she'd paced it. Cameron had been quiet ever since she'd come out. Calling out his name had only brought 'shh' as a reply. Maybe he was trying to sleep. She was bored and hungry. And she couldn't hear a single sound from downstairs. Larry had said to bang on the floor and he'd come. Her hand flattened across her stomach. She still couldn't decide if she was hungry enough to want to spend time with Larry, but she had to keep her strength up if she was going to escape. Starving wouldn't help.

"Cameron?"

"Shh."

She glared in the direction she thought his voice had come from. "Damn it, why won't you talk to me?"

"Tired. So very tired. Let me rest, Shelby. Give me some time to rest."

His voice sounded empty. She wanted to rush to his side and check he was okay. It was an effort, but she stayed still. "Sorry." Time stretched out again. She tried counting but when she reached the thousands she kept losing track. There was nothing to do in the dark. It wasn't a very entertaining friend. She smiled as she pictured a shadowy clown trying to entertain her. She sighed. Is this how people went mad? Odd visions, no contact, talking to herself in her head. At least it wasn't out loud, but then Cameron would probably tell her to be quiet. She sighed again and her stomach rumbled. Maybe she should try and get Larry's attention. She rolled to her side and sighed.

"I bet you always ask 'are we there yet' on long drives."

Shelby smiled, sitting up and facing where she thought Cameron's corner was. "I'm hungry."

"No."

"That wasn't a question."

"But it will be. Don't call him. The less time you spend with him the better. He's crazy. You can't trust him."

"How do I know I can trust you?"

"You don't, but you should know you can't trust Larry. Stay away from him, Shelby. Promise me."

"I'll try, but I'm starving. Even drinking water from the tap didn't help. And you're not helping. Talk to me. Distract me."

"This is all very one sided. How about you distract me?"

"You're the one who doesn't want me to call Larry." She agreed it was a bad idea, but she also wanted to hear the rest of his story. "So what happened next? You were picking up a rolling body, whatever that is."

"A car body without an engine. And we picked it up. Damn thing had a snake hiding under it. You can imagine how impressed it was when we started to winch the car onto the trailer."

Shelby shuddered. "I don't like snakes."

"It was only a carpet snake so nothing to worry about."

"I don't care what type it was, I don't like any of them."

"Can't say I'm a fan of them myself. Anyway, we dumped the body at John's place, down the side of the house near the work shed and in front of the ute, after I'd moved my car. Then we took the trailer back to his work."

"At the wreckers."

"Yeah." He fell silent for several minutes. "I must have looked at that bloody card a million times. Trent was in IT. Trent Hawley. I talked myself out of ringing a million times, but I had to know. It took me three days before I was actually able to dial his number…

Chapter Nine

"Hello." The tone was casual, a touch of question in it.

"Ah, Trent?"

"Speaking. Who's this?"

"Ah, I met you the other day when I was returning Simon's watch-"

"Gorgeous. How could I forget? I've been waiting for you to ring."

"You have?"

"How could I not? Tell me when you're free."

"Uhm, the thing is... I'm not... that is..." Cameron closed his eyes and stopped pacing his bedroom floor. "I'm sorry, this probably wasn't a good idea-"

"Don't hang up, I tend to rush things. I get impatient. Let's meet up for drinks, no pressure."

Trent laughed, a deep drawn out sound. "Talk about rushing. I don't even know your name."

"Cameron Morgan."

Trent swore. "Tell me you're not Bryce's nephew he talks about all the time."

"I'm sorry."

"Yeah, me too." He swore again. "Who am I kidding? I'm not that sorry. I still want to see you. Your uncle will probably beat me to a pulp if I lay a single hand on you, so how about you do all the laying on of hands."

"I don't... I'm not... well..."

"Get to the point, remember my lack of patience?"

"I'm not gay."

Trent laughed again. "Neither am I. I happen to be human and I have a major weakness for gorgeous guys."

Cameron had no idea how to answer that comment.

"Are you still there?"

"Yeah."

"I know interest when I see it, Cameron."

"I wasn't... I'm not..." he stared down at his wrist where Trent's fingers had been.

"Why'd you ring?" The previous warmth was leached from Trent's tone.

"I needed to know something."

"You want to ask me something?"

"No." Cameron frowned, renewing his pacing. "I want to see you, but not… well, I just need to know something."

"You're confusing me."

Cameron wanted to tell him he was just as confused, but he held back the words. "Can I see you? I need to know something. Maybe we can meet at… uhm… maybe your place."

There was a long silence before Trent spoke. "How old are you?"

"Eighteen."

Another long pause. "When do you want to come here?"

"Whenever. Now? I don't know."

Trent laughed. "I certainly know how to pick them. All right, gorgeous, come on over. I'll text my address to the number you rang from."

"Okay. Bye."

"I wouldn't choose the word bye." His voice dropped. "See you soon." Trent disconnected.

Cameron eyed his phone, wondering if he'd made a big mistake. Less than a minute later his phone beeped. He stared at the message. Trent wasn't that far away, he could be there in half an hour. He read over the address again and slid his phone into his pocket.

Maybe it was a mistake, but he had to know. And there was only one way to find out. He grabbed his car keys from the desk and strode through the house, heading for the front door.

When he reached Trent's house he sat in his car, staring through the window that was starting to fog up from his breath. His hands gripped the top of the steering wheel. The house was ordinary. Lowset, painted block, a small patio, a couple of shrubs along the front of the house. Ordinary. Nothing at all to be worried about. Yet his stomach kept doing back flips and he couldn't bring himself to loosen his grip on the steering wheel.

He leaned forward, his forehead touching the back of his hands that ached from holding on so tight. All he had to do was open the door and cross the street. Simple. Then why couldn't he do it? He sighed heavily and began to think about starting the car again. It was a mistake. He shouldn't have come.

When his phone rang, Cameron reared back. His heart raced as he stared at the number displayed. After the amount of times he'd looked at Trent's card he quickly recognised it. The phone continued to ring and he swallowed hard as he answered. "Yeah."

"Are you coming in or going to admire me from afar?"

Cameron couldn't stop a smile forming as he looked towards the house. The front door was open and Trent was part shadow from the light behind him. One hand rested on his hip, the other held his phone to his ear. You look good from afar, he wanted to say, then closed his eyes as he leaned his head back. He barely managed to hold back a groan. This was crazy. He had to leave.

"You were the one who asked to come here."

Cameron had no answer. He opened his eyes and turned his head again. Trent's hand was now pressed against the door frame.

"I don't need this bullshit. Come back when you get your shit together and grow up. I don't need some screwed up kid in my life."

"I'm not a kid."

"You're five years younger than me, Cameron. I thought you were twenty when I first saw you." Another pause. "I can't do this again. I need someone who knows who they are. Someone who isn't ashamed of themselves."

"I know who I am."

"Do you?" The words were whisper soft.

Cameron felt a shiver go through him. Still holding

the phone to his ear, he pulled the keys from the ignition and opened the car door. Gaze on Trent, he locked the car, ended the call and slid the keys and phone into his pocket as he crossed the street.

Trent slid his own phone into his jeans' pocket and crossed his arms over his chest as he waited. He stepped back when Cameron reached him.

Cameron looked past Trent, but his gaze was drawn back to the man in front of him. He met the dark blue eyes that warily watched him. He wanted to reach out and reassure Trent, but he had no reassurances. Not even for himself. Especially not himself.

Trent's lips twisted into a wry smile. "You were more talkative in the car. Or is it the phone that makes you talkative? Want me to ring you?"

A fleeting smile crossed Cameron's lips. "I'm sorry, I shouldn't have come." He started to turn away.

Trent reached for him, his hand holding onto his wrist. "What did you want to ask?"

Cameron couldn't face him. The warmth of Trent's hand shot through him and he closed his eyes, trying to think of something to say. Something other than the words that clawed to escape. He drew in an uneven breath and pulled away. Trent let him go, but still he couldn't turn around. "I needed to know–" he broke off, alarmed by the rusty sound of his voice. He cleared his throat. "I'm sorry." It was a broken whisper as he broke into a run, fumbling for his car keys.

"Cameron."

He ignored Trent. There was no way he could answer with how tight his throat was. Reaching the car, he jumped in, catching the seat belt in the door and having to try again to close it. Then he was halfway home, not knowing how he'd got there, his brain a confusing swirl of emotions, unspoken words and a screaming 'no'.

A flash of light drew his attention and he swore as he realised he'd just sped past a speed camera. He swore again, hitting the steering wheel with the palm of his hand. Now he'd lose his licence. Pulling up in front of his home, he turned off the ignition and leaned against the headrest. His phone rang and he stared at the display. He couldn't answer. What could he tell Trent?

The phone fell silent and still Cameron stared at it. He wished his head was equally silent. He swore. It didn't help. He dropped the phone onto his lap and rubbed his eyes. This wasn't happening. He wouldn't let it. The phone started to ring again.

Cameron stared at it a moment longer before he

answered roughly. "Damn it. Why you? I don't want this. I'd rather be asexual like I thought I was." He hit the steering wheel again. "This can't be happening." His voice became a plea.

"I rang to see you got home okay. I won't bother you again."

Cameron swore when Trent disconnected. He quickly rang and waited for Trent to answer. It rang out. He stared at the blank screen before deciding to send a text.

I'm sorry.

And he was. About everything. The way he felt, what he said, the impossibility of it all. Asexual. That's what he'd be. He didn't need anyone. The front light went on and he hurriedly hopped out of the car. His father stood at the door and watched him stride towards him.

"What were you doing?"

Cameron held up his phone. "Someone rang." He grinned, trying to act natural. "I guess Mum was right when she told me I couldn't multitask."

Steven glanced at his watch. "You know you're not meant to be out this late on a school night. It's nearly ten."

"Sorry." He was getting sick of that word. Maybe

he should get it tattooed on his forehead to save himself having to say it. "I'm heading to bed now."

Steven nodded as he locked the front door. "Hurry up then. You don't want to be tired tomorrow afternoon at practice. It'll be a tough game this weekend."

"Yeah." He hurried to his room, grabbed a change of clothes and quickly used the bathroom. Back in his room he stared at his phone. Maybe it was a rebellion thing, a subconscious rebellion against his father.

Dropping onto his bed he sighed heavily. It was just after ten. Bryce would still be awake. He rang his uncle and waited for him to answer.

"This better be good. You're interrupting something… hmm… we'll say interesting. Oh and Simon keeps telling me to say hello from him."

"How did you know you were gay?" Cameron frowned as he heard something crash, swearing and then a hurriedly whispered conversation. "Uncle Bryce?"

"Sorry. Now you want to start this conversation again? They usually start with hey, how're you going. Work up to the weather then drop the bombshell."

"Whoa. This isn't about me. I was asking… I was just asking. That's all."

"Just asking, huh? For a friend?"

"Forget it."

"Wait. Ouch." The words became muffled. "Stop it Simon. You can't talk to him. And stop hitting me. You hit like a girl. Damn it!" Then clear again. "What's going on, Cameron?"

"Can't I ask a simple question without getting the third degree?"

"I was sixteen-years-old watching porn with my mates and they were all raving about the chick and I couldn't stop watching the guy. Now can I give you the third degree?" The words were muffled again. "Simon, enough. You can't talk to him."

"No you can't. And you might as well put Simon on the phone. You know he'll ring me after we hang up."

"Here he is." The phone was silent for a moment and a whispered conversation was held in the background before Simon spoke.

"Darlin, I'm so happy. Are you having a coming out party? Can I plan it?" There was a sharp slap. "Stop trying to hush me, Bryce."

"I'm not gay."

Simon continued as if he hadn't spoken. "I always knew it. I have a radar for these things. I know some darlin men that'd be perfect for you, would you like to meet some of them?"

"Simon-"

"Oh, oh, I have it. I know the perfect one."

"Simon." Exasperation forced the word out.

"He only came to Brisbane recently. He was in Sydney. Messy break up, but you don't want to hear about that. You have to meet him. You'd be perfect together."

"Simon. I'm not-"

"Trent. He's divine. If I weren't madly in love with your uncle I'd be chasing after that one. Although he'd never be interested. He likes you more masculine looking types."

Hands shaking, Cameron hung up. He stared at the phone in his hands, his breath coming fast. He felt light headed and tried to gulp more air. His chest didn't feel like it could expand enough. Dropping the phone on his bed, he staggered to his feet. The phone rang and he backed away from the bed until he hit the door. Covering his face with his hands he closed his eyes.

"This isn't happening." Half plea, half demand. He shook his head and took a step forward, hand outstretched towards his phone. He couldn't bring himself to answer Bryce's call. Then it stopped. It started again almost instantly. His gaze was caught by the tremble in his hand. He made a fist, but it didn't help. The phone continued to ring and he forced himself to answer.

"What?"

"What's going on, Cameron?"

He tried to ignore the concern in his uncle's voice. "Simon wasn't listening and he wouldn't shut up."

"Come and see me after school tomorrow."

"Can't. I've got practice."

"After that."

"I've got other plans."

"Cameron-"

"I have to go. I'll call you another day, Uncle Bryce."

The sigh was loud and clear over the phone. "Goodnight, Cameron."

"Night."

He dropped the phone on his bedside cabinet and stood there staring at it. This was all a mistake. He'd ask John's cousin to set him up with one of her friends, or better yet, he'd be asexual. He needed no one.

Chapter Ten

When he continued to remain silent, Shelby started to worry. "Cameron? Where are you? Let me sit beside you."

"No."

"People do need other people. Not sexually. Well, that too, but friends are also important. Let me sit with you."

"Drop it. Just drop it, Shelby. Please."

She ached at the anguish in his voice. Ached to wrap her arms around him and hold him like her mother had held her when she was little and upset. Arms wrapped around tight so you felt like there was no way you could fall apart with how tightly you were held together. "Cameron-" her tone was filled with his anguish.

"No." He cut her off, the word harsh. Then his

voice changed, becoming a plea. "If you care, just drop it, Shelby. I need space."

She wrapped her arms around herself. "What if it's me that doesn't need space?"

"I'm sorry."

Silence fell between them.

With nothing to hold her attention, hunger came back with a vengeance. Rising to her feet she paused a moment as she got her bearings. She strode across the room and grinned as she found the bathroom. She was more cautious in here, but she was finally getting the hang of the dark. Cameron was right. It was the light she had to fear.

Turning on the tap she drank several mouthfuls, wishing it were something more filling. She rested her hands on the edge of the vanity. A chocolate thick shake so thick she could barely get it up the straw. And cold. Icy cold. Cold enough to make her brain freeze. Her stomach rumbled and she had another mouthful of water.

She turned the tap off. It hadn't helped, only made her stomach ache from too much liquid. She pressed her hands against her stomach as she thought of Cameron alone in the other room. There had to be a way to draw him out. She thought of how he spoke about John earlier. And the way he had teased John about his car. With a smile she shuffled her feet over the tiles until she reached the door.

"Did John ever name his car?"

"What?"

"You were trying to think of a name for his car." She frowned. "Some Holden thing."

Cameron chuckled. "Blasphemy. It's a HQ one tonne ute, not some Holden thing."

"Okay." She drew the word out. "But I thought it was a Holden."

"HQ Holden one tonne ute."

"Does the HQ stand for something?"

"High Quality."

"Really?"

"Nope." Cameron chuckled. "Just a prefix. The model."

"Oh." She struggled to think of something else to keep the conversation going. "So why a HQ… ahh… oh hell. I forget the rest of the name of the ute."

"HQ is fine. Or you could even call it a Q."

She smiled at the affection in his voice. It sounded like John wasn't the only one into the car. "Why that car?"

"Ute."

She rolled her eyes even though he couldn't see her.

"Ute." She had the childish urge to poke her tongue out at him. "Why?"

"Because when he has his opens, John can legally put a three-fifty Chevy in it."

"Oh. Okay." She guessed she failed at sounding like she knew what he was talking about when he laughed. "It's an engine. Right?" It had to be. Engines always had numbers. Usually small ones like four or six or eight.

Another laugh. "Yeah. I'll give you half a point for that answer, but not just any engine. It's-"

"Ah, Cameron?"

"Yeah?"

"Do you think we can skip the lecture? I really don't want to know anything about cars other than you put oil and petrol in them and turn the key."

"Don't forget the water."

"What water?"

"That goes in the radiator so you don't cook the engine."

"Okay, that's it. When I finally get a car I'm getting myself a boyfriend who'll do all that boring stuff." She paused. "Actually, skip that plan. He'd probably be a car nut and want to talk about cars all day. I'm going to get a mechanic to do that and a boyfriend who likes parties, movies and shopping."

"I hope you won't be upset when he wants to bring his boyfriend shopping."

It was Shelby's turn to laugh. "Liking to shop doesn't make a guy gay."

"Nope, but there's a good chance he is."

She was still smiling. "Does your uncle like to shop?"

"His boyfriend does. Uncle Bryce suffers a shopping expedition occasionally."

"There you go, being gay doesn't make you like shopping."

"I didn't say that. I said if a guy likes to shop he's probably gay. And when you say shop, I'm guessing you don't mean hardware and auto shops."

Shelby laughed. "Absolutely not. Real shops. Ones with clothes and stuff in them."

"Real shops, huh? So what's a hardware? Fake?"

"No, worse. Boring." She shook her head. "How did we end up talking about hardware shops?" She was still smiling, relieved to hear the laughter in Cameron's voice.

"We were agreeing that if a guy likes to shop he's probably gay."

"Nope, that was your theory."

"Then name one guy you know who isn't gay who likes to shop."

She frowned. "I'm sure there are some out there. I just don't know a lot of guys."

"I do and not a single straight guy I know likes to shop. Or if they do they certainly don't admit it."

"There you go. Even you think straight guys might like to shop."

"No, I said they'd never admit it. If you don't let yourself like something, that's the same as not liking it."

Shelby yawned. "I'm sure there's a flaw in your argument, but I'm too tired to figure it out. And hungry."

"Don't think about it." There was a warning in Cameron's tone.

"Think about what?"

"Calling Larry."

"I wasn't, but now I am. Thanks." Her tone was dry. "Cameron?"

It took him a moment to answer. "Yeah?"

"What about you?"

"I have no idea what you mean."

"Aren't you hungry?"

"Not for food."

She hesitated. Did she really want to know when he used such a harsh sounding voice? Yeah, of course she did. Her words were soft and hesitant. "What are you hungry for?"

"Not today. Later. Now what are the addresses I made you memorise?"

She sighed. She was tempted to press the matter but let the conversation drop and told him the addresses then asked him to say hers. They were correct. Not a single mistake, but it didn't help. They were still stuck in a completely dark room in a house that could be anywhere. All she knew was it couldn't be Brisbane or any other town. She hadn't heard a single car the entire time she'd been locked up.

Chapter Eleven

"Shelby. Wake up. Don't speak. Just wake up."

Cameron's voice brought her back from the nightmare that had gripped her dream. "What?" She struggled to focus.

"Shh, Larry's at the door. Remember, don't tell him I'm here."

She sat up abruptly, rubbing sensation into the arm she'd been lying on. She reached out, trying to feel where Cameron was. His whispered voice had seemed so close. Her hand encountered nothing, only darkness. Then greyness entered the room as the door swung open.

She suppressed the urge to greet Larry excitedly, demanding food. Then wondered why she shouldn't. Wouldn't he expect that? Didn't he say his Melissa always missed him? Maybe she could use it to her advantage. Her gaze was drawn to the gun. She'd have to be careful.

"Daddy?" She struggled to her feet. "I missed you. Why were you gone so long?"

"Mellie." There was joy and relief in his voice. "Come downstairs. I got the photo albums. It took me longer to get them then I thought it would. I couldn't go until after work and I had to wait until your mother went out. You want dinner?"

"Yes." She hurried to his side, smiling up at him in case he could see her expression with his torchlight. "I'm starved."

Larry chuckled. "That's my girl, never a dainty eater. There's plenty of roast left over from last night, then we can look at the albums. How's that sound?"

"Good." She watched as Larry locked the bedroom door and was tempted to tell him to leave it open, but she didn't want him to wonder why. Maybe he already had an idea Cameron was still in the room. "Can I have a mattress to-"

"No."

"But-"

"No. Now come on." Larry gestured towards the steps with the gun when Shelby continued to stand there. "Dinner."

She bit back a sigh. It looked like she'd have to do a

lot more work to gain his trust. He didn't even want her behind him on the stairs. Did he think she was going to push him down them? She glanced back at him, meeting his wary gaze. Maybe. She turned and headed down the steps.

In the kitchen she looked around. This time she needed to take something back with her to help them escape. "Can I help you get dinner ready?"

Larry shook his head. He pointed to the seat she'd used last night. "Sit down."

She wanted to argue. Her gaze dropped to the gun. No. Arguing probably wasn't a good idea. She nodded and pulled out the seat. Once she was sitting, Larry bustled around the kitchen. Plates were taken from a cupboard, food from the fridge, cutlery from a drawer. Shelby watched where everything was. Next time she'd be prepared. She wasn't going to miss a single chance.

Once the leftover roast was heated in the microwave, Shelby wolfed down the food and asked for more. Larry grinned and heated up another plateful.

"It's always been your favourite meal. You used to ask if you could have it every night."

Shelby returned his grin. "It's only this good when you cook it."

"That's because I slow cook it just the way you like."

"Thanks, Daddy." She speared another potato onto her fork and ate it. Her gaze avoided the gun and she tried to tell herself she was Melissa. There were moments when she actually felt like Melissa and they scared her less than being herself. In the light, only Melissa was safe.

Larry rose from the table. "I'll do the dishes then we can go into the lounge room and look at the albums."

"I'll do them." Shelby smiled. "I mean, you did the cooking, so I should do something."

Larry's eyes narrowed. "You hate doing dishes."

Shelby wanted to look away from his gaze. She held it, keeping her smile in place. "Yeah, but I love you more than how much I hate doing dishes. You take such good care of me, Daddy." She held her breath, waiting. Time stretched out endlessly.

Then Larry smiled and strode around the table to put his arms around her and draw her to his chest. "You're such a good girl, Mellie." He stroked her hair. "Such a good girl."

She tried to relax. It took all her willpower to return his hug. I'm Mellie. Melissa. I have to be Mellie. She repeated the name over and over. When she thought it was safe, she started to move back. "I'll do the dishes, Daddy."

"Not tonight. This was our celebration meal. You stay in your seat and I'll do the dishes." He patted her shoulder before he turned and collected the gun from the table. She heard the sound of it being placed on the bench.

Shelby felt her heart plummet. She wanted one of those knives and there was no way she could take it without him noticing. Doing the dishes would have given her a chance. She forced herself to relax. It was impossible. Sitting was hard enough, especially since she had to sit with her back to him. She wanted to watch what he was doing. How did she know if he was still in a good mood? She couldn't, not unless she could see him. She listened as the cutlery and crockery rattled against the sink, then the sound of the water draining away. She jumped when he placed his hand on her shoulder.

"Come on Mellie, let's look at the albums."

Her heart continued to race as she nodded and rose from her seat. Her gaze dropped to his right hand, which held the gun, and she wondered if he slept with it. She couldn't think like that. Mellie. She was Mellie. Then her heart skipped a beat. How stupid was she? Her feet slowed. She was about to sit down with Larry and look at photos of Melissa and he'd see his mistake. There was no way she could do this. "Daddy…"

"What's wrong, Mellie?" Larry stopped in the doorway of the lounge room.

"Maybe we should do this tomorrow. I'm so tired."

"Just a couple. Look." He pointed to an open album on the coffee table. "It's one of my favourite photos of you." He pressed against the small of her back. "Go on. It was a good idea. There's so many wonderful memories in those albums."

Her gaze dropped to three more albums sitting on the carpet. Her feet slowly crossed the space and she stood between the lounge and coffee table. But she couldn't bring herself to look. There was a strip of coffee table visible at the edge of the open photo album, clear varnished pine with several dints and a couple of marks. They were arc shaped, the rest of the mark hidden by the album.

"What do you think?" He tapped the page. "This one, right here. It's my favourite."

She stopped breathing as her gaze rose to meet Larry's. He was smiling. Green eyes met hers. She saw only acceptance and belief. Her gaze dropped to the photo album. A man held a girl around the chest, his fingers linked, her back against his chest as they were caught mid spin, her legs cutting through the air, both laughing. Shelby's legs gave way and she sat heavily on the lounge chair, her gaze still fixed on the album.

She recognised Larry's eyes. They were on the girl he held in front of him, love and laughter filling the clean shaven face. And the girl. Shelby couldn't believe it. She had looked so similar at that age. Melissa's face was more oval, but they had the same colour hair, rounded cheeks and brown eyes. The expression was different. Where many of Shelby's photos made her look serious, this photo made Melissa seem vibrant, happy and like she was about to share the funniest joke ever with her father. Shelby couldn't stop a smile forming. She reached out her hand and ran her fingers across Melissa's face. How could the girl look so much like her?

She dragged forward her own memories. She wasn't Melissa. It wasn't possible. She was Shelby West. She was seventeen-years-old and had a brother. An annoying brother who was two years younger. Kyle. Not Robert. And parents. They might not be together, but they were still her parents. Katherine and Aaron, her parents. Shelby West's parents. And she was Shelby West.

"Well, Mellie? What do you think?"

She wanted to yell at him. I'm Shelby. I'm me. She pressed a hand against her lips, trapping the words. A deep breath didn't help. She looked up at Larry whose smile was starting to fade. She had to say something. Fast. "We were so happy."

Larry's smile returned in a flash and he sat beside her, draping an arm around her shoulders, the gun resting on her arm. "It'll be like that again, I promise. I'll find Robert and things will be the same. Just the three of us. I'll never let either of you go. We'll be together forever." He reached out and ran a finger down her cheek. "Don't cry, honey. Don't cry. Everything's going to be all right. There's no reason for tears."

She dropped her gaze, trying to ignore the gun against her arm. "I missed you."

Larry tightened his arm around her. "I know honey, but that's all over. Everything's going to be all right. I promise."

She nodded, unable to speak past the tightness of her throat. Her cheeks felt wet and cold and now she wished she hadn't eaten so much. Her stomach churned and she felt sick. "I… I'm tired."

Larry dropped a kiss on her forehead. "I'll take you up to your room. We can look at the albums tomorrow night after dinner."

"Okay." She hated how small and lost her voice sounded, hated how it echoed what she felt. She rose to her feet, her legs feeling rubbery and as if they belonged to someone else. Someone like Melissa. Trudging beside Larry she chanted her name over and over in her head until they stopped at the bedroom door. Looking up at Larry, she waited for him to unlock it.

"Goodnight, Mellie." He smiled, reaching out to wipe her tears away with his thumb. "You can't imagine how happy I am we're together again. I love you, honey."

Her mouth dried as she opened her mouth to answer. Nothing came out. She nodded, fear drying up her tears as his smile disappeared. She had to speak, had to be Mellie. A breath shuddered out of her. "Love you, Daddy."

The smile returned and he swung the door open. Turning her by her shoulder, and with a gentle push at the small of her back, he sent her into the room. The door locked behind her.

Shelby sank to the floor, her hand pressed against the timber of the door. "Shelby West." She whispered her name and her hand became a fist. "Shelby West." It was slightly louder this time.

"Shelby?"

She smothered a shriek with her hand. Turning, she leaned against the door, her breath coming fast. "You scared the crap out of me."

"Sorry," Cameron said. "What's wrong?"

"I saw a photo of her. It could have been me. I could be Melissa."

"You're not. You're Shelby West. You're not Melissa and I'm not Robert."

"Let me sit next to you."

"No."

"Why not?"

"Shelby. Enough."

"I'm lost, Cameron. I don't know who I am."

"You're Shelby West."

"You don't know that. It's only because I told you." A shuddering breath tore out of her. "What if I'm as screwed up as him? I could be crazy, insane. Maybe the people I think are my family are a foster family. Maybe I'm really Melissa."

"Crazy people don't think they're crazy. They think everyone else is."

"You didn't see that photo. It could have been me."

"It wasn't."

"How do you know?"

"Because I'm not Robert. It took me long enough to figure out who I am. There's no way I'm going to let anyone steal that from me. I'm Cameron Morgan. You're Shelby West."

Chapter Twelve

"Cameron?"

"Yeah?"

"How long have I been asleep?"

"I don't know."

"I'm hungry. Aren't you?"

"No."

"Why not?"

"Have a drink of water." There was irritation in his tone.

She sighed. "Water just makes me feel like there's an ocean sloshing around inside me." She rose to her feet and crossed the room, her hand stretching out at the last second to meet the doorway. She smiled. It was victory. This was becoming her place. The dark. The bedroom. The bathroom. Nearly every inch was hers. Only one corner Cameron kept for himself. She was tempted to sit down beside him, take his hands and make him let her near, but they had so few choices she didn't want to take that last one from him.

After drinking too much water, she returned to the bedroom. "Cameron?"

"Yeah?" There was still irritation in his voice.

"What if I slept an entire day? How would I know?"

"Larry would wake you. For some reason he only offers dinner. That's how I kept track of the days to start with, but it gets hard after a while. Too many of them to keep track of."

She sat down, her back against the wall beside the door frame. "Did John's cousin set you up with a girl?"

"Yeah." The irritation was replaced with weariness.

"What happened?"

"We barely won the game that afternoon. The competition was as tough as I'd expected. Then we went to a movie in the evening. John, Jeremy, myself and three girls that John's cousin had rounded up. The girl Jeremy was with had the most annoying giggle. John's girl wouldn't stop talking and her sentences were filled with the word 'like'. Mine started off quiet. I can't even remember the movie because I was focused on what I was meant to be doing, but no matter how hard I tried I couldn't stop thinking about Trent. John grunted answers to his date every few minutes, Jeremy kept trying to get close to his girl and she kept pushing him away and mine kept leaning in and putting her hand in the popcorn whenever I did. I wanted to run out of the cinema."

When he remained quiet, Shelby asked, "Did you?"

"Did I what?"

"Run?"

"No, but I should have. We went to Southbank after the movie. For a walk. Jeremy walked ahead, holding his girl's hand. She turned to John's girl and started talking to her until her and John began to walk beside them. The girl I was with slowed down."

"What was her name?"

Cameron laughed mirthlessly. "I couldn't tell you. John's girl introduced them and all the 'likes' distracted me. Later, when I realised I'd forgotten her name, it seemed rude to ask." He sighed. "She slowed down to a crawl...

* * *

"They're getting ahead of us." Cameron gestured to John, Jeremy and the two girls.

His date turned to face him, coming to a stop. She reached out and took his hand. "I enjoyed the movie, thanks for taking me."

"That's okay." He looked at a point over her shoulder. When she leaned forward and pressed her lips against his, he wished he'd been paying better attention. Her arms came around him and he wanted to push her away. He pulled back and she pressed forward.

"What's wrong?" She frowned, reaching out to press a hand against his chest.

Cameron shook his head. "No." He took another step back. "John will leave us behind if we get lost." He looked in the direction his friends had taken. John had borrowed his boss' van so they could all go in one vehicle.

The girl smiled and stepped closer. "I don't mind. We'll find another way home."

Cameron captured her hands as they ran up his arms. "I'm sorry. I enjoyed tonight, but…" his voice trailed off. "I just don't…" Everything he thought of to say would hurt her.

"What's wrong?"

Cameron winced at the tone. It felt like an accusation. "I guess I'm old fashioned. I like to be the one making the moves." He almost shouted in relief when she smiled, tilting her head to look up at him through her lashes.

"I'm not in the least old fashioned." She took a

step closer. "I'll give you some time, but you take too long and you'll just have to get over your old fashionedness."

"Ah, okay." He took a step back. Why hadn't Jeremy got this one? He'd much rather the one that kept pushing him away. He gestured in the direction his friends had gone. They were no longer in sight. "We'd better hurry and catch up."

She slid her hand in his. "I should warn you, I'm not very patient."

Her comment brought back Trent's words. Once again he heard the echo of Trent's laugh in his head, a deep drawn out sound that Cameron felt through his entire body. He wanted to pull away from the girl, tell her she was wasting her time. Instead he lengthened his stride.

"Are we in a race?"

"Something like that." He almost smiled. John's girl would have been so proud of his ability to add the word 'like' to a sentence.

"Slow down. I can't run in these heels."

He slowed slightly. Ahead he could see the other four. The distance was decreasing.

"Can I have your number?"

"No."

"Why not?"

"I thought you were going to give me some time."

The girl laughed. "I did."

The sound grated and he wanted to tell her to shut up, to leave him alone. Catching up with the others, they followed behind them. He remained silent. It wasn't her fault. Not her fault that every time he closed his eyes he could see Trent, that every night he dreamed of him. Why couldn't he find the girl beside him even slightly interesting? He'd given up on the idea he was asexual. Nope, not with the dreams he'd been having. But why now? He was eighteen. Bryce had known when he was sixteen. What was wrong with him?

"Are you ignoring me?"

"Huh?" He turned to the girl who'd jabbed him in the ribs. "What?"

"I asked you a question."

"Sorry." Cameron was relieved to see they'd reached the van. He waited for John to unlock the door, trying to keep his thoughts from turning to Trent again.

"Well?"

Cameron frowned and stepped back so Jeremy and his girl could get in the back first. "Well what?"

"Your number. You were going to give me your number."

"Oh." He climbed into the van. There was no way in hell she was getting his number.

The girl pressed up close to him on the seat. "Charlie said you play a lot of sport."

"Yeah." He was never going to ask John's cousin, Charlie, to set him up on another blind date. He should have learned that the first time he fell in with Charlie's constant need to have everyone in pairs. He shifted over slightly, but the girl followed so he was pressed between her and the interior of the van.

Her hand dropped to his thigh. "What's your favourite?"

He looked out the window, wishing John would drive faster. How much longer before they could ditch the girls? He couldn't even remember which one's house the girls were staying at. All he knew was that they'd get rid of them all at once. Behind him he heard Jeremy ask his girl for her number. "Favourite what?"

"Sport. Cricket? Football? Soccer?"

Her hand felt uncomfortable on his thigh. Hot and sweaty, even through the denim of his jeans. "All of them. Even the ones you didn't name." He wanted to tell her to shut up, but it wasn't her fault. He was the one who'd let Charlie set him up. When the van slowed, he looked through the front window and barely stopped himself from swearing when he saw the red light.

The girl frowned. "You have to like one of them more than the rest, everyone has favourites."

"Why?" In the front of the van John and his girl were quiet. How had he got stuck with the talkative one?

"I don't know, it just is. Everyone has favourites."

He shook his head, relief hitting him as the light turned green. "Why do I have to have a favourite? Why can't I like them all as much as each other?"

"Because you can't."

The words annoyed him. He looked out the side window and wondered what she'd do if he pushed her hand off his leg. He almost cheered when they turned into the girls' street.

As they pulled up, the girl rubbed his leg. "When are you going to give me your number?"

He moved her hand and unbuckled so he could cross the floor of the van to slide open the door. He crouched by the opening, keeping his hands to himself. Pushing her out the van probably wouldn't be a good idea.

As soon as she stepped out of the van she turned to face him. "Well? When?"

"When I ring you."

"You don't have my number." She reached for her minuscule handbag. "I'll write it down for you."

Cameron waited for Jeremy's girl to climb out of the van before he answered. "No thanks." He slid the door shut, trying not to smile at her slack jawed expression.

John's girl glared at him through the van window. "Like, the arsehole is brushing you off!"

"Sounds like we'd better leave." John glanced over his shoulder then pulled out onto the road. "Before they come after us with pitchforks."

"What's wrong with you?" Jeremy demanded.

Cameron sat in his seat again. "You didn't have to put up with her."

"I would've taken her number," Jeremy said.

"You'd take any girl's number," John said. "I'm glad that's over. I swear I'm going to start saying no to Charlie." He swore. "Who am I kidding? Charlie is relentless. Like a dripping tap."

"You're still an idiot." Jeremy hit the back of Cameron's seat.

Cameron turned to glare at him, then smiled. "I didn't see anyone trying to force their number on you."

"Arsehole." Jeremy crossed his arms over his chest.

"Yep." Cameron turned in his seat. The girl's

expression came back to him and he had to agree with Jeremy. He closed his eyes. He didn't have a clue what to do. Holding back a sigh that'd only have Jeremy hassling him, he pulled out his phone. He needed to talk to Bryce. Checking the time first, he sent a text.

Can I come over? Cameron stared at his phone as he waited for a reply. The light faded then went dark before it came.

I was wondering when you'd stop avoiding me.

Was that a yes or no?

Of course it was yes.

Cameron slid his phone into his pocket and leaned forward. "Drop me at Uncle Bryce's?"

John glanced at him in the rear view mirror. "Sure."

"Why are you going there?"

Cameron hated the tone of voice Jeremy always used when Bryce's name was mentioned. It wasn't anything overly obnoxious, only slightly. But it still made him want to punch him. "Because there's orgies going on at their place and they thought I might like to join the younger guys."

"It wouldn't surprise me," Jeremy muttered.

"Bastards. Where was my invite?"

Cameron laughed at John's teasing tone. "I'll tell them you're devastated you weren't invited."

"I'll get over it if I can be pit crew at Bryce's next race."

"When do I get to go to a race with you?" Jeremy asked.

Cameron shrugged. "When Uncle Bryce invites you."

John pulled up outside Bryce and Simon's home. "Do you need a lift later?"

"Nah. Uncle Bryce will take me home." Cameron started to hop out of the van then stopped and turned to John. "Tell Charlie not to give my number to anyone."

John grinned. "Especially if they're wielding pitchforks."

Cameron chuckled and stepped onto the footpath. He gave a single wave, as Jeremy climbed into the front, then headed to Bryce's front door. His knock was answered immediately.

Chapter Thirteen

Simon dragged him inside, kissing one cheek as he patted the other. "You poor darlin. Come inside. Do you want a drink?"

Cameron shook his head. Simon wore a multi-hued silk dressing gown that was loosely belted and gaping to show his smooth chest. His blond hair was fashionably cut and his pale blue eyes were filled with worry. "I like your dressing gown."

The worry evaporated and Simon spun, showing off the garment. "Your darlin uncle bought it for me." Simon lowered his voice to a conspirator's whisper. "And so he should, he's always leaving that watch lying around. He doesn't appreciate me the way he should."

Cameron quickly spoke, not wanting Simon to go off on one of his tirades. "Where is Uncle Bryce?"

"Tinkering in the garage." Simon rolled his eyes

as he drew him along the hallway, stopping at the lounge room doorway. "Where else?"

Cameron smiled.

"I told him you'd arrived. As soon as he cleans up he can come inside. He keeps telling me he's done playing with messy engines, that he only drives them. Yet every time I turn around, what do I find?"

Cameron turned at Bryce's chuckle. Water still clung to his uncle's arms and face, a towel slung around his neck. He was relieved Bryce wasn't wearing a colour clashing dressing gown like Simon. He was dressed in his old faded jeans and a t-shirt. "Can we talk?"

Bryce nodded. "Do you want something to drink?"

"You're too late asking. He's already declined," Simon said.

Bryce smiled at Simon, giving him a kiss as he walked past into the lounge room. "Don't wait up for me."

Simon snorted. "As if." He flounced away. "No one ever wants to talk to me."

Bryce grinned as he turned back to Cameron. "He'll get over it." He draped an arm around Cameron's shoulders, walking further into the room. They were a similar height. "How've you been?" Bryce stopped in front of the leather lounge suite choosing an armchair for himself and gesturing towards the other chair past the coffee table.

Once he was seated, Cameron shrugged, then smiled. "Enjoying the weather we're having lately."

Laughter burst from Bryce. "Thanks for the warning. Now you can hit me with the bomb."

"I think I'm gay."

"Really? What makes you think that?"

"There's this guy. I can't stop thinking about him. I even dream about him."

"Simon's going to hate missing this conversation. Is the guy hot?"

Cameron shrugged again. "I guess." He leaned forward, resting his arms on his knees. "But why now? I mean-" he broke off to lean back in the chair, the leather creaking. "I don't know what I mean."

"Have you ever been turned on by another boy before?"

Cameron shook his head. "No. No one."

"No one? What about a girl?"

He shook his head again.

"That doesn't make you gay."

"Then what does it make me?"

"Interested in a person. Not a boy or a girl, a person."

"But that person is a boy so technically that makes me gay."

"No." Bryce shook his head. "Technically that makes you the walking dead."

Cameron frowned. "How do you figure that?"

"When your father finds out he's going to kill you."

Cameron swore and dropped his head in his hands. "I'm going to leave the country, get a new identity."

Bryce laughed.

Cameron looked up at his uncle. "It's not funny."

The laughter faded. "I know." He stood and crossed the lounge room to sit on the edge of the coffee table, reaching out to momentarily rest a hand on Cameron's shoulder. "Simon would love to create a new identity for you, but with the direction his art's been taking lately, you wouldn't fade into a crowd."

A smile quickly turned into laughter and then tears. "How do you do it?"

"By knowing who I am. No one else's opinion matters. It's all just labels. I'm me. Not a label."

"How do you know who you are? Who you really are, not just who you think you are."

"Learn to listen to yourself. How you feel about things, how you react. But a big part of it comes with age."

Cameron swore. "I've got to get old before I know who I am?"

"Old! Watch it kid, I'm not old."

Cameron smiled weakly. "So am I gay?"

Bryce stared at him for a moment. "Does the label really matter?"

"I don't know." He shrugged. "Maybe." He knew it would matter to some people, but he had no idea if it really mattered to him. "I guess not."

"Good. Because you're you, Cameron Morgan. Anything else is irrelevant."

"Dad won't think so."

"That's his problem."

"And mine."

Bryce nodded. "Maybe." He paused a moment. "You know you've got a bed here if you need it." He winced. "You're always welcome, well, you will be once Simon gets over the shock of having only one room for his art."

"Thanks."

"Who is he? Do I know him?"

Cameron hesitated. "Trent."

"Not Simon's Trent."

Cameron nodded.

Bryce swore. "I hate it when he's right. There's going to be no living with him for at least a month."

Cameron shrugged, causing the leather of the armchair to creak again. "Sorry. I didn't exactly choose Trent."

"Yeah, I know. So how did you meet him?"

Cameron grinned, making his uncle wait a few seconds before he answered. "When I dropped your watch in last time you left it at our house."

Bryce grimaced. "Promise me you never tell your parents that, neither of them. As far as they're concerned you met him somewhere else. Somewhere I'd never even think of going."

"The topic won't come up."

"Why not?"

"Because I can't tell them. Ever."

"Oh no you don't. You can't do that to Trent. What does he say?"

Cameron looked away.

"Well?"

He rose to his feet staring down at his uncle. He shook his head and started to walk away.

"That's it? Conversation ended. Are you going to avoid us again?"

Cameron turned to find Bryce had followed him into the hallway. "I don't even know if I'll see him again."

"So what was it? A one night stand?"

"No." The word exploded from him. He shook his head. "Nothing like that."

"Then what happened? We haven't seen Trent since Tuesday. What happened?"

"Tuesday?" He felt his stomach lurch. "Four days ago?"

"What did you do?"

Cameron stepped back from the anger radiating from Bryce. "Nothing."

"Before that he was over here nearly every day."

Cameron turned away from the accusation in Bryce's eyes. "I didn't... he said... oh shit." He hurried towards the front door. "Tell Simon I said bye."

"Where are you going?" Bryce held his hand on the front door as Cameron started to open it.

He held his uncle's gaze for a moment before he said softly, "I don't know." He tugged on the door and Bryce let it go.

"Cameron?"

"Yeah?" He kept his back to Bryce.

"Do you need a lift somewhere?"

He shook his head, "No." He strode towards the footpath, turning in the direction of Trent's house and broke into a run. He was an idiot. He hadn't thought how his moment of stupidity would affect

Trent. He pushed himself harder, as hard as he'd run if he were trying for a goal. The pound of his feet hitting the ground sounded like 'idiot'. Each step. Idiot. Idiot. Idiot. And they were right.

When he reached Trent's house, seeing a light still on at a window, he pounded on the door. He bent forward, resting his hands on his knees as he tried to steady his breathing, straightening as the door opened. Trent's sleepy look evaporated when his gaze fell on Cameron. "I'm sorry."

"For what? Waking me?"

"No. Well, that too. I thought you were awake. There was a light on."

"What are you sorry for?"

Cameron couldn't meet his gaze any longer. He dropped his gaze, but the bare expanse of chest was distracting. His gaze fell lower to the black pyjama pants Trent wore. Bad idea, even more distracting. His gaze flew back to Trent's. "Uncle Bryce said you haven't visited them since... since..." his gaze slid away to a point past Trent.

"Not everything is about you."

"I'm sorry. I shouldn't have come here that first time. It was just... I haven't... I never... not even..." his rambling came to a sudden halt. His gaze met Trent's and he forced himself to speak the words

Trent deserved. "I thought I was asexual, then I saw you." Silence fell, broken only by Trent's sudden indrawn breath. He continued to hold Trent's gaze then looked away, dropping his voice. "I'm sorry." He started to turn away.

"Wait." Trent reached out and grabbed his upper arm. "Come inside."

Cameron shook his head. "I can't."

"You can't tell me that and run off." Trent's lips curved slightly as his gaze roamed down and then up again. "Although I don't think you should give up running. It's done wonders for your physique." Trent's hand loosened its grip in favour of a caress.

Cameron clenched his hands to keep them from reaching for Trent. He shook his head. "I can't. My father would kill me if he knew I was here."

"Talk. Come in and talk." Trent's lips twisted into a wry smile. "Maybe I'll learn you're an absolute prick and you'll stop invading my dreams."

Cameron closed his eyes as he tried to ignore the images from his own dreams that rose before him.

"Cameron?" Trent's hand reached his shoulder, his fingers grazing Cameron's neck.

He reached up to remove Trent's hand and Trent slid his fingers between his, tugging him forward. "I can't." The words sounded weak.

"For a little bit. Just to talk."

There was nowhere else he had to be. His parents thought he was staying at John's. Bryce wasn't likely to mention he'd seen him. No one was expecting him tonight. He let Trent pull him inside and close the door behind him.

Chapter Fourteen

The door opened, sending a splash of dim light into the room, making Shelby jump to her feet. "Daddy." She sent a glance to Cameron's corner. Had he heard him speaking? "Is it dinner time already?"

Larry nodded and stepped out of the doorway.

She breathed a sigh of relief as he locked the door and pointed to the stairs with the light of his torch. Cameron's voice always softened when he talked about Trent and this time it had been quieter than usual. Her heart began to drop back to a normal pace as she hurried down the stairs, trying to focus on the now. She had been lost in Cameron's story.

In the kitchen, the table was set, steak and vegetables on plates, steam rising from them. Her gaze arrowed in on the knives. The stainless steel glimmered in the dim kitchen light.

"Sit down, Mellie."

His tone sounded distant and she wondered if he'd heard Cameron and was waiting to catch him when they least expected.

She turned to him. "I missed you so much today. Why can't we spend more time together?"

Larry's expression softened. "I wish we could too, honey." He transferred the torch to the hand with the gun, reaching out to pat her cheek. "But I have to work." He grinned as he gestured towards the table. "Someone likes to eat too much."

Shelby laughed. "I must have got it from you."

He laughed with her, then covered his mouth when he yawned. "I thought I was fit, but these long hours are going to take some getting used to."

"Where are you working?"

"On one of the local farms. It's hard to get cash work these days. Everyone wants to know who you are."

"It's safe for you? Working there."

Larry nodded. "For now. When I find your brother we'll move away from here, maybe go to WA."

Her grip on the Melissa personality slipped. She struggled to stay in character. Western Australia was too far away. It had to be over four thousand kilometres. She wanted to tell him there was no way she'd go that far with him. Her gaze flickered towards the gun. What choice did she have? She had to go where he told her. "When will you look for Robert?"

"I get Saturday off. I'll look for him then."

She nodded as she had another mouthful of her food. Saturday. Five days. They had to leave before then. Cameron couldn't hide from him forever. Her grip tightened on her knife as she cut into her steak. Tonight. She had to find something tonight. "I'll do the dishes tonight, Daddy. You look so tired." She smiled at him.

Larry reached across the table and clasped her hand that held the knife. "You're a good girl, Mellie. What would I do without you?" His smile held sorrow. "You're my life. You and your brother are my life."

Her heart lurched at the thought of taking that from him, but he wasn't her father and she wasn't Melissa. She had to remember that as well as forget it when she was with him. She placed her fork on her plate and covered his hand with hers. "I can help you look for Robert."

He shook his head. "No. It's not safe. I can't let them take you away from me again." He pulled away and yawned. "Eat up, Mellie. I'd say we won't be looking at photo albums tonight."

"Saturday. On your day off. We can spend the day together then, just you and me."

"I really should look for your brother. The sooner I find him, the sooner we can leave."

Shelby thought of the girl in the album. Her head at an angle as she stared up at her father. He'd been the source of her joy. What would that girl have said? Years without her father, how would she have reacted. "But we've hardly spent any time together. Didn't you miss me as much as I missed you?"

A weary smile crossed his face, to be quickly replaced by another yawn. "We'll spend Saturday together, but the Saturday after belongs to your brother."

She grinned at him. "That sounds fair." She'd gained them an extra week. Cameron would be safe a little longer, but she didn't want to take that long to escape. If she could, she'd leave tomorrow. She rose to her feet, gathering her empty plate.

Larry's hand went to his gun. "What are you doing?"

"The dishes. Are you finished with your plate, Daddy?"

He finished off his meal then slid it across the table.

Shelby picked it up with a smile. Her hands shook as she rinsed the plates under the tap before she began to fill the sink. In the cupboard below the sink she found detergent. Bubbles filled the water and she washed everything, placing them in the draining rack, each second feeling like an eternity. With a quick glance towards Larry, she took the tea towel from where it hung at the front of the stove and began to dry the dishes, stacking them on the bench and leaving the cutlery until last. Once the cutlery was dry, she opened the drawer, her heart racing and her mouth dry. As her hand reached for the drawer, she bumped against it and deliberately dropped the cutlery onto the floor. The pound of her heart echoed in her ears.

She sent an apologetic smile Larry's way. "Lucky it wasn't the plates. Maybe your tiredness is catching." She stooped to pick up the cutlery, tucking a knife under her dress and sliding it in the side of her knickers. As she rose to her feet, she quickly tossed the cutlery in the drawer, hoping the elastic of her knickers was strong enough. Another quick smile to Larry. "I promise I won't drop the plates." She turned back to the dishes, unsettled by his steady gaze. Had he seen her? Wouldn't he have already said something?

Gathering the plates she moved across the kitchen and opened the cupboard. She felt the knife slide down a little as she walked. Her heart skipped a beat and she fought the urge to hold it in place. She turned to face Larry, the tea towel still in her hands as she leaned against the bench. "You look so tired, Daddy. You're right, we'll leave the albums for another time."

Larry slowly rose from the table and picked up the gun and torch. He didn't speak, only nodded and turned the torch on.

Shelby left the tea towel on the bench and pushed away from it. She didn't want to take any more steps than necessary. As she slowly crossed the kitchen she felt the knife slide down a little more. Her hand itched to press against it, but she couldn't. Then she was past Larry and headed for the stairs. The knife kept slipping, a millimetre at a time. Holding her breath, Shelby took the first step. She hugged the wall on her right, the side with the knife. Then she was on the stair that creaked, hoping the noise covered the catch in her breath as the knife slid further down.

Larry walked beside her and in the semi-darkness Shelby finally felt safe enough to press her arm against the knife. Cameron was right, the dark was their friend. She eyed the torch beam that shone a path up the stairs, glad it was on the side away from her. Not much further, almost at the top. She wanted to run up the stairs. No, that might make the knife fall. She wanted to go extra slow. But that'd make it longer before she could hide in total darkness.

"You're quiet, Mellie." Larry paused at the top of the stairs to look at her, the beam of light falling on her face.

She blinked in the light, squinting as she raised her left hand to shield her eyes. "I thought you might be too tired to talk."

"Never. Not for you, Mellie."

She nodded, then forced a smile to her lips. "Thank you Daddy, for working all these long hours to look after me."

Larry smiled back at her, drawing her forward for a hug. "I love you Mellie."

She had to let go of the knife and it slid a little more. Only the top of the handle was caught. Hugging Larry she tried to remain relaxed. It was almost impossible. She didn't dare breathe. Then she was pulling away from him, her arm pressed against the knife again.

He walked to the door and unlocked it, standing back so she could enter. "Night, Mellie."

"Night, Daddy." She held his gaze in the hope he wouldn't look down and see how her arm was pressed against her hip and leg. The moment she stepped into the room, she moved to the side, her hand grabbing the knife and pulling it free from its anchor. The door closed and she slid down the wall, her body trembling as she clutched the knife. The more she tried to stop the trembling, the harder she shook. Then she was sobbing, both hands gripping the metal handle.

"Shelby? What happened? What did he do?"

"I've got a knife." She could barely bring herself to speak the words. She was terrified he'd somehow hear and take it away. "We're going to escape. I've got a knife."

"The bathroom window, above the toilet. He never goes in there."

"It's so small."

"It's big enough."

Shelby tried to rise to her feet, but she couldn't. Her body still trembled. "Tomorrow. When he's at work."

"Hide the knife, just in case."

She nodded even though he couldn't see her in the dark, then crawled along the floor, unable to rise. Reaching the toilet, she slid it behind the plumbing, against the wall. The light never reached this far. It'd be safe. "I've got a knife." She whispered the words to herself, barely able to believe them. She grinned. "I've got a knife. We're going to escape." She crawled out of the bathroom, the cold tiles not helping to stop the trembling, and curled up on the floor at the bathroom door. Like a guard dog. I'm Shelby West and I have a knife. She thought the words several more times before she dropped off to sleep, still trembling.

Chapter Fifteen

"Shelby. Wake up."

She sat up abruptly at Cameron's demands. "What's happening?" She kept her voice at a whisper in case Larry was outside.

"I think I heard him drive off. You need to work on the window."

She stretched and groaned at the aches in her body from the hard floor. "I really wish I had a mattress."

"Sorry."

"That's okay, I might have done the same." She stumbled to her feet and staggered into the bathroom. After splashing water on her face she felt more awake. She looked in the direction of the toilet, grinning. "I have a knife," she whispered. Crouching down, she reached behind the plumbing, her fingers curling around the cold metal handle. It wouldn't be much defence if she wanted to attack someone, but hopefully it'd lever the plywood off the window.

Ages later when she'd barely managed to make the plywood budge, Shelby growled in frustration. "We're never going to get out of here."

"Don't you dare give up."

"I don't even know how long this has taken me. It feels like forever. Why don't you take a turn?"

"I can't."

"Why not?"

The silence stretched out before Cameron finally answered. "I haven't the strength."

Fear raced through her and she stared at where the bathroom door was, wishing she could see in the blackness. "What's wrong with you? Are you sick? Hurt?" Then she realised that each night when Larry fed her, Cameron was left locked in the room. "You need food, don't you? I'll steal some for you tonight."

"No." The word was an explosion. "Don't be crazy. Don't you dare risk it. Just get the ply off the window and then no one will be stuck in this room."

She sighed, wanting to argue, but his words made sense. "Talk to me, Cameron, take my mind off this. Tell me about Trent. What happened when you walked into his house?" She flexed her hands, massaging cramped muscles before she attacked the window again.

"We talked. All night. I don't even recall falling asleep. But I woke up beside him on his couch, his head on my shoulder and his hand on my chest as I half reclined…"

* * *

Cameron froze when he realised he'd been reaching out to run a hand through Trent's hair. Early morning light spilled across the room to show Trent's eyes were still closed. He shouldn't be here. He should never have entered the house. It was crazy. It couldn't go anywhere. He started to slide away.

Trent murmured in his sleep. His fingers curling around Cameron's shirt as he snuggled in closer. Cameron couldn't move. Didn't want to. He wanted to wrap his arms around Trent and spend the rest of the morning lying there with him. No, the entire day.

Trent's eyes flickered open and he smiled sleepily. "Hello gorgeous."

His stomach clenched at the look in Trent's eyes and a shiver went through him when Trent's hand lazily moved across his chest. He didn't know if he should push him away or draw him closer. He was torn. He wanted this so much he ached. His entire body. Yet the thought of what his father would do terrified him. Images of his father and Bryce flickered through his mind, years of negative images. Even after all these years his father still couldn't accept Bryce. He wouldn't become another argument between his parents.

The sleepiness fled from Trent's gaze. "What's wrong?"

Cameron hesitated before he restarted an unresolved conversation from last night. "I can't have both you and my father in my life. How can I make that choice?"

"You're his son. He'll eventually accept. It's different with Bryce, he's only his brother-in-law."

Cameron shook his head. How could he explain his father belonged to an earlier century? Obviously the few comments he'd made last night hadn't helped. "You don't know him, he never changes his mind. And he never admits when he's wrong."

"Then he's not worth your effort."

"He is, he's my father. He's been there for every one of my games. Cheered me on, even when I lost. He taught me every sport I know, how to drive and took me fishing when I was younger. He's a hard man who has rigid beliefs, but I've never doubted that he loves me." He pulled away from Trent and rose to his feet.

Trent looked up at him from where he lay on the couch. "It isn't love if you have to be a certain person to keep that love."

"I can't do this." He ran his fingers through his hair, turning away from Trent.

"Do what?"

What choice did he have? Trent hadn't been willing to accept the suggestion he'd made last night. "Be anything more than friends."

"Friends." The word was hard and bitter. "I can't be just friends. You ask the impossible of me."

Hearing Trent move across the room, Cameron turned to find him within arms reach. He clasped his hands behind his back, his fingers locked tightly together. He slowly shook his head. "That's the only other offer I can make." His words were soft, an apology threaded through them.

"How can you stand there and say that?"

"You're asking me to give up my family for you. To destroy my life."

"Then you can't feel the way I do."

"It's just lust." It had to be. It couldn't be anything more. A month, a few months and the relationship would end.

Trent shook his head. "I've known lust, this is different. I want to know every inch of you. How you feel. How you think. I want to be so close I wouldn't have a clue where one of us ends and the other begins. I think about you. Dream about you. Last night was perfect. And you can't tell me that was lust. I've never met anyone before where everything clicked. Everything."

He ached. Ached to cross the small gap between them and pull Trent close, tell him he felt the same. But he couldn't. He knew what pain the friction between his dad and Bryce caused his mum. How could he do that to her? And his father. How could he tell him? Why couldn't Trent understand? "I'm sorry. I can't offer more."

"Can't or won't?"

"Can't. I can't destroy the people I love."

"So you'll destroy yourself instead."

"Trent." He couldn't help it, he reached out to him.

Trent stepped back. "I can't be hidden away like a shameful secret again." He shook his head. "I can't. I know I'm worth better than that, even if it took me a long time to realise."

"It wouldn't be like that."

"It would. You want to visit me in secret. I don't

deserve that. I don't deserve being treated like something worthless."

Cameron was desperate to make him understand. "You don't know my father."

"Maybe not, but I do know me. I want someone who's willing to be seen at my side, happy to introduce me to their friends and eventually take me home to meet their parents. Someone who's proud to call me their boyfriend. I'll never stand by again and let someone deny our relationship."

"I'm sorry."

"So am I." Trent turned away. "I think you should go."

Cameron stared at Trent's back. Lowered head, slumped shoulders, tapering down to narrow hips. His hands clenched into fists. "I'm sorry." He whispered the words before he walked to the front door. A noise behind him had him turning.

Trent strode towards him, a determined glint in his eyes. "I want to haunt your dreams like you haunt mine. I want you to wake a hundred times every night and reach for someone who isn't there." He reached out, one arm encircling Cameron's waist, the other threading through his hair at the nape of his neck.

Cameron opened his mouth to protest, but Trent's

lips met his. Need rushed through him. Fierce, desperate need. His hands clutched at Trent, all protests forgotten, only demands left behind. When they finally broke apart, Cameron stared at Trent, desperate to reach out for him. "You already haunt my dreams." His voice was raw. It took all his willpower to turn and open the door. He nearly didn't make it when he heard the jagged sound Trent made behind him. Closing his eyes he stepped outside, letting the door shut behind him. Deep shuddering breaths didn't help. He wanted to shout.

He broke into a run, making for the bus shelter around the corner. It was empty. He slammed his fists into the wall of the shelter. The pain couldn't compete with the pain already ripping through him. With a wounded groan he slumped onto the seat, his head resting against the side of the shelter.

Cameron swore, wanting to hit something else. Smash it. Instead he sat there, breathing hard as he fought the urge to lash out again. He didn't have a clue how long he sat there before he saw a bus headed towards him. Once he read the destination on the front, he staggered to his feet and hailed the bus. As he made his way to a seat at the back, he kept his gaze on his feet, not wanting to meet the gaze of the handful of people travelling on the bus. He dropped his head into his hands and wondered how he was going to survive the feelings that tore at him. Why couldn't he have been asexual? It would've been so much easier.

Chapter Sixteen

Shelby wiped at the tears on her cheeks and the knife dropped to the tiles with a clatter, her hands cramping from clutching it for so long. "Cameron." She felt his pain, wishing there was something she could say to comfort him. "Tell me things changed. Please."

"He haunted my dreams. I haunted his street." A loud shuddering breath escaped him. "After school. I'd turn up and watch his house. I ditched so much practice. He'd sometimes see me and stand at his front door and watch. We'd stay like that for ten to fifteen minutes. In the end I'd walk away, head to the bus shelter and home. I couldn't stop myself. Every day I'd tell myself I wouldn't, that I had to stop, but every day I did the same."

"Why didn't you give in? You obviously wanted Trent badly. Why?"

He didn't answer straight away. "I didn't want to

destroy my family. One little sentence and I'd ruin the lives of the people I love. Mum. Dad. They'd never get past that. And Trent didn't want someone who'd make him hide who he is. I didn't want to do that to him, not after what he went through with his last boyfriend, but I couldn't stop going there. I had lost my licence and hated catching the bus, but even that didn't stop me. I kept telling myself how friggin stupid I was, that I was acting like an addict."

"You love him?"

"That night we talked he was telling me a story about his mum, then he laughed. He has the most amazing laugh. I was completely lost. I think that's why I panicked so much the next day. I already knew I was lost. Completely and utterly lost. There I was, eighteen-years-old and thinking I wanted to spend the rest of my life listening to that sound. I was terrified. Excited. So friggin high with the feelings that swamped me I wanted to grab him and never let go. I didn't. I made some stupid comment and the moment slipped away. I shouldn't have let it. All that time I wasted standing out the front of his house when I should have grabbed hold of him right then and never ever let him go."

"Did you? Did you ever end up grabbing hold of him? Did you fix your mistake?"

"Some mistakes can't be fixed. Ever." There was a moment of silence before Cameron continued. "I lost weight. Not a heap, but enough for Mum to ask if I was okay. I couldn't pay attention in class. I've never been that good at school. Sport has always been my thing. And when I wasn't acting like some lovesick idiot out the front of Trent's house I was helping John on his car."

"The one you kept naming." Shelby smiled, tears still making her lashes feel stuck together.

Cameron chuckled. "Yeah. I-" he broke off at a sound outside the bedroom door.

Shelby was out of the bathroom and facing the door in seconds. A glimmer of light shone underneath it. She rubbed at her eyes, trying to slow the beat of her heart as she waited for the door to swing open. Melissa. I'm Melissa. Larry's Mellie. She chanted the words over and over in her head. The door swung open.

"Daddy." She spread her arms wide, taking a step forward, trying desperately to ignore the gun.

"Honey." He reached for her.

She threw herself into his arms, her head against his chest as she gripped the sides of his shirt, trying to hold onto Mellie's character equally as tight. She wanted to yell at Larry to leave her alone. Cameron needed her. But she couldn't. Rejecting Larry might be one of the last things she ever did.

It was Larry who drew away this time. "Are you all right, honey?" He shone the torch into her face and she shielded her eyes, nearly closing them. "Have you been crying?"

"I missed you. It's lonely waiting for you. All day alone. In the dark."

He reached out and wiped at her cheeks. "Shh, honey. You're safe here. No one can find you and take you away. Everything will be different when we move, you'll see. No one will ever find us then."

She nodded, unable to speak as panic threatened to overtake her. They had to leave, before he took her even further from her life.

"Come on, honey." Larry guided her from the room, locking the door. "Come and have dinner."

Shelby obediently headed for the kitchen, wondering when Larry would stop locking the room. She paused in the doorway. The table wasn't set yet.

"Sit down." Larry gestured towards the table. "Dinner's nearly ready. I was late home."

She crossed the room and dragged out her chair.

Larry opened the cutlery draw and pulled some out.

Shelby stood with her hand on the back of the

chair, her gaze drawn to the drawer. She swallowed, but her mouth remained dry.

Larry stopped partway through closing the drawer. Placing the cutlery from his hand on the bench he pulled out the knives. He turned to Shelby. "Where's the knife?"

Her heart rose in her throat, making her want to clutch at it. She stayed still, her hand tightening on the chair back. "What knife?" She frowned, trying desperately to hold onto Melissa's character. "You just put them all on the bench." She pointed to them, relieved her hand remained steady even though her legs threatened to buckle.

"Where's the knife?" His voice rose and he took a step towards her. "There's one missing. Where is it?"

Her breath came fast as she glanced at the knives held at his side. "I don't know." Her voice was small. "I dropped the cutlery. But I thought I got them all. Remember? Last night. Maybe it's still on the floor." She slowly lowered herself to the floor, looking under the table, flattening out so she could peer under the stove.

"Get up."

"I need to find the knife."

"Now!" The word cracked through the room.

She scrambled to her feet.

"Where's the knife."

Each word slammed against her and she shivered at the look in his eyes. "I was trying to find it." She gestured to the floor. "You wouldn't let me." A shuddering breath, her gaze caught by his. "Daddy you're scaring me." A half step forward. "Let me find it." The words soft, a plea filling them. "Please. I know I can find it. It has to be here somewhere."

He dropped the knives into the still open drawer and seemed to shrink as he ran a hand across his forehead. "Come here, honey." He tightened his arms around her as she staggered into him. "I couldn't bear to lose you. Tell me you want to stay with me, that you don't ever want to leave."

Shelby clung to Larry, tears shuddering through her. "I never want to leave. I miss you when you're gone." Another shudder ripped through her. Fear, relief, confusion. "I love you, Daddy."

"Aw, honey." His hand stroked her back, solid and comforting. "Don't ever be scared of me, Mellie. I couldn't bear that. I love you. You're my life."

"I love you too." She clung to Larry, sobs shaking her body, tears coursing down her face to dampen his shirt.

"Shh, it's all right. Everything's all right. Don't cry Mellie, don't cry, honey."

His words made her cry harder.

He reached out with one hand and pulled the chair towards them. Sitting he dragged her onto his lap like a little child, rocking back and forth as he patted her back. "Aw, honey, you're killing me here. You know I can never stand to see you in tears. I tell you what, after dinner we'll have ice cream. I've got double choc chip. I was saving it for Saturday night, but we'll have it tonight. What do you say? No more tears?"

She tried to stop. It was impossible. "I n… need to use… the bathroom." She drew away from his shoulder, wiping at her eyes with the back of her hand.

"That's the plan. Wash your face and after dinner we'll have ice cream." Larry helped her stand and led her to the downstairs bathroom. "Go on." He guided her in. "I'll be right out here waiting for you." He stepped back and closed the door.

The room was plunged into near darkness, a slight glow highlighting the edges of the door. Shelby tried to stop, but sobs continued to shudder through her as she locked the bathroom door. Her hands ran along the wall beside the door. Finding the switch, she turned it on. The room stayed dark.

It didn't matter. The dark was her friend. It was safe. Turning around she reached for the vanity she'd seen before the door had closed. The cold porcelain edge met her fingers and she patted her way to the tap. Cold water washed over her hands and she splashed her face. Leaving the water running, she slid to the tiles, her forehead pressed against the vanity cupboard.

It rushed in on her that she was alone in a new part of the house. Her sobs finally slowed and she opened the cupboard, sliding back out of the way. Her hands patted the empty space and she gritted her teeth to hold back the words she wanted to scream. Her breath continued to shudder in and out as she quickly catalogued the room. Bars on the window, a thick towel, soap, a bottle that was probably shampoo a scrubbing brush and a disposable razor. None of them could help.

There was a knock on the door. "Mellie?"

She turned off the tap, trying to calm herself. Another shuddering breath followed by hiccups. She wasn't ready to face him.

The knock was louder this time and he tried the handle. "Mellie."

"One… one minute." She stared at the back lit door, her fingers twining and untwining. She couldn't do it, not one more minute. It was impossible. The disposable razor came to mind. She stopped mid breath. No. Her breath came out in a rush. She wasn't going to give in. She could do this. A deep breath and she reached for the door, unlocking and swinging it open. A weak smile was all she could manage. "I'd really like some ice cream."

Chapter Seventeen

Larry smiled, relief evident. He reached out and clasped her shoulder. "Not till you've had dinner."

She sighed heavily. "If I have to."

He chuckled as he put his hand at her back and guided her to the kitchen. "I've lost count of the amount of times you've wheedled dessert out of me before dinner. Can we have an upside down dinner, you'd beg." He smiled down at her as they reached her chair. "But not tonight. Dinner first, all right?"

"We can have an upside down dinner Saturday." Her smile came easier this time.

"Maybe. Now sit down and I'll dish up."

It wasn't until dinner was served and they were eating that Shelby realised Larry didn't have his gun. As she ate and half listened to him, she tried to think where she'd last seen it. Then it came to her. It was on the bench behind her. She was between Larry and his gun. Her food was halfway between her mouth and plate.

"Mellie?"

She put the food back on her plate. Think. Think, you idiot. She tried for a smile. It felt fake. "We should look at the albums after dessert. You aren't too tired, are you?"

Larry smiled. "I'm never too tired for you, Mellie. After dessert."

She nodded and picked up her fork again. But she couldn't get her mind off the gun. How quickly could she move? She'd have to turn, but he had to come around the table. And what if he'd moved it while he'd been dishing up dinner? What if it was no longer there? Then her plate was empty and she rose, turning to take it to the sink. Her gaze fell on the gun and she took a step towards it.

"Mellie?"

She froze.

"Here."

She turned to find he'd risen from the table and held out his plate. She reached for it as he took a couple more steps. As she turned back towards the gun, Larry came closer and reached past her to pick it up. A scream threatened to break free. She held it back as she took the last few steps to the sink and placed the dishes in it. She had to be more alert so she didn't miss any other opportunities. When she saw Larry take bowls from the cupboard she crossed to the chest freezer and started to open it.

"Get away from there!"

She stumbled back at the anger in his voice, turning to see him charge across the room to her. "I… I was only t… trying to help."

"Of course you were." His voice was calm as he grabbed hold of her shoulders. "Of course you were." He patted her cheek then turned her towards the table. "You sit down, honey. I'll get the ice cream."

With a nod, Shelby did as she was told. She sent quick glances towards Larry and the chest freezer. She noticed her hands were shaking as she sat down and she held them in her lap, her gaze fixed on the table. As soon as she was in the bedroom she was going to work on the window. She wasn't going to sleep until they were free. She couldn't cope with much more of this or she'd be begging Larry to shoot her. Unless she forgot who she was.

Larry scooped ice cream into two bowls and placed one in front of Shelby before he sat down. "I remember the first time you had chocolate ice cream. You were not much more than one. You'd pulled a bar stool from the breakfast bench to the fridge freezer and there was food scattered all around the kitchen floor. You were in the middle of it, ice cream smeared all over you and a big grin on your face. It was one of those cardboard type containers and you'd crumpled the lid getting it off."

"Who doesn't like chocolate?"

Larry chuckled. "We put the bar stools up so you couldn't get into the freezer again. Every day after that you'd stand at the fridge and stretch towards the freezer and open and close your little hands like you could somehow make the door open and the ice cream fall into them with your determination."

Shelby grinned, the image clear in her mind. "It should have." She scooped another spoonful of the creamy dessert into her mouth, letting it slowly melt on her tongue. "Milo would be so good sprinkled over this."

"I think you're getting worse every year with your chocolate addiction."

"You can never have too much chocolate."

"So you keep telling me."

His words jarred her and her smile faded. She quickly had another mouthful of ice cream.

"I've got Chocolate Quick in the cupboard. Will that do?"

Shelby shook her head. "No. It's okay."

"I'll get Milo before Saturday."

She nodded, finishing her ice cream. She wanted to escape to the bedroom, but she still had to look at photos with him. When she rose and headed to the sink, she couldn't help looking at the place where the gun had sat.

"I'll do dishes later, Mellie. Let's look at the albums."

Shelby nodded and walked with him to the lounge room. One of the albums was open on the coffee table. A different one to last time and she wondered if Larry had sat here, alone, looking through them.

They sat together and Larry turned pages, reminiscing. She watched as Melissa grew from a chubby baby to a mischievous toddler. They both laughed when they came across the photo of Melissa covered in chocolate ice cream. More pages were turned and Melissa continued to grow. A gap tooth grin in one, pigtails in another, but always a glint in her eyes that made her look like she knew a joke no one else did. And if you were lucky, she might share it with you.

Larry turned another page and Shelby stabbed her finger on a photo. "Oh, my god. My bike."

Larry chuckled. "When you unwrapped that on

your sixth birthday you screeched so loudly I thought my ears would bleed."

Shelby stared at him. "Yes." The word was a whisper as she tried to figure out what was real. "Every time we went to the department store I hoped you'd buy it for me. I'd look at it and think, that's my bike. I want that bike."

Larry chuckled again. "And you didn't stop at thinking. Do you love me daddy, you'd say as you ran your hands over that bike. Don't you think I'd look good on it? I'm gonna be six soon. And you'd smile at me and I knew I couldn't disappoint you." Larry reached out and held her hand, a soft look in his eyes. "They only had one left. Another woman was looking at it when I went in but I snatched it up and bought it." He grinned. "And she wasn't quiet about how she felt about me taking it from under her nose."

Shelby laughed with him, a sense of unreality descending over her. "I'm tired." She forced a yawn. "Can we look at more tomorrow night?"

"Sure thing, honey." Larry rose to his feet and held out his hand to her.

Shelby stared at it a moment before she took it and let him pull her to her feet. "Tonight I..." her voice trailed off as she tried to think how to apologise for cutting their night short.

"I know, honey. It meant a lot to me too. If your brother was here, it'd be perfect."

She could only nod and look at his hand that still held hers.

His hand tightened on hers. "We can't stay here forever, it isn't safe. I don't want to, but maybe we should move on. I think she's being more careful with your brother now I have you."

Her gaze flew to his, confused. Didn't he think Robert was still in the house? "You want to leave before you find Robert?"

Larry nodded. "I can't let her take you from me. Maybe I have to accept I'll only be able to have one of you." He reached out to pat her cheek. "You and me, honey. Forever."

"When?" The words came out as a whisper.

"We can have our day together later. This is more important."

"When?" She spoke it louder this time.

"I'll try and find Robert Saturday. One last time. We leave Sunday, with or without him."

Five days until they left. She nodded mechanically, a roaring sound filling her ears. Larry smiled at her and turned her towards the stairs. Then she was looking at the bedroom door and hadn't a clue how she'd arrived there. Five days. Larry shook her shoulder and she faced him.

"Mellie?" Concern filled his eyes and his tone.

She shook her head, trying to clear her thoughts. "Sorry. I just… Robert-" she broke off, looking away from him.

"I feel the same." He crushed her to him. "It's killing me to make this decision, but I can't lose you. We have to leave before she finds you and takes you away again."

"How can she? If I said I wanted to live with you, they'd let me. I'm old enough."

"Aw, Mellie, I wish it was that easy." He drew back to look down at her, his hands resting on her shoulders. "I don't know how she did it, but she convinced them I'd killed you and Robert. I was only doing a couple of k's over the speed limit. Five at the most. That roo came out of nowhere. The last thing I remember was you screaming. Then I woke up in the hospital. They wouldn't let me see either of you, tried to tell me you were both dead. It was impossible. We weren't going fast enough. And I lived, didn't I? It wasn't that bad an accident, but she made them believe her. She'd finally got her wish to keep you all to herself. She looked after you, didn't she?"

She could only nod. "Mum makes sure we have everything we need."

"I'll give Cynthia that. She's always been a good mum, but she had no right to keep you away from me." His hands tightened on her shoulders. "You're mine too. Both of you are."

Fear hit her at the look in his eyes. "Daddy, I'm tired."

"Of course you are. It's nearly midnight." He patted her cheek. "I love you, honey."

"I love you too." She smiled up at him. "We'll look at more photos tomorrow."

He grinned. "You always did like hearing about yourself. Centre of attention all the time. Haven't you noticed there's a million more photos of you than your brother?"

She laughed and tossed her hair back. "That's because I'm the best." She spun and bounced into the bedroom, tossing over her shoulder. "Night, Daddy." She was still smiling as the door closed.

Chapter Eighteen

"Shelby?"

It took her a moment to realise Cameron had spoken. Arms wrapped around herself, she sank to the floor. "I'm Shelby West." Her words were uncertain, hushed.

"What happened, Shelby?"

"I… she… we had the same bike, for our sixth birthday. Pink and white, with a bell. We say the same things. How do I know I'm not Melissa? How?"

"You're not. You know you're not."

"I don't know anything. How can we be so alike? She could be my twin. Explain that to me. If I'm not Mellie then why do I look a lot like her?"

"When I first started school there was a kid who looked so much like me I punched him because I thought he'd stolen my face."

"What happened?"

Cameron chuckled. "John pulled me off him, dragged me to the bathroom and showed me I still had my face." He chuckled again. "We'd taken one of Uncle Bryce's horror movies to watch. It was about some creature with no face of his own who stole other people's faces to wear. When the whole story was finally dragged out of us, we were in so much trouble. Bryce couldn't stop laughing. He kept telling me he was going to steal my face and wear it when he was misbehaving so I'd be the one who got in trouble, not him. It became a bit of a joke after a while." He was silent a moment. "When Larry thought I was Robert, it reminded me of that. As if Robert had stolen my face, because it's my face, no one else's."

At the mention of Robert's name, fear spiralled through her. She staggered to her feet. "Robert."

"What?"

"If he doesn't find Robert Saturday he's taking me away from here. Somewhere we'll never be found. We have to leave. We've only got five days to escape. No. Four days. Because he's taking me away in five."

"You can do it, I know you can."

She walked slowly towards the bathroom. "What if I can't?" She paused in the doorway. "What if I'm stuck with Larry? Forever."

"Even if he took you to the other side of the country you'd still find a way to escape."

"But you won't be with us. What if he leaves this door locked when he goes? You'll never get out. You have to tell him you're here."

"No."

"I can't go without you. Who'll remind me who I am?" She picked up the knife from where it had fallen earlier and was relieved Larry hadn't entered the bathroom. She had to be more careful with it. "We have to get out of here before then. I can't go with him. I just can't."

"Shelby-"

She tried to pry the plywood away from the window. "No." The knife slid, she grazed her knuckles and the knife clattered to the tiles. She wanted to scream. Or cry. She wasn't sure which. "Let me sit with you, Cameron." When he didn't answer she panicked. "Cameron? Cameron!"

"Please stop asking me. I need space. I can't-" he broke off momentarily. "Just don't ask me."

"Why?" The word burst from her.

"Why don't you put that stubbornness into getting the ply off the window?"

She stared into the darkness. "There are bars on the downstairs windows, even the one in the bathroom.

How do you know there aren't any on these windows?"

"Why would he board them up if there was?"

She bent and ran her hands across the tiles until she found the knife. "I don't know." Her fingers closed around it and she rose to her feet. "He's not sane. He can't be. If he's sane, neither of us are."

"Maybe we're all insane."

"Probably." She worked the knife in behind the plywood and levered. The knife started to bend and she held her breath. The plywood moved and her hands began to tremble in excitement. The nail held, but the knife snapped. She swore.

"What happened?"

"The knife snapped." She continued to clutch the handle. "I can't do this."

"You can."

"I can't. You're just going to have to try. I'll steal some food for you."

"Don't, it won't help me."

Shelby started to argue then closed her mouth, a hand pressed against her lips. "No."

"What?"

"He hurt you, didn't he? When he shot you. I mean, I know you were hurt, but it was more than a graze, wasn't it?"

"Don't worry about it, there's nothing you can do. Focus on getting out of here."

"How bad? Let me help you. Please, Cameron, can't I come and find out how bad?"

"Shelby. Enough. Stop hassling me." His words were sharp. "Just get the bloody ply off the window."

"Fine." Her words were equally sharp. She jabbed at the plywood with the broken knife, the blade about half its original length. Then the nail gave a little more and she reached out to run a finger along the edge of the plywood. "It moved. Cameron, I can fit my fingers between the ply and the window."

"I said you could do it. Now don't stop. I doubt you're that skinny, even with only one meal a day."

She laughed. She couldn't help it. They were going to get out of here. Pulling her fingers out of the gap, she levered with the knife again, sliding it along a little further up the side of the window. She worked at the plywood until her fingers began to cramp and she had to stop and massage feeling into them.

Sitting on the cold tiles near the toilet she leaned her head against the side of the vanity and closed her eyes. She could fit her entire hand in the bottom section now, but not towards the top of the window. She still had a long way to go. Continuing to massage her hands, she fell asleep.

* * *

Shelby woke as light hit her eyelids, forcing them open. She pushed away from the toilet lid that she was using as a pillow and scurried backwards, her first thought was of Larry and his torch. Her gaze was drawn to the light coming from the bottom corner of the window. Even knowing it wasn't Larry didn't stop the fear. Scrambling to her feet, breath coming fast, she stumbled from the room, slamming the door. She leaned against it, her hands covering her eyes as she tried to hold back her sobs. She couldn't stop shaking as she slid to the floor, her back pressed to the door.

"Shelby? What's wrong?"

"The sun." Her words were muffled by her hands across her face, her fingers keeping her eyes closed.

"You're going to have to say a few more words than that if you expect me to know what you mean."

"I can't go in there, I just can't."

"Why not?"

She couldn't answer him. How the hell was she going to explain the sun shining in her eyes had freaked her out? She continued to tremble, trying to stop. One of her arms crossed at her waist, the other at her shoulder and she held on tight as she kept her eyes closed. The dark was her friend, the light the enemy.

"Shelby?"

"I just can't, Cameron. Don't make me go in there."

"What about when you need to use the toilet?"

"Great, now my bladder feels full."

Cameron chuckled. "You only have to open the door and you'll find a toilet."

She held her breath. It didn't stop the trembling. She let out a long shuddering sigh. "I can't." Her voice was soft, pleading. "I'm terrified of the sun."

"Shelby-"

"No. I don't want to hear it. I know I sound crazy, but-" she broke off, remembering how it had felt being woken by the light shining on her face, thinking Larry was standing over her with his torch. When Cameron fell silent she gritted her teeth. It was worse. Now she felt alone. "Talk to me. If I can't be at your side at least talk to me."

"About what?"

"How long did you haunt Trent's street?"

"Weeks. Long tortuous weeks. Every afternoon after school and more often on the weekend. Sometimes even late at night." He chuckled, the sound a mixture of bitterness and irony. "I even got to know a couple of the neighbours by sight. There were two of them with dogs, which they walked of an afternoon. A smile and a nod and on they'd walk. I'd jog past, or continue to watch Trent's house if I was already across from it. I have no idea what they thought."

"That you were a stalker?"

This time his laugh came freely. "I never thought of that. But Trent didn't tell me to stop. If he'd asked me to stop I would have. I don't know how, but somehow I would have. It's not like he didn't know I was there."

"Why did you do that to yourself. Why didn't you forget him?"

"I tried. Then I'd find myself on the bus headed back there. You can't imagine what it was like. And then I had an idea, a compromise. It took me days to get up the nerve to go through with it. Every minute I wasn't at school or haunting Trent's street I was helping John on his car. Jeremy seemed to always be there. He's on all my sports teams. He can play any sport, and play it well. After practice and matches we sort of started hanging out. Then he'd come over to John's with me. He was one of those mates you're not sure how you ended up with in your life. They somehow plant themselves there while you're distracted."

"I know the type. The ones you usually end up

having to figure out how to get rid of without all hell breaking loose."

"Yeah, that's the type. Anyway, I got to the stage where I thought I was putting it off because I was procrastinating. Afterwards I wondered if it was because I already knew how he was going to respond…

Chapter Nineteen

"I'm gay."

"Okay." John's gaze returned to the rolling body. "I'm going to use this panel, it's better than the original one."

"What the fuck do you mean, you're gay?" Jeremy demanded.

John grinned at Jeremy. "Didn't realise you were so slow." He turned to Cameron. "Grab me a spanner. We'll take these panels off first."

Cameron started to walk back to the tool shed, but Jeremy grabbed him by the shoulder and spun him around. He shook the hand off his shoulder. "What?" The word came out sharper than he planned.

"Since when are you gay? You work on cars, you're good at sports and you like chicks. I've seen you checking them out. You can't be gay."

John started to laugh, not even stopping when Jeremy sent him a glare.

"Well," Jeremy demanded.

"I've probably always been gay." Cameron shrugged, not bothering to say that the girls he'd checked out had been pointed out by Jeremy first. "Probably."

"And that's why you've been hanging out with us?"

Cameron took a step back. "Get real. You're not my type. Besides, I'm interested in someone else."

"Don't worry about it, Jeremy. We'll get a carton later and I'll help you drown your sorrows."

Jeremy spun towards John, his fists coming up. Cameron grabbed his arm before he could swing. Jeremy shook him off with a snarl. "Don't touch me."

Cameron froze at the venom in his friend's voice. "Jeremy?"

"Stop being a prick," John said.

"Screw you," Jeremy snarled at John.

John grinned. "You're looking at the wrong person when you say that." He waved towards Cameron. "He's the one who's gay."

Jeremy gestured towards John with his middle finger before he turned back to Cameron. "So it's all been a lie? The sports? Working on cars together. Checking out hot chicks. All a lie."

Cameron shook his head. "I'm still the same person."

Jeremy shook his head. "No you're not. You're a liar." He stalked off.

Cameron stared at Jeremy's retreating back, wanting to run after him, wanting to explain. He turned to John. "How about you? Have you got anything you want to say?"

"Yeah." John's expression went neutral. "Where the hell is my spanner?" A split second later he grinned.

Relief rushed through Cameron, but he had to be certain. "I tell you I'm gay and you want me to get you a bloody spanner."

John shrugged. "Do you think I can remove the nuts with my bare hands? I know I'm good, but I think that's a little beyond even me." His eyes narrowed. "You are still going to help me fix her up, aren't you?"

"Yeah."

"Good. So why are you still standing around? Spanner." He threw his hands in the air and started forward. "Do I have to do everything myself?"

"No questions? Jeremy had plenty."

"I keep telling you Jeremy is an arsehole." He flashed a grin at Cameron. "I'm always right. You should listen to me. Time to get back to work or she'll never be on the road."

"Sally."

"No name."

Cameron grinned. "Lucy."

John strode towards the work shed, gesturing behind him with his middle finger.

Cameron continued to grin as he followed, grabbing a spanner for himself. By the time they had removed all the panels John wanted to use and sanded them back, the light was fading.

John started to gather up tools. "Guess we should call it a night. I've got an assignment due tomorrow and I haven't even started. The weekend's never long enough."

"Might be 'cause you spent most of Saturday working at the wreckers."

John shrugged. "The old girl isn't going to fix herself." He wiped his hands on a rag of indeterminate colour. He eyed his hands. "Give me a minute to wash up and I'll give you a lift home."

"Thanks. I'll cover," Cameron paused and glanced over at the ute, "Kylie."

"You want a ride, or you walking?"

Cameron grabbed the tarp and started to cover the ute. "You want help to fix Penny?"

"No. Name. Are you thick or something?" John shook his head and headed for the laundry.

Glancing down at the marks still on him, Cameron joined John in the laundry to wash the dirt and grease off his hands and arms. "You know you're going to name her. You'll give in eventually."

"I'll gag you first." They strode towards John's sedan that was parked out the front. "Everyone would thank me." He grinned at Cameron over the roof of his sedan. "Might even earn an award."

"Screw you." Cameron hopped in the car.

As soon as he was seated John eyed Cameron up and down. "Nah. You're not my type." He paused. "Although you don't get bored when I talk about the old girl." He grinned. "You going to tell me about the guy you're chasing?"

Cameron returned the grin. "That comment's probably more appropriate than you think."

"Yeah? Why's that?" John pulled onto the road.

"I seem to be doing a lot of jogging to his house these days." He kept to himself the part about jogging away from the house before he even spoke to Trent.

"Is that why you're losing weight?"

"Shit, it must be worse than I thought if you noticed."

"Nah, Charlie asked me why you've lost so much

weight." John laughed. "She's gonna be pissed she wasn't the one to find him for you."

"Thank god. We wouldn't last a minute if Charlie had a hand in it."

John pulled up in front of Cameron's home. He turned his head and met Cameron's gaze. "You should have told me ages ago."

"Told you what?"

"That you're gay."

Cameron frowned. "Why?"

John grinned again. "We could've got rid of Jeremy a lot sooner."

Cameron laughed as he got out of the car. He leaned back in. "You picking me up tomorrow morning?"

"Yeah. See ya."

Cameron nodded, shut the door and strode inside. His father greeted him not far from the front door. His heart sank when he saw the piece of paper his father held. The best defence was a good offence wasn't only true in sport. "What were you doing in my room?"

"Were you going to tell us about this?" Steven shook the paper.

Cameron shrugged. "It didn't seem important."

"You lost your licence and you didn't think it was important?"

Cameron snagged the paper his father waved under his nose. "Stay out of my room. I don't invade your privacy." He pushed past his father, heading for his room.

"You're grounded."

Cameron spun to face his father. "What?"

"You heard me."

"I'm eighteen."

"You're still grounded."

Cameron glared at his father. He opened his mouth to argue, then shook his head and walked away. There was no way in hell he was going to be grounded. What could they do? Throw him out? He grinned. Maybe they'd rethink that if he said he'd move in with Bryce.

He placed the paper on his desk and paused. He was tempted to ring Trent. No. He'd wait until he could see him. This was something he had to say to him face to face. Decision made, he showered and got ready for bed.

For the first time in weeks, he had a good night sleep. His father glared at him over the breakfast table, but it did nothing to ruin his mood. That wasn't ruined until they arrived at school. When he and

John reached the usual place they hung out at before school, Jeremy and several of the team were sitting around talking and joking. They fell silent as Cameron came close.

"Fuck off fag," Jeremy hissed.

"Find somewhere else to sit," the boy beside him said.

Cameron froze.

John laughed. "We were playing a trick on you, Jeremy." He pointed at him, grinning. "You should have seen him run home, his hands behind his arse as if we were going to rape him."

There was laughter around the group.

Jeremy rose to his feet, hands curling into fists. "Bullshit. He was serious."

"Nope, just a little experiment. He didn't believe me when I said you were homophobic. We thought he'd be the logical choice for the trick because of his uncle." John's hands went to his hips. "Score a point for me. I was right. Again."

"Bastard." Jeremy swung at John who ducked out of the way.

Cameron, finally able to move again, leapt forward to his friend's defence and grabbed one of Jeremy's arms. "Back off, Jeremy."

"Yeah, Jeremy." John grinned. "Or we're gonna

have to kiss you." He made exaggerated kissing actions. "Give me some tongue, Jere. Come on darlin." The last sentence was a perfect imitation of Simon.

Cameron laughed. So did the rest of the crowd.

Jeremy shook him off, glaring at him before he stormed away.

"So you're not really gay?" one of the boys asked.

John moved towards him with a lumbering movement that was a cross between a bear and a zombie. "It's me who is darlin. Come and get some." Grabbing the boy who struggled and laughed, John wrestled him to the ground. John eventually let him go, sitting on the ground, pulling one knee up to rest his arm on. "I think I'll go back to girls. They're less effort."

"What about the one who accidentally punched you in the jaw for kissing her?" Cameron held out his hand to help John to his feet.

"She wasn't a girl, she was an alien. Anyone that clumsy couldn't have been human," John said.

"It still brings tears of pain to my eyes every time I think about that date," one of the boys said.

"Tears to your eyes! It makes me want to cross my legs every time I remember it." John shook his head.

"I'd rather be gay than get within fifty metres of her. What a hazard."

Cameron joined in the joking, feeling half removed from the group. He'd hung out with these guys all through high school. He thought he knew them. Obviously not as well as he thought. When the bell rang, the group broke up and they headed towards their different classrooms. Cameron fell into step beside John.

"Thanks."

John shrugged. "They're dickheads."

"Yeah, but school would have sucked even worse if you hadn't done that."

John stopped and met Cameron's gaze. "I didn't do it just for you. Part of it was revenge. That little prick had no right to do that. If Jeremy hadn't stirred them up, most of them wouldn't have given a shit."

"And the other part?"

"Bryce."

Cameron frowned. "Uncle Bryce?"

John nodded. "He took me to my first speedway meet. He introduced me to cars. He's a legend and if I turned out just like him I'd be happy." He grinned. "Minus the boyfriend of course."

Cameron laughed. "Of course." They fell into step again, heading to class.

Chapter Twenty

Shelby grinned. "I like John. I hope you didn't forgive Jeremy."

"Not a chance. And yeah, John's a good guy. He's been my best friend forever. And I want you to tell him that if you leave without me."

"I'm not leaving you behind."

"Don't be a bloody idiot. If you get the chance you go. Don't wait for anyone."

"What if it's daytime?"

"Then you think of that gun Larry carts around and you make yourself run."

Shelby shifted. "I'm nearly wetting myself and I still can't make myself open this door."

"Don't forget there's no change of clothes if you piss those ones."

Shelby momentarily closed her eyes. Even the thought of opening the door made her body start trembling. But Cameron was right. She rose to her knees and opened the door a crack. The light made her close her eyes. It wasn't as bad. She could see a red glow through her eyelids as she crawled towards the toilet, pushing the door shut behind her.

The entire time she was in the bathroom she kept her eyes closed, shaking so hard she was surprised she didn't wet herself before she managed to get to the toilet. Then she was in the bedroom again, pressed against the closed door. She drew in a shuddering breath. "I can't do that again. I can't."

"What do you plan to do? Live with Larry forever?"

"No. But Cameron-" she broke off, covering her face with her hands. She swore. "Both ideas scare the crap out of me."

"Then sleep. Work on the window when the sun goes down."

"What if I sleep too long?"

"I'll wake you. Sleep."

"I've already slept."

"Pick. Work on the window or sleep."

She started to shake again. She swore. This was ridiculous. She could do this. Forcing herself to her feet, she grasped hold of the doorknob. She couldn't bring herself to open it. Her hand remained frozen and her eyes stared at the darkness of where the door was. Still unable to move, she lowered her gaze and her heart leapt. A faint light crept in under the door. Fear exploded. Larry would see it. If he came before dark he'd see it. She threw the door open and flung herself across the room, slamming her palms against the plywood until it was nearly back in place. The darkness settled around her.

"Shelby! What are you doing?"

"He'd see. The light. Under the door." She collapsed onto the toilet. "He'd see." Her words became a whisper.

"Can you pry it open again?"

"I don't know." She sunk her head into her hands. "I don't know anything." Sliding to the floor, she lay back, staring at where the ceiling should be. For all she knew there was a gaping hole above her.

"You okay, Shelby?"

"I don't know." The cold seeped into her body. Not for the first time she wondered how long Courtney had waited for her before she'd tried ringing. And how long before she'd rung her mum. She would have freaked. Would John have freaked if he'd waited for Cameron who hadn't turned up? "What does John look like?"

"What?"

"Your mate. What's he look like?"

"Strong."

She couldn't help smiling. "What does strong look like?"

"Like they can carry a lot of weight. Not just physical weight."

"What colour are his eyes?"

"Oh, you want the stuff everyone notices. He's about my height. Green eyes, brown hair, grease under his fingernails, as Bryce always points out, and a scar on his right shoulder. I tackled him when we were kids and he landed on a rock."

Green eyes, like Larry. She shuddered, trying to focus on other details. "How tall are you?"

"Six foot."

"Now I feel short."

"How short are you?"

Shelby smiled. "Five six."

"Midget."

She laughed, a reluctant sound that held a touch of fear. "What are the things not everyone notices about him?"

"He's loyal. Why do you think he goes on all the dates Charlie arranges for him. It's because she thinks she's a matchmaker. And the scar on his shoulder, everyone thinks he fell off a swing. We were told not to muck around near the garden beds because they're edged in rocks, but we did. There was a birthday party I wanted to go to that weekend and I didn't want to get grounded. I was nine and he was eight and he promised he'd never tell."

She tried to get comfortable on the tiled floor, but it was impossible. "Did he?"

"Never. You're the only other person who knows."

"You're lucky."

"Yeah." Cameron paused. "You'll get to meet him, but you have to give him a chance."

"You sound worried."

"He can be a bit abrupt with people when he first meets them, just until he decides if they're worth his effort. He'll soon see you are."

"You'll have to meet Courtney. She's my best friend, but I haven't known her forever like you've known John."

"I'd like to stay friends with you forever."

Shelby sat up. "You say that like it won't be possible."

"I say that like someone who knows there aren't always possibilities."

"Cameron." His name was a sigh as she pushed herself off the cold tiles and returned to the bedroom. "Let me sit with you."

"Maybe soon. Not today. But soon."

"Really?"

"When you get out of here you have to remember how to get back. You have to show the police where this place is."

"You'll have to remember. I can get lost in a car park."

"Take note of where the sun is. Or the stars if it's night."

"You do that."

"Shelby, stop arguing. We have to think of every possibility."

"Didn't you say there aren't always any?"

Cameron laughed. "John'd throw that comment back in my face too."

"Then stop being an idiot." She yawned. "I'm actually tired."

"That doesn't surprise me. You were up a long time last night."

"I'm going to rest for a few minutes. Don't let me sleep too long."

"I'll wake you when it's time."

"Okay." The word was spoken around a yawn.

Chapter Twenty-One

"Shelby. Wake up. Larry's headed up here," Cameron whispered.

She struggled to sit up, pushing her hair out of the way. "You said you'd wake me when it's time. I was going to work on the window."

"It's time to have dinner. Then you work on the window. Try and ditch Larry early."

Shelby nodded. Before she could speak again, the door opened and she looked up at Larry, torch and gun in his hands. She wanted to scream, instead she pulled on her Melissa personality.

"Daddy." She hurriedly rose. "You're home." Arms outstretched she threw herself into his waiting arms.

"All day I waited to get home to you. If it wasn't for the thought of you waiting for me, I couldn't stand working for those arseholes. They think they own me along with every blade of grass on their property."

"Forget about them. They aren't worth thinking about. But I am, and I'm hungry." She was surprised to find the words weren't true. When had she stopped feeling hungry all the time?

"You're right, honey. They aren't worth it. Come on, dinner it is. Only salad and cold meat tonight, it was too late to make anything else." Larry locked the door once she stepped into the hallway.

She was tempted to ask him why he locked it, but she didn't want to risk upsetting him. Remaining silent, she walked beside him down the stairs. In the kitchen she automatically sat in her seat and started to eat the food set out for her.

Larry sat across from her. "The past five days have meant so much to me."

Shelby stared at him. "It's only been five days." Shock filled her voice. "It seems longer. Like forever." An eternity.

Larry smiled. "It will be forever. You, me and hopefully Robert."

"How will you find him?" She wanted to make sure he didn't search the bedroom then decided it might be best to steer him away from thoughts of Robert. "How did you find me?"

Larry chuckled. "Cynthia's not as smart as she thinks she is. Using false names and trying to hide the two of you from me, but I found you. I watched. I waited. I figured out the pattern. Then I brought you home. I know where Robert is. But there's no pattern. And I can't wait forever for it."

Shelby frowned. No pattern? If he knew Cameron was in the bedroom then what sort of pattern did he need for that?

"I know, honey. It hurts me too that we might not be able to take him with us, but I can't risk her getting you. She's had you long enough. You're all mine now."

The look in Larry's eyes made her want to run. To scream and hide in the dark. She fought back the urge. "I missed you Daddy."

Larry reached across the table and patted her hand. "I know honey. I know." He smiled. "I bought Milo today, for Saturday's dessert."

"You're the best." She grinned at him.

Larry answered her grin with one of his own. "So you always say when you get your own way."

"I don't only say it then. I always say you're the best." She tried to sound offended.

He chuckled. "Yep. And what did you say to me when I wouldn't let you get your nose pierced?"

Shelby floundered. Her smile faded. What had she said? Panic flared at that thought and she quickly corrected herself. What had Melissa said? "I didn't mean it. How could I? You're the best."

"If you say so."

"I do." She nodded decisively and had another mouthful.

Once dinner was over, she helped clean up the kitchen, avoiding the chest freezer and sending frequent glances to the gun Larry still carried around. Would he ever stop carrying it?

"You want to look at the albums?"

She couldn't think of any reason they shouldn't. Not one she could be sure wouldn't upset Larry who looked so hopeful. "Sure. I love hearing you tell me about the photos. It reminds me of everything."

"I love remembering." Larry guided her to the lounge room where they sat at the coffee table. "Every moment of my life that's worth remembering has you kids in it."

"What about when you were a kid?"

Larry's face hardened. "You know I don't like to speak about my parents. Ever."

"I know, but there must have been something, a single moment that's worth remembering. That's all I wanted to know about."

"Not until you and Robert were born. Everything before that wasn't worth living through once, let alone reliving it." He picked one of the albums up off the floor and started to flick through it. "Ahh, look at this one."

Shelby wasn't sure how much time had passed before she called an end to the night, but they managed to look at one and a half albums. She had to stop before she became Melissa. Forever. She not only looked like her, she was now gaining her memories and half the time wasn't certain which memory belonged to who.

Once they stood in front of the open bedroom door, Larry asked, "Which one's your favourite photo?"

She didn't even have to think about it. "The one of you swinging me around."

Larry laughed and pulled her into the bedroom as he tucked his gun into the back of his jeans, still holding the small torch. "You're too old." But he turned her and encircled her chest with his arms, spinning around the room, the torchlight sending random paths of light throughout the room.

Surprise held Shelby silent for a moment. It didn't last. She laughed, her head leaning back on his chest as they spun around the room. Cameron was forgotten. The gun. Everything. She was Melissa, being spun around in her father's arms. Then they were stopping.

Larry laughed again. "Time for bed, honey." He dropped a kiss on her cheek. "I'm getting too old for that."

"No you're not." She followed him to the door. "You'll never be old."

Larry reached out and patted her cheek. "Not long now and we'll be somewhere really safe. Love you, honey."

"Love you too." With a smile on her face she watched as the door swung shut. Once it closed she sat on the floor, leaning against it.

"Shelby? Shelby."

She swore as her smile evaporated. "I'm losing myself. Oh god, Cameron. What if he'd seen you? I didn't even think of you hiding in here."

"He didn't, it's okay."

She leapt to her feet. "No, it's not. I can't get caught up like that again. We have to get out of here. I have to stay focused." She dashed to the bathroom and grabbed the knife from behind the toilet plumbing. "We have to escape, before I forget who I am. Before he finds you and before he drags me across the country."

"Stop panicking."

"I can't help it. I'm going crazy. Do you know how easy it is to be Melissa? She's me." Shelby frowned. "Or I'm her." She pushed the broken blade under the edge of the plywood. "Maybe we're one. You know, like those twins that absorb the other twin in the womb."

"No. You're Shelby West. I know you, just like I know me. We're not his kids. I swear."

"It seems so real. Picture after picture of me in the album. I feel like Shelby is the lie when I look at them."

"Melissa is the lie. You'll see. When you get out of here your parents will know you. And Courtney. She'll know you."

"If we ever get out of here." She levered another section of the plywood.

"How are you going with that window?"

"It's easier this time. Well, the parts I've already done are easier."

"See, you'll get there."

"Maybe." Silence fell between them for a moment. "You never told me what telling John you were gay had to do with your compromise."

"It took me a couple more days before I could finish sorting out the compromise. Dad hounded me about losing my licence and Mum begged me to stay home for a couple of days. I felt so guilty about what I planned to do that I gave in. By Wednesday I couldn't last another minute without seeing Trent. I hadn't seen him since Saturday. I paced my room all afternoon. I didn't even turn up for practice. By the time dinner was over I'd had enough. I walked out the back door. I had my phone and wallet, what more did I need? My sneakers were at the back door and I pulled them on and headed for the bus stop. It took ages to arrive. And every stop it made I felt like shaking the driver and telling him to keep going. To get me to Trent's house now…

Chapter Twenty-Two

Without hesitation Cameron strode to Trent's front door and knocked.

It took several minutes for Trent to answer the door. He stared at Cameron. "I hope you don't think it's my turn to stand on the other side of the road like an idiot."

Cameron shook his head. "I can give you everyone in my life, but my parents."

Trent stared at him a moment. "That's the last comment I expected to hear when I opened my door."

"I know it's not perfect, but that's all I can give you. I won't hide you from anyone else. I'd be proud to introduce you to my friends."

"What happens if your parents find out?"

"I'll deny it. Deny you, deny me, everything."

"And you think I'll be happy with that?"

Cameron shook his head. "I'm not happy with it. But I told my best friend about you. Uncle Bryce and Simon know. They're all who matter to me. I'm giving you more than half of them."

"I'm a fucking idiot."

"No, you're not."

"Yeah, I am." Trent eyed him up and down. "Come here." His lips slowly curved into a smile. "I want to drag you inside like I've been tempted to do so many times."

Cameron grinned as he crossed the last few steps between them. "Drag me."

Trent laughed, a deep drawn out sound.

Cameron closed his eyes as he let the sound wash over him. His hands pulled Trent to him. "God I've missed that sound."

"What sound."

"Your laugh." He opened his eyes, a smile forming. "You can't imagine what that sound does to me."

Trent grinned. "How about you tell me."

"How about I show you?" Cameron stepped forward so Trent was forced to step back. He pushed the door closed behind them and glanced around before his gaze was drawn back to Trent. "I have very fond memories of this spot."

"Want a replay?"

"Shit yeah."

★ ★ ★

Shelby swore as the knife slipped.

"Are you okay?"

"Yeah. No. I don't know." She wanted to curl up in the corner and stop thinking, but that wouldn't get them out of here.

"Take a break."

"I have to keep going. I'm so tired that if I stop I'll fall asleep. Keep talking to me. Keep me awake. I'm nearly there. Not much longer and I'll have the ply off and we'll be able to get through."

"What do you want me to talk about?"

"Trent. Tell me everything about you and Trent. I need to hear something good."

"Nearly everything about the next few months was good. He met John. He wasn't keen on the old girl, but he liked John. Said it was such a waste he's straight."

Shelby giggled. "Courtney says something similar when she meets a hot gay guy."

Cameron laughed. "If I had to pick one memory from my life that meant the most to me, I'd beg to pick two."

"Which two?"

"John lying his arse off to save me from getting

into trouble when he got hurt on the garden bed and Trent laughing. I couldn't spend enough time with Trent. The days he joined John and me while we worked on the old girl were the best days of my entire life." He chuckled. "Not that Trent helped, unless you call him suggesting removing our shirts would make us feel more comfortable was his idea of helping. He kept saying he was going to bring a beach chair and a cocktail and recline there all day admiring the view. John treated him the same as he did me."

"I can hear in your voice how much you care for both of them."

"There are so many good memories." He chuckled. "Like the time we got the seat in the old girl and John kicked us out of the cab because he's going to be the first one to make out in his own vehicle. And when we were choosing paint, all of us had opinions. John of course didn't listen. He must be finished the old girl by now. He was so close when I last saw him."

"How did you spend so much time with them? Weren't you grounded?"

"We found a compromise. Well, Mum found one for us. I improved my grades, stopped skipping practice and went to all my games. If I didn't the grounding would be enforced." He paused a moment. "Trent came to every one of my games. Sometimes with John, sometimes with Uncle Bryce and Simon." Another long pause. "Uncle Bryce kept telling me I should tell Dad, that he'd find out eventually and things would be worse. But I couldn't. There's no way in hell I could ever tell him. My throat freezes at that thought."

"How did you manage to spend so much time with Trent? Where did your parents think you were?"

He chuckled softly. "With John. Even the nights I stayed at Trent's, John covered for me. He didn't hassle me to tell my parents. He knew how they'd react. Well, how Dad would react. Mum would accept, just like she accepts Bryce. I think she'd be sad there'd be no grandkids though. She still gets a bit clucky at times. It can be so embarrassing when she's drooling over some stranger's baby."

Shelby laughed. "My mum does that too. But that's not as bad as when she starts comparing baby stories with the stranger. I hate it when she gets to the really embarrassing stuff like toilet training."

"Yeah, Mum does that too." Cameron laughed. "And she wonders why I don't go shopping with her. It's not just because I hate shopping."

"How did you end up here, Cameron?"

"Simon told me that I didn't need to worry about

telling my parents. The moment they saw us together they'd know because it was written all over our faces. I asked John. He laughed at me. Said I looked like a lovesick idiot and the looks we gave each other were bad enough to rot an entire classroom of kid's teeth. So I kept catching the bus when John couldn't give me a lift. And we kept our distance at games."

"Did he catch you at a bus shelter too?"

"It was my birthday. A Saturday. I'd spent the night with Trent and promised Mum I'd be home by ten. Larry wandered into the shelter and did that whole forgot his glasses trick like he did to you. I didn't suspect a thing. I was still grinning after leaving Trent's place. He said he'd been asked to go back to Sydney by his old boss and asked me to move in with him once I finished school, that he didn't care where he lived. Here or Sydney, as long as it was with me. I said yes. Told him we could move to Sydney where we could tell everyone. We had so many plans." Cameron fell silent.

"You could still go to Sydney with him."

Cameron spoke as if Shelby hadn't. "I love him so much it hurts to think about him. You'll tell him for me, won't you?"

"You can tell him yourself when we get away from here."

"My parents are important to me, but not like Trent, John and Uncle Bryce. Life would've been colourless without them."

"Oh. My. God."

"What? What's wrong?"

"Nothing. I could get out this window. It's big enough I could get out. And there's no bars."

"Go."

"What? No. If I can just fit through you won't be able to. I need to get the ply completely off."

"Shelby."

She waited for him to continue, but he didn't. "What?"

"Even if you completely remove it I won't fit."

"What?" She shrieked the word then pressed a hand against her mouth and hoped it hadn't been loud enough to wake Larry. "Then why make me work on this one? Why?"

"Because Larry would've caught you if you'd worked on the one in the bedroom. You have to tell them where to find me. Bring them back here. Please, Shelby."

She started to tremble, the knife falling from her hand. "I can't. Not on my own. Don't make me, Cameron. It'll be day in an hour or two. Already the sky has some grey in it."

"Think of the gun. Of Melissa. Do you want to be Mellie forever? To let Shelby die so Mellie can live?"

"No."

"Then you have to go. Now."

"Cameron-" her voice broke and she took an unsteady breath before she continued. "I can't leave you behind. How could you even think that?"

"Because you have to. Think of my family. Think of Trent and John. It's been two and a half weeks. You have to tell them where to find me. Please."

She nodded, her hands pressed against her chest. "Can you help me out the window?"

Silence stretched out. "I wish I could. Look at the stars. Take notice of landmarks. And trust no one. You have to make it home safe."

A broken sob escaped and she pressed her hands against her mouth. She closed her eyes and tried to picture her family. She could only see Larry. A shudder ran through her. "Okay." The lost sound crept back in her voice and she tried again. "Okay." It was a little better but she could still hear the fear in her tone.

Shelby stood on the toilet lid once she found the knife she'd dropped. Another deep breath and she started to wriggle through the window, letting the knife fall to the ground below. Several times she nearly fell, but managed to catch herself at the last moment. Then she was clinging to the side of the house. "Don't let him catch you, Cameron."

"Don't let anyone catch you, Shelby. And let them know where to find me. Promise."

"I promise."

"Tell John I know what he should call his ute."

"What?"

"When he finds me I'll tell him. Now go, quickly."

Chapter Twenty-Three

She lowered herself as far as she could. Her arms outstretched and burning she tried to see the ground below. It was impossible. Darkness filled the world. A scattering of clouds obscured the moon and most of the stars. Closing her eyes she let go, relaxing her body in the hope it'd hurt less.

Hitting the ground, she bit back the words that wanted to pour out and lay there gasping for breath. She needed to move. Aches and pains bombarded her and she hissed as her body protested the movement. Her hands skimmed across the ground until she found the broken knife. Rising to her feet, she stared up at the darker shadow of the house in a world of near darkness. Unable to call out to Cameron, she turned her back on the house and stumbled away.

Shelby glanced around, looking for landmarks. Everything was shadows, the stars and moon hid behind clouds. Her foot caught on something and she fell, rolling. She swore under her breath when she collided with a tree and came to a sudden stop. It took a moment before she could rise, still tightly clutching the knife. She pressed on, staggering and stumbling in the dark until she fell again, shrieking as she rolled down an uneven slope to land in a creek. It was impossible. How was she meant to find her way when she couldn't even see?

Gasping and struggling to rise she floundered in the water. She tried to get her bearings, her hand almost cramping from how tight she held the knife. Shivering from the cold water, she could see nothing but darkness in every direction. How was she meant to find her way back to Cameron? She wanted to return before she lost her way, but she had to keep going. Cameron wasn't the only one back there.

The slippery rocks beneath her feet made it hard to wade through the waist deep water. Then it grew shallower and she hoped she might be nearing the banks. No such luck. Shelby shivered and crossed her arms, the knife pressed against her side. The sky began to lighten further and a darker shadow rose up to her right. She headed for it and found herself clinging to a tree on the banks of the creek. More colour filled the area and she started to shake harder.

She had to find help before the day began. Still clutching her knife she left the creek behind, pushing through the scrub that stretched out around her, wincing at the twigs and rocks beneath her feet.

Random bits of conversations with Cameron came back to her. His address. Trent. John. She stumbled, wanting to stop. There was nothing but gum trees and scrub. How was she meant to find her way? She forced one foot in front of the other. Cameron needed her.

The sun was starting to tint the sky with colour when she stumbled onto a road. She wanted to cry then hide in a hole somewhere and wait till it was dark, but she couldn't. Cameron was relying on her.

Let them know where to find me, he'd said. And she'd promised.

She crept along the side of the road, her head swivelling as she tried to make sense of her surroundings. A car sounded behind her and seeing it was a dark colour she stood and waited, trembling.

The car came to a stop, a door opened and a man half rose. "Are you okay?"

His voice sounded so much like Larry's she panicked. With a scream, Shelby ran, crashing through the scrub, becoming disorientated. The day started to brighten and she stumbled back into a creek. The same one or a different one, she didn't have a clue. She tried to focus. Cameron needed her, but all she wanted to do was run and hide. Looking in both directions, she saw where the creek flowed under a bridge. A dark tunnel beckoning to her.

Gasping sobs and shivers kept her huddled under the upside down u shaped concrete that formed the low bridge. She tried to tell herself Cameron waited for her to bring help, but her body refused to move. She had promised to bring help, but no mental pep talk could force her from under the bridge.

The day was spent drifting in and out of sleep as she struggled to keep her head from going under water, the occasional sounds of cars crossing the bridge waking her. Each time she tried to force herself to climb out of the creek and clamber up onto the road, but what if it was Larry looking for her?

Exhaustion and cold pulled at her and it was only the thought of Cameron that kept her from collapsing. Over and over she repeated his name, her name and the names and addresses of those he wanted contacted.

When shadows started to fill the world, Shelby crept out, shivering. Her skin wrinkled and cold. It might be mid spring but the water had felt icy in the darkness beneath the bridge. Body aching, head drooping, she followed the road. Time spun out, becoming meaningless. She was nearly asleep on her feet.

She didn't realise anyone was there until she felt hands touching her arms. Then she struggled, screaming and striking out with her broken knife. They were around her. Behind her. In front of her. There was no way she could run.

"It's okay." A lady held out a hand. "I've called the police. You'll be home soon."

Home. No! She couldn't let them take her home to Larry. "Don't take me back there. Please. Don't take me back."

"I've seen your picture. On all the news reports."

She spun to face the man behind her. Breaths coming in gasps she kept turning, trying to keep watch on all of them. It was impossible. But they didn't move. They stayed out of arms reach. She continued to clutch her knife, watching warily.

When the police arrived she continued to hold her knife, pressed against her chest, refusing to let go. They tried to help her into the back of the police vehicle but she pulled away from the hands. They watched as she fell onto the back seat without help.

"We'll take you to the hospital. Everything will be fine," one of the officers said gently.

Shelby shook her head. "No. I don't need a doctor. Cameron. I have to find Cameron. Larry still has him."

"There was another kid with you?"

Shelby nodded. "We have to help Cameron." When the officer continued to stare at her, she said, "Please. I'm okay. Just a few scratches from escaping, but Cameron's hurt." She couldn't stop shivering.

With a nod, the officer closed the door making her feel trapped. She wanted to smash the window, instead she sat frozen, unable to move. Even when the police officer told her to buckle up she could only stare at him. He turned away first. She felt a small victory as she huddled against the door.

Her parents were at the police station waiting for her, Kyle beside them. She shrank back when they tried to pull her to them. Her father flinched away when she pushed at them. He put his arms around her mother instead. How many times had she rung him over the years, needing him to be there for her? And this is what it took. Bitter laughter welled up, but she didn't let it escape. Shelby stared at her parents. It didn't seem real. None of it. And the lights. There were too many lights and nowhere to hide from them.

She had to focus on why she was here. "Cameron."

"Are you ready to talk to someone, Shelby? The officers who brought you in said you mentioned there was another child with you."

She turned towards the female police officer. "Cameron Morgan. You have to find him." She recited his address, repeating it while the officer wrote it in her notebook as she fought the urge to hide from the lights.

"Why don't you come this way and tell us what happened?"

Shelby glanced towards the three people who waited for her, huddled together. She wondered where her father's girlfriend was. The police station was probably more than she was willing to face. How would she explain being in a place like this to her snobby friends? She turned to the officer and nodded, shaking her head when they asked if she wanted her family with her.

They listened while she spoke. Short sharp sentences. The bare facts. She didn't want to talk to them at all. At least they'd darkened the room for her, but only after she'd handed over her knife. They'd also offered her a blanket, but she'd refused. She didn't want to be trapped by it. A net to hold her.

The female police officer she'd first spoken to

entered the room and sat beside her. "Are you sure that was the name and address, honey?"

Shelby leapt from her seat, backing away from the officer as panic swamped her. "Don't call me that." Words of pleading trembled on her tongue, but she refused to let them spill. She had to hold it together. They had asked her again if she wanted to see a doctor. She didn't have time to waste on doctors.

"Shelby. Are you sure that's the name? Cameron Morgan."

Her body remained tense. She wanted to flee, instead she nodded.

"Are you sure you saw him?"

She shook her head. "I already told them," She pointed to the other two officers in the room. "We were kept in the dark. I only ever saw Larry."

"We found him the day you went missing."

"You found him? He's safe?" She frowned, confusion mixing with fear.

The officer shook her head. "We found his body."

"What does that mean?" She heard the rising note in her words as she took a step backwards. "Where is he?"

"I'm afraid he didn't make it." The words were gentle.

"No." The word exploded from her. "You have to find him. Larry still has him."

"He's gone. I'll get your parents for you. They can take you to the hospital. Have a doctor see you."

"No."

The woman had risen to her feet. "Then where do you want to go?"

"I want to find Cameron."

"We used DNA to confirm the body. I'm sorry, Shelby, but when you're locked up like that with no light, sometimes the mind plays tricks on you. I'm sure the hospital will be able to recommend a psychologist your parents can take you to."

Shelby glared at the officer. She couldn't believe they wouldn't help her. Someone had to listen. His family. She looked down at herself. It'd freak them if they saw her like this. Wet, dirty, rips in her dress. She'd have to go to her house first. Then she could see Cameron's family. "Where's my mum?" She had to help Cameron. There was no way she was leaving him with Larry. The police had obviously made a mistake.

"This way." The officer strode ahead of her and Shelby followed, shading her eyes from the glare.

She couldn't focus on the conversation between her parents and the officer. All she wanted to do was run. Run and hide. When her father reached towards her, she drew away, unable to meet his gaze, his words an unintelligible mix of sounds. When he gestured towards the exit, Shelby nodded and followed her family outside.

She was relieved to find it was night. There were lights, but nothing as bright as the sun. She could do this. Go home, get cleaned up and visit Cameron's family. Getting into her mum's car, she huddled against the door, ignoring the constant glances her brother sent her and the argument between her parents in the front of the car. Her mother wanted to take her to the hospital, but her father argued that she'd refused to go. Knowing him, he probably was glad of any excuse not to sit around wasting time at the hospital.

A couple of times they had tried to talk to her, but she wasn't interested. She couldn't let anything distract her from getting Cameron out of that house. Someone had to go after him. If the police wouldn't, then his family had to.

When they reached the house Shelby made her way to the bathroom. She took a change of clothes. Black jeans, black shirt. If she couldn't have the shadows she needed, she'd wear them. Once she was clean she reached for the bathroom light with a trembling hand. She squinted at the brightness, a stab of fear hitting her. A glance in the mirror showed her more than she wanted to see. She turned off the light. Gone was the serious look and the rounded cheeks. Her face had a hollow haunted look, her once fitted clothes now loose on her.

Returning to her room for shoes and socks, she rushed to the window and clutched the sill, her legs buckling and causing her to collapse onto the carpet and lean her head against the wall. It was too late. Day was coming. She couldn't go anywhere.

There was a light rap on her door.

"Yeah?" Still sitting on the floor, she turned to face her bedroom door as her mother swung it open.

"Are you hungry, Shelby?"

She thought of the roast dinner, steak and vegetables, and salad and cold meat she'd been fed this week. They all reminded her of Larry. "Soup."

"Okay. It won't be long."

While her mother went to heat up some tinned soup, Shelby stripped her bed and hung the sheets and bedspread over the curtain rod to block out the grey light entering her room. Her curtains weren't going to be thick enough to keep out the daylight.

When Katherine returned, she paused in the

doorway with a tray of food and stared at the window of the darkened room.

Shelby watched her mother, waiting for her reaction.

There was none. Katherine finally crossed the room and handed over the tray with the bowl of soup, cutlery and glass of water. She then left the room and Shelby had enough time to eat before she returned with new sheets and a bedspread.

"What?" Shelby demanded when her mother continued to watch her.

"We were so terrified." Katherine stepped forward, her hands outstretched.

"Don't touch me." She could understand why Cameron had wanted his corner all to himself. Every time they reached out to her she felt trapped.

"Shelby–"

She handed back the tray. Only the bowl was empty. "I need sleep."

Katherine stared at her a moment longer, the tray in her hands. "Call me if you need me." She turned and walked away.

Shelby closed the door and locked it. The light wasn't on. She had eaten by the light from the hallway and even that had been too bright. She lay on her bed, cringing at how soft it was. Taking a pillow with her, she lay on the floor, sliding under her bed. It was safest there. The light couldn't get her.

Chapter Twenty-Four

A burst of light woke Shelby and she screamed, scurrying out from under her bed to see her mother crouched beside it.

"I'm sorry. I'm so sorry." Katherine turned off her torch, her voice shaking as she rose to her feet. "I couldn't find you. I knocked, but when you didn't answer I had to unlock your door."

Shelby squinted at Katherine, the glare from the hallway making her shield her eyes. "Shut the door." The words came out harsher than she'd planned.

Katherine hesitated before she closed the door. "I've made an appointment for you to see someone tomorrow. They've slotted you in since it's an emergency."

Shelby looked towards her alarm clock. It was just after three. From the light in the hallway it had to be afternoon. "Is it still Friday?"

"Yes. Now about your appointment-"

"When's the appointment?"

"Ten a.m."

"I'm not going."

"Shelby-"

"I'm not going." Her voice firm, she turned her back to her mother. Tuning out the words that continued to fall behind her, she assessed her room. She needed a better place to sleep. Crossing the room she opened the built-in wardrobe. It was narrow and she had far too many clothes hanging in it. There were also shoes lying in the bottom. The clothes could go on her bed, the shoes under it. She wondered how hard it'd be to put a lock on the inside of her wardrobe door so no one could open it. She began to take out her shoes and clothes, leaving only the contents on the shelves.

"Shelby." Katherine grabbed her by the arm when she started to return to the built-in.

Shelby froze, expecting to find a gun at her mother's side. Her hands were empty and she shook her mother off, fighting back the urge to run. "Don't touch me."

"We were so worried about you."

Shelby looked at Katherine. Even in the dim light forcing it's way through the covered window she could see the shadows under her eyes and the weight she'd lost. There was nothing she could say. She didn't know what her mother wanted, but she had nothing to give. It took everything she had to keep moving, to not shut herself in her wardrobe and scream until she lost her voice. She stepped to the side and continued to empty the wardrobe.

"Can I help?" When Shelby still didn't answer, Katherine tried again. "Is there anything I can do?"

Shelby dumped the contents from her arms and stared at Katherine. She knew her mother only wanted to help, but she felt crowded. "Yeah." Her voice was soft. "Leave me alone." She watched Katherine a moment longer before she continued with her task. Behind her she heard a half muffled sob, but she couldn't help her mother. She had to focus on helping Cameron. Still removing clothes from the built-in, she heard her bedroom door open and close. When she turned back with another armful of clothes, the room was empty. Dumping them on the bed, she eyed the covered window and wondered if she'd be allowed to paint the glass. She doubted it.

By the time the sun was nearly set, Shelby had emptied her built-in and put her pillow in one end. She pulled out a pair of dark sunglasses and a broad brimmed hat, hoping they'd be enough to get her through the last light of the day. Snatching the car keys from the kitchen, Shelby found her family huddled in the lounge room. The talking stopped when they saw her.

"I'll be back later." She held up the keys before she opened the front door and slipped outside. Once she would've laughed at their stunned expressions. Now she hurried, got in the car and started it. She couldn't let anything distract her from saving Cameron. As she drove down the street she glanced in the rear view mirror and saw her father come running onto the road, waving at her to come back. Shelby ignored him and kept driving.

At the first red light, she entered Cameron's address in the GPS. It took her about twenty minutes to drive there. She was surprised they lived so close to each other. Maybe she'd seen him somewhere without even knowing how important he'd become to her.

Pulling up in front of the house, Shelby stared at her hands. They shook slightly and she wished she still had her broken knife. She removed her hat and sunglasses, wanting to look as normal as possible for his family. Her hands shook harder. She could do this. Cameron needed her to do this. She thought of him, locked in the dark room, alone since yesterday morning. That thought drove her from the car and to the front door.

She waited for someone to answer her knock. A tall man, broad shouldered in faded jeans and a well-worn t-shirt opened the door. Behind him hovered a woman, looking enough like him for them to be siblings.

"Can I help you?"

"Are you Bryce?"

He nodded. "Who are you?"

"Shelby. I was-" she broke off to swallow. It was harder than she'd thought it would be. "The police, they told me-" she closed her eyes momentarily and took a deep breath. "I was kidnapped by Larry too. Like Cameron."

Emily let out a cry and pushed past Bryce. "Come in. Please." She tugged on Shelby's hands.

Shelby wanted to shake her off, but she didn't want to alienate these people. They had to help her find Cameron. She gritted her teeth and let Emily pull her into the house and lead her to the kitchen before she drew away from her.

"Can I get you something? A drink?"

"No." Shelby shook her head, looking around. Thankfully it was nothing like Larry's kitchen. There were no bars at the windows for starters.

"Who's this?"

Shelby warily eyed the man who entered the kitchen, waves of anger pouring off him.

Emily reached out to the man. "Steven, this is Shelby. She's the girl the police told us escaped. The one who gave them information that should lead them to finding the-"

Steven interrupted, his words filled with anger. "It's too late now. It won't help him."

"But it might help some other kid, some other family." Emily's hands clasped together then unclasped again. "It might spare some other family this pain."

"How did she manage to escape and not our son?" Steven gestured towards her.

"Cameron helped me. He told me what to do."

Steven rounded on her. "He's dead. Understand? He couldn't help himself let alone you."

Shelby shook her head. "I know him. Why won't anyone believe me?"

"Because he's dead." Bryce's words were as harsh as Steven's had been. Emily made a whimpering sound and Steven pulled her close as he glared at Shelby.

"He can't be. We talked. For hours. He told me everything. About all of you. And Simon. About his friends. John, Jeremy, Charlie." Her gaze met Bryce's.

"Trent." Her voice softened like Cameron's always did when he spoke the name.

Anger flushed Bryce's face and he strode towards her, roughly grabbing her arm. "Enough. Haven't we suffered enough?" He dragged her towards the front door.

Shelby tried to pull away from him, fear making her want to run. But she couldn't run, somehow she had to convince them Cameron needed their help.

"Bryce." Emily reached for her brother, but her husband held her tight, murmuring to her.

Shelby looked back at them, stumbling as Bryce propelled her forward. He stopped once they were on the doorstep, the door closed behind them. She forced herself to hold his gaze, reminding herself this wasn't Larry. "You were the one he always turned to when he needed advice."

"Stop it." Bryce shook her. "Why are you doing this to us?"

She desperately tried to hold back her fear. Bryce had to help her. "He was in that room with me. He was all I had in there."

"He wasn't. I had to view the body. And do you know why? Because there was no way I was going to let his parents see him. That sick bastard removed his head and hands. A birthmark and a couple of scars was all I had to recognise him by."

She blinked, trying not to let the tears fall as her stomach flipped and nausea crawled at the back of her throat. "I'm not crazy. I know I sound it, but I'm not. He was there. Why won't anyone look for him? He can't be dead, he can't be."

The anger fell away from Bryce and he put his arms around her. "Shh." He ran his hand down her hair, like he was soothing a young child. "You're safe. They'll catch him."

Feeling trapped, she wrenched away from him. "I don't care about Larry. I should never have left Cameron behind."

"Is there someone I can call to come and get you?"

Shelby shook her head. "No." The only person she wanted to see right now was still with Larry. She didn't know how Larry had done it, but Cameron was still there and no one believed her. Maybe Larry was right and his kids really were alive. The police could obviously be fooled. She gestured towards her car. "I don't need a lift."

"You can't drive like this."

She shrugged. "I got here okay, didn't I?" She started to walk away.

"Let me drive you."

She turned back to him, shaking her head again. "When I first met him, he made me memorise three addresses. John's because he's been his best friend forever. Trent's because he loves him. And his parents' address. He told me he wouldn't need to give me your address because you'd be here. You're always there when you're needed."

"Shelby-" he broke off and cleared his throat. "He can't have been there with you. I saw his body. The day Larry took you I was viewing his body."

"No." She continued to shake her head. "You're wrong. You have to be."

"If I thought there was any possibility he was still alive I'd be tearing this country apart looking for him."

Shelby stared at him a moment longer, blinking back tears, trying to breathe past the lump in her throat. She turned away, walking towards the car, wishing it was night already. The dark was her friend. It was safe. But nowhere was dark anymore. There were too many lights. Even in the night. She climbed behind the wheel of the car and started the engine. Looking out her window she saw Bryce still standing there, watching her. She'd really thought his parents would help. That Bryce would help. Maybe John would believe her.

Chapter Twenty-Five

She put John's address in the GPS and waited for the map to load. It didn't take long for her to reach his house. She parked out the front, clearing the two addresses from the GPS. The day was drawing to a close, stars showing in the sky, very little natural light left. She started towards the front door then heard music coming from the side of the house. The sound drew her towards the back of the house and she stopped in front of the orange ute parked near a work shed. The windows were down and music pounded around her. She reached out to touch the door.

"Don't even think about it."

Shelby spun to see a figure step into the light spilling from the work shed. Cameron had been right. He did look strong. And not just because of the broad shoulders and muscles she could see. His shirt hung from one of his hands and he wore only low-slung jeans. He had messy brown hair and when he took another few steps she noticed his green eyes. A moment of panic was followed by relief as she realised they were a different green to Larry's.

"Don't think about what?" She spoke up loud enough for him to hear her over the music.

"Touching the paint. You might as well sand it every time you do that."

Shelby glanced over her shoulder at the ute. Her gaze was drawn to the bench seat and she couldn't resist smiling as she remember Cameron telling her John wouldn't let him make out there. Her smile faded as she turned back to him. "You're John."

He nodded, reached past her to turn off the music then stepped back. "Who are you?"

"Shelby West."

"Should I know you?"

She shook her head and stared at him. There had to be a way to make him believe her. Coming straight out and telling his parents hadn't worked. "You have a scar on your shoulder."

"You're a bit odd, aren't you?" He glanced down the side of the house. "Where'd you come from?"

"I know how you got it."

John stared at her. "What's really going on?"

"It's on your right shoulder and you got it when

you were eight. You told everyone it was from falling off a swing."

"That's because it was."

Shelby shook her head. "It was Cameron's fault. He tackled you and you landed on the rocks around the garden bed. You lied for him so he didn't have to miss out on a birthday party."

"How do you know that? We never told anyone." John covered the ground between them. "Tell me."

Shelby felt a tremble go through her body as John towered over her. She tried to remind herself Cameron trusted him, but she wanted to run and hide. "No one will believe me. They keep telling me he's dead. He helped me escape. He asked me to tell everyone where he is, but they won't listen." She blinked, but it didn't stop the tears from forming.

"No." The word was a sigh and John stepped away from her, the shirt falling to the ground. "Cameron's dead. They found his body." He hesitated. "Most of it."

She shook her head. "I spent five days with him. Five days locked in a dark room with only the sound of Cameron's voice." It had seemed so much longer. An eternity. "He told me about you. About Trent." She gestured towards the ute. "About the old girl." A watery smile appeared momentarily. "About trying to name her."

"You were with him before he died?" He reached out towards her.

Shelby stepped to the side, shaking her head. "The police told me I was kidnapped the day they found what they think is his body. But it can't be. They have to be wrong. I can tell you so many things. We talked for hours and hours. Well, mostly Cameron talked."

"About what?"

She smiled. "When he told you he was gay." Her smile became a sad laugh. "You asked him for a spanner. He was so worried about telling you. It took him days to work up the courage. But I think it was mostly because Jeremy was there. And you making everyone laugh at Jeremy when he set some of the team against him was a brilliant plan. You mean the world to him."

"He can't be alive. What's your name again?"

"Shelby."

"He can't. The police don't make mistakes like that. I'd give anything for him to be alive. Anything. But it's not possible."

"He told me if he had to pick one memory from his life that meant the most to him, he'd beg to pick two. You lying to save him from getting into trouble and

Trent laughing. He said the days he spent here with you and Trent working on the old girl were the best days of his life. You have to help me find him."

John shook his head. "What you're saying is impossible. I want him to be alive more than anyone else in the world. Except maybe Trent."

Shelby met his gaze, mentally pleading with him, feeling safer as the darkness settled around her. "He said to tell you he knows what you should call your ute. When you find him, he'll tell you."

John staggered as if he'd been hit. His hand reached out and grabbed onto the shed's doorway. "It's not possible. Maybe they're wrong. Maybe you were there before he was found. You escaped, right? Maybe the bastard killed Cameron after you left."

"I don't know what to think. I was taken last Saturday. I escaped yesterday."

John swore. "They found him Saturday." He stared at her a moment. "Why can't the police search where you were held?"

"It was dark when I escaped. I got turned around. I need someone to go with me and help me find the place. My parents told the police I can't go back there. You don't need to believe me, just help me find where Cameron and I were locked up."

"Okay. I can do that. Where do we start?"

She was tempted to ask him why he was going to help, but she didn't want him to rethink his decision. "There's a slight problem. Well, there's actually two."

"You sure there's only two?"

Shelby ignored his sarcastic question. "I need to get the location of where I was found from my parents. But I don't think I should go home and get it because they might not let me out again."

"Why not?"

She hesitated. "They think I've lost my mind."

John laughed abruptly. "Great. I'm going to let some crazy girl take me to some unknown destination so we can find the place where she was locked up." He met her gaze. "So crazy girl, where have you hidden your axe?"

"I knew I shouldn't have told you. You're not going to help me, are you?"

"I'll help."

Had she heard correctly? "You will?"

"Yeah, but think about everything you've told me and I'm still willing to help. What's that say about my sanity?"

For the first time in days a small measure of feeling safe mingled with her constant fear. "Cameron was right. You're loyal."

He held up a hand. "Don't go making comments like that and we'll get along fine."

She nodded then stopped. "I've thought of another problem."

"What? You need to stop off and sharpen your axe before we go?"

"No. I need to return my mum's car. If she asks the police to look for me, they'll know what car I'm in."

"That's easy enough. I can follow you and when you ditch the car at your mum's place we'll use mine."

"And we have to do this at night."

"Why?"

She couldn't say the words while he watched her. Looking at her feet, she forced them out. "I can't be out in the sunlight." Her gaze flew to his face at his laugh.

"Why? Do you burst into flames?"

She shook her head.

He stared at her a moment longer and when she didn't explain he shrugged. "Okay, crazy girl, nights only." He bent and picked up his shirt. "Give me a minute to lock up the old girl and let my parents know I'm heading out."

She nodded and watched as he wound up the windows and locked the car. He started to head to the back door of the house then stopped and turned to face her.

"Did you want to come in?"

She shook her head. "No. I don't do very well with people anymore. Or bright lights."

"You'll be here when I come out?"

She nodded.

John watched her a moment longer before he walked away. She noticed the white scar on his shoulder before he stepped out of the light and headed for the back door. When he came out, he had a black knapsack slung over one shoulder, his shirt was on and he tossed his keys in his hand.

Shelby headed for her car and when she was about to get in, John grabbed hold of her door. She looked up at him and waited for him to speak.

"Do you want my number in case we get separated?"

"I don't have a phone. I can give you my mum's address."

"Okay."

She sat in the car and rummaged in the glove box until she found a scrap of paper and a pen to write the address on, then handed it to John.

He pushed it into a back pocket of his jeans. "I'll see you there."

Chapter Twenty-Six

Shelby closed the car door when he stepped back and started the engine. She waited until John started his car before she pulled onto the road. Once they reached her house, she threw the car keys under the front seat and ran to John's car.

"Go. Quickly. Someone's opened the front door."

"Why do they think you're crazy?" John drove away from her house.

Shelby turned to watch her father stop beside her mother's car and peer inside before he looked up the street. "Turn here." She gestured to the intersection coming up.

"Well?"

"Why do you think I'm crazy?" She emphasised the word 'you'.

"You see dead people."

"I don't. He was alive. I talked to him. And I never

actually saw him. We were kept in the dark." She pointed again. "Turn right up here."

"Where are we going?"

"To a public phone."

"You can use my phone."

"I don't want my mum to have your number."

"It's set to private for numbers not in my phone book." He held the phone out.

Shelby took it and dialled her mum. "Mum–"

"What are you thinking? Haven't we been through enough? Come home, Shelby."

The word home caused a shiver to run through her and her other hand tightened on her leg. "I can't. Not yet. I need you to get me the location the cops found me at. Email it to me."

"What phone are you on? Give me the number and I'll text the location to it."

She felt like telling her mother, nice try. "I don't know the number. You'll have to email it to me."

"No. Come home and I'll think about getting it."

"I can't. I'll call you later. But I won't be home until after I get that location. And your car keys are under the driver's seat." She hung up before Katherine could speak again.

"I'm guessing there's another problem," John said once she hung up.

"Yeah." She looked out the window, still holding the phone. "Where are we going?"

"To Trent's."

"Why?"

"Would you rather go back to my place and have my parents give you the third degree?"

"No."

"You can tell Trent we're going to look for the place you and Cameron were held, but don't tell him you talked to him. I don't think he'll be able to handle it. He's really cut up about losing Cameron."

"You want me to lie to him?"

"I don't care what you do as long as you don't destroy him. He's barely holding on."

She wanted to say she knew that feeling. Instead she nodded. When they pulled up in front of Trent's house, she recognised it from Cameron's description. Then she noticed all the lights on in the house. "I can't go in there."

"Why?"

"All the lights are on."

"Are you serious?"

She nodded.

"I'll ring him and ask him to turn some off. Will that work?"

"And the front light."

"Okay." He held out his hand and she returned his phone. He got out of the car as he made his call.

Shelby sat there a moment and watched as he walked around the front of the car. He paused mid stride, nodded, then waved at the house. She looked towards the house in time to see a curtain twitch back into place. When he slid his phone into his pocket and continued towards her door, she got out of the car.

Dizziness hit her and she stumbled, reaching out for something to steady her. John grabbed her and she pulled away, backing up against the car as she stared at him, breathing fast through her mouth.

He held his hands up. "It's okay. I was only trying to keep you from falling."

She took a shuddering breath, slowly straightening, warily watching John. "I'm sorry, it's been a while since I've eaten."

"You're hungry?" He dropped his arms to his sides.

"Probably." She shrugged. "I think I've forgotten how to feel hungry."

"Come on, crazy girl. Let's see if Trent can make you something to eat." He gestured towards the house.

Shelby looked over to see the front door was open

and a man stood framed in the hallway light. "I can't go in there."

"What now?"

"The light. Behind him."

John sighed. "Okay. I'll get him to turn it off. Wait here." He strode to the house and a moment later the light was off.

Shelby walked towards him before he could return for her. She stopped in front of Trent, her gaze roaming his dimly lit figure. This was the man Cameron had loved and yet when he reached out towards her, she shrank back.

John stepped between them. "She has some personal space issues, Trent. And she's hungry."

"I turned the light off in the lounge room. If you want to wait in there I'll get something for her to eat." Trent sent her a glance past John's shoulders before he left them at the front door.

Shelby reached out and lightly touched John on the back of his arm. When he turned to face her she tried to smile. "Thanks."

"What happened? Did he hurt you? The one who kidnapped you."

She shook her head.

"Your bruises?"

"From when I dropped out of a second floor window to escape."

"What did he do? He must have done something."

"Larry didn't need to do anything. He had a gun."

John started to reach out to her then stopped, letting his arm fall to his side. "Sorry I called you crazy girl."

Shelby momentarily smiled. "I think I must be. I prefer that name to the silent looks and awkward comments from my family. I'd rather be called a freak than be treated like one."

John grinned. "Maybe I'm crazy too. That makes perfect sense." He gestured inside. "Come on and I'll show you where the lounge room is. That's if I don't kick my toe in the dark."

"It's not dark."

"Not everyone has cat eyes like you."

When they reached the lounge room, Shelby asked, "Can I use your phone again?"

"Sure." He handed it over.

The phone was picked up before it barely rang. "Shelby? Is that you?"

"Yeah."

"The psychologist said we can give you her number and–"

"Mum, all I want is the location. Can you email me the location?"

"Will you come home then?"

She couldn't help flinching at the word home. "Yes." She would, once she'd found Cameron.

"All right."

"Thanks."

"Don't hang up."

"I'll call you later. Once I get the location. Bye." She hung up, dropping into a lounge chair, unable to stop shaking.

Trent came into the room with a plate of sandwiches. "Are you okay?"

"Yes." She looked up at him. "No." She shrugged. "Maybe."

John took the plate from Trent and offered it to Shelby with a quick smile before he turned to Trent. "Don't worry about it. Once we figure out which institution she prefers we're going to have her committed. I'm booking in for the room next to her."

She took the plate. "Will you tap on my wall in the night?"

"Do you know Morse code?"

She shook her head in answer to John's question.

"Me neither. Guess we should learn that first."

Her shaking slowed and she had a bite of food. She

was tempted to reach out to John and thank him for distracting her, but she couldn't do it. The light touch she'd given him at the front door had been difficult enough.

Trent continued to stand over her. "Can I get you anything else?"

She wished she could tell this sad sounding man it was his laugh Cameron loved the best. What if he could never laugh again? They had to find Cameron. "You can ask me questions if you want." She wasn't sure she'd be able to answer them.

"John said you were kidnapped by the same man who took Cameron."

"Yeah."

"Why'd he do it?"

"He thought we were his kids. He wanted to love us, keep us safe and never let us be taken from him again."

"Where are his kids?" Trent sat down.

"I don't know, but we're… I'm pretty sure they're dead. Melissa and Robert. They were killed in a car accident."

"I can understand how losing your kids can send you off the rails," Trent said. "But why you. Why Cameron?"

"We look like them. He was the one driving. He couldn't accept he'd killed them."

John swore. "Then why'd he… why hurt Cameron?"

"Because Cameron fought him. There wasn't a single item left in the bedroom he locked me in. They had all become weapons. Even the mattress." She smiled slightly. "He barrelled Larry with it. And the blanket, it was a net. Even though Larry had a gun, Cameron still fought. Still refused to give in."

Trent began to sob and John dropped onto the arm of the chair beside him, awkwardly patting his back. "Hell. You know I never know what to do or say when you start to cry. Would it make me a complete bastard if I asked you to wait until I leave?"

"What am I going to do without him? How can I feel like doing anything other than cry? I don't even know what the word laugh means."

"Your laugh is one of Cameron's two favourite memories."

John swore.

Shelby clapped a hand over her mouth.

Chapter Twenty-Seven

"You weren't going to do this." There was anger in John's voice.

"It… I…" Shelby started to shake again, shrinking into the chair.

John swore and was instantly in front of her. "I'm sorry." He started to reach for her, his hands centimetres from her own. He dropped one arm to his side and ran a hand through his hair. "Give me some piece of shit car and I can fix it. Turn it into a show car if you want. I can't fix this. I haven't a clue what to do. Why'd he send you to me?"

"I don't know." Her words were whisper soft.

Trent joined John at her feet. "You spoke to Cameron? You were with him before he… before?"

"I don't know."

"What did he say? Did he talk about me?"

Shelby looked to John. "You have to fix this. I don't know what to say."

"Please." Trent reached out to her, but John grabbed his arm before he could touch.

"We don't know what happened, Trent. There's some confusion over the time frames."

Trent pulled away from John. "What does she think happened? Was she there?"

"The police think she wasn't kidnapped until Cameron was… until after."

"I'm trying to find the house Larry kept us in."

"I'm coming too," Trent said.

"Trent-"

"No." Trent jabbed a finger at John's chest. "You're going. I am too."

She looked from one to the other. "I don't know if I can find it."

"What do you need?" Trent asked.

"I need to check my emails."

Trent rose to his feet. "I'll turn my computer on for you." He started to walk away.

"No lights."

Trent stopped near the doorway. He kept his back to her. "Why? What happened?"

She clasped her hands together. "The dark's safe. The light brings Larry."

"Did he keep Cameron in the dark too?"

She stared at Trent's back. "The dark's a friend. Cameron taught me that." She watched Trent until he nodded and then walked away.

When they were alone, John rested his hand on the arm of her chair. "I won't let him get you again."

"He has a gun."

"I've got a cricket bat in my car boot. Well, technically it's Cameron's but he'd think hitting Larry with it was a good cause."

"I shouldn't ask you to come with me, but I can't do it on my own." She hesitated and her words were a whisper. "I'm scared."

John reached for her again then swore. "I'm sorry. I don't mean to keep trying to grab you."

Her fingers tightened on each other then she pulled them apart. Her hand hovered above John's that was still on the armrest. Silence filled the room. How many times had she begged Cameron to let her be with him when he was hurting? It had hurt her as much not to be able to comfort him. "I'm sorry too." She forced her hand to drop the last few centimetres. The warmth of John's hand radiated into her own cold hand. She hadn't realised how cold her hand was until she had the comparison.

"You don't have anything to be sorry for."

"I keep pushing you away. I'm sorry. I know how that feels."

"Who pushed you away?"

She shook her head. "You won't believe me."

"I want to. You can't imagine how badly I want to."

She felt his hand tense under hers. "I don't know what's real anymore. Voices in the dark. Me. Melissa. Maybe my escape's a dream and I'm still there, locked in the dark waiting for Larry to let me out for a few hours each night. Long enough to eat and wonder who I really am."

"Don't worry, crazy girl. I know exactly who you are."

"Who?"

"Whoever the hell you want to be."

She tightened her grip on his hand, wanting to pull him to her and feel his comforting warmth through her entire body. But she couldn't bring herself to get that close.

"The computer's on."

Shelby looked up to see Trent in the doorway. "Okay."

"And the lights are off. Can I use a torch?"

"No." The word burst from her and her fingers bit into John's hand.

"What about a candle?" John removed the empty plate from her lap and put it on the floor.

"I don't know."

John placed his other hand over hers. "How about we try. If you hate it we can blow it out."

She thought about it, her body tense, her breathing jagged. "Okay."

John continued to stare at her as he spoke. "Get a candle, Trent."

When the tiny flickering light was brought into the lounge room Shelby tensed further. Then a shuddering breath of relief filled her lungs and she reached out to grasp John's shirt as she made a fist against his heart. This time the dizziness she felt was from relief. "Candles. We can have candles." She felt her eyes water.

"That's good, crazy girl. I'd hate to have a naked birthday cake next month."

"It's your birthday next month?"

"Yeah. November. I'll be eighteen." John paused. "You still want to use the computer?"

She nodded and let go of his shirt. He continued to hold her hand between both of his. When he stood up, he pulled her with him. "She didn't say when she'd send me the location."

"It doesn't matter how long it takes. I've got nothing planned for the rest of the weekend."

When they reached Trent's study, Shelby's gaze was drawn to the photo Trent placed the candle near. "Is this him? Is this Cameron?" An athletic looking boy grinned out of the photo.

Trent nodded and reached out to run a finger across the top of the frame. "When I think of him he's always smiling like this."

"You can see how much he cares for the person he's looking at," Shelby said.

"I took the photo," Trent said.

She nodded as she sat at the desk, wishing she'd brought her sunglasses with her. "Can the brightness of the computer be turned down?"

Trent reached out to press a couple of keys. "I'm sorry. I didn't think of that."

Shelby pulled up the web page she needed. "That's okay." She signed into her email account and glared at the lack of emails from her mum. "She hasn't sent it yet."

John shrugged. "So we'll wait. What do you want to do?"

"I don't know."

"I've got a stack of DVDs if you want to watch something," Trent offered.

She shook her head. The brightness of the computer screen was bad enough. She didn't think she could handle the television.

"You look tired. Do you want to have a rest and I can wake you in an hour to check your emails?" John suggested.

"I don't know if I can."

"You can use the bigger spare bedroom," Trent said.

"I'll show you where it is." John held out a hand to her.

She nodded and rose from the chair, taking his hand. When they reached the spare room, she stared at the bed. It was an ensemble. No room to sleep under it. She started to turn away.

"What's wrong?"

She stared into John's green eyes, the candle flame flickering in them. "You're going to think I'm even crazier than you already do."

"Try me."

"There's no space under the bed."

John's gaze was drawn to the bed. "I guess that depends what you want to fit under there."

She looked down at the carpet beneath her feet. "Me." The word was a whisper.

"Nah, you're not that skinny."

She turned away.

"Shelby."

"Yeah?" She looked down the hallway.

"Why do you need to sleep under the bed? What's wrong with the mattress?"

"It's too soft. And if I'm under the bed the light can't get me." She turned to face him.

"Sunrise is hours away."

"There's still light bulbs."

"That I can fix." John strode into the room and removed the light bulb.

"There's one in the hallway."

A few seconds later he placed both bulbs on the bedside drawers in the spare room. "Now what?"

"What if you fall asleep and the sun comes in?"

"I wouldn't. But what if I throw the blanket over the curtain rod?"

Shelby nodded and watched as John made the room safe. "Thank you."

He flashed her a grin. "Anything else you want me to do? If it's stand on my head I have to warn you I've never been very good at that. Back flips I can do. Handstands, not so much."

"You can do a back flip?"

John chuckled. "Yeah."

"How did you learn that?"

"Picture five guys, a beach and several bottles of tequila. I bet if someone had thought to record it all we'd have had a YouTube hit."

Shelby laughed softly. "Was Cameron there?"

"Of course. It was about a year ago."

She ached to tell him how much his friendship had meant to Cameron, but he didn't want her to talk about the impossible.

"You going to take a nap now?"

She nodded and walked to the other side of the bed where she lay down on the floor. As she curled onto her side John's indistinct figure came to sit against the wall beneath the window. "You don't have to stay in here."

"I promised to keep you safe."

Her throat tightened. "No wonder you were so important to Cameron."

"Sleep, crazy girl." His voice was soft.

Chapter Twenty-Eight

Shelby stared at John's shadowy form several more minutes before she closed her eyes. Sleep came quicker than she expected and she was caught up in disjointed dreams. Endless corridors, dark rooms and torch light cutting through the dark as she tried to avoid it. Then Larry was in front of her, Cameron at her side as they stared down the barrel of the gun. A scream escaped as she tried to reach out for Cameron.

"Hush, crazy girl. You're safe. Everything's safe."

"Cameron?" She felt warm skin and hard muscles as arms encircled her. The beat of a heart sounded against her ear.

"It's John. Shh, you're safe."

She couldn't stop trembling, cold and hot at the same time.

"Don't cry, Shelby."

She heard the rumble of his voice against her ear.

"I'm not," she whispered, then realised her cheeks were wet. "He's not dead. He can't be."

"I want to believe you. I really want to believe you."

"What time is it?"

"Last time I looked it was nearly four."

"I have to check my emails. You should've woken me." She pulled away. His arms tightened momentarily before he let her go.

"You left your email account signed in and I've been checking regularly. There's no emails from your mum, unless the one with the subject 'Meet hot Russian girls' is from her."

"Unless she's been taken over by aliens I'd say it isn't." She sighed heavily. "Why hasn't she sent it yet?"

"I don't know. You could ring her and ask."

She shook her head. "No. That's probably what she wants. When she sends it I'll ring, just like I told her."

"Think you can get some more sleep?"

"What if I have another nightmare?"

"You want to tell me about it?"

She shook her head. "No."

"What can I do?"

"Talk to me?"

"I have no idea what to talk about other than the old girl."

Shelby grinned. "Isn't that your method of getting rid of blind dates?" When she heard his sharply indrawn breath, she winced. "Sorry. I didn't mean to say that. I know you don't want to hear-"

"It's okay. I shouldn't have stopped you from talking about him."

"Tell me about your car."

"Ute."

She rolled her eyes. "Car. Ute. It's got wheels, hasn't it?"

"It's got more than wheels."

She lay on the carpet, a slight smile still in place. "Then tell me what it has got. I could do with some more sleep."

John chuckled. "Nice to know you expect me to bore you back to sleep. Are you trying to give me a self esteem problem?"

"Is that possible?"

"Haven't you heard that a guy's ego is related to their vehicle? If you're calling the old girl boring you must be calling me boring too."

She smiled at the lighthearted tone of his voice. "Thank you."

"For what?"

"For caring enough about a stranger that you'd try and distract her when she wakes up screaming."

"That part wasn't a problem. It was being called another guy's name that destroyed my self esteem."

"I was dreaming about him." She reached out a hand and John moved closer to take it. "And Larry."

He lay down beside her, his face centimetres from hers, his arm bent to pillow his head. "I won't let him get you. Go back to sleep."

"Tell me about your ute."

He chuckled. "Okay."

"Thank you." Her words were quiet.

"I already had my sedan, but that was only because it was cheap and I wanted a car the day I got my licence. Something I wouldn't care if it got dented. Or people sanded the paint off with their fingers when they played in the dust on it."

"How was I to know? I'm not a car nut," she muttered.

"When she came into the wreckers I knew I had to have her. She was missing panels, needed a new interior, had been in an accident and didn't even have a tray. But I could see what she'd look like the moment I saw her. Mum freaked and said I wasn't turning her yard into a wreckers, Dad laughed and said not to look at him when I got stuck fixing her up.

Cameron said with the way I was talking about her it sounded like she needed a name." He laughed softly. "My boss said there is a sucker born every minute and why did he always end up employing them. I started looking for the parts I needed the day I brought her home."

Shelby smiled as she listened to John begin describing each part he found. She let his deep voice surround her in the softly flickering light and guessed there was a candle on the bedside drawers. Her eyes closed and she continued to hold his hand, his warmth seeping into the coldness that seemed to permanently surround her. And to think she'd thought it'd be a hot summer. She was still smiling as she drifted back to sleep.

Chapter Twenty-Nine

"Shelby."

"Hmm." She kept her eyes closed, trying to go back to sleep, her hand drawing the warmth it held to her cheek.

"Crazy girl. Wake up."

"John?"

"Yeah." He chuckled. "Who's hand did you think you were trying to steal?"

Shelby became aware of his hand tucked under her cheek and she let it go. "Sorry."

"I'm not complaining, just wondering."

"It was the warmth I was stealing. Not your hand." She sat up.

John sat up too, reaching out to press the back of his hand to her cheek. "Do you want a blanket?"

"No. They make me feel trapped." But she guessed

she needed to get used to them again sometime before winter arrived.

"I've got a hoodie in the car. I can get it for you."

Before Shelby could answer, John's phone beeped and he checked the message, chuckling.

"Who is it?"

"Trent. He said if we didn't hurry up he was opening your email. He's not very patient I'm afraid."

"Trent's been checking for the email?" She frowned. "I thought you were."

"I tried. You wouldn't let go of my hand. I turned down the brightness on my phone and sent a message to Trent to keep checking for you."

"What time is it?" She rose to her feet and stretched, wincing as her bruises let her know they were there.

John stood up and glanced at his phone. "Twenty to five. Nearly sunrise."

Shelby closed her eyes and took a deep breath before opening them again. "Why did she leave it so late to send?"

"Does she know how you feel about sunlight?"

"Yes." Her voice was a whisper. "I bet she did it deliberately." Pain filled her voice. How was she meant to look for Cameron in daylight? Drawing in a shuddering breath, she pushed down the panic. "Let's see if she sent the location."

John nodded and walked with her to the study, pausing to pick up the candle as they passed the bedside drawers. Trent was pacing the floor of the study and stopped when they entered. He hovered at Shelby's shoulder as she opened her email.

Relief washed over her. "We have a location to start from."

"You want my phone so you can ring your mum?"

"Yeah." She took John's phone and quickly dialled. It was answered instantly. "What took you so long?"

"Come home, Shelby."

"I can't. It'll be daylight shortly."

"Then come home. You won't want to be out now."

"If that's your plan it's backfired. I can't get home before sunrise. I'll see you after dark."

"Shel-"

She hung up and handed the phone to John. She stared at the email. "How do we find where I was? I can't go out there."

"Let me have the seat. I'll use Google Earth to try and find the area." Trent sat in front of the computer as soon as Shelby had moved. He looked up at her. "Is there anything you can tell me to help find it?"

Taking a deep breath, she recounted her escape from Larry. Only the moments after she left the house. She couldn't bring herself to tell them how she'd left Cameron behind.

Trent nodded. "It might take a bit of time to find the areas to check. If you're hungry John will show you where the kitchen is. I've covered all the windows for you."

"Thank you."

Trent reached out towards her then stopped midway. "Will you tell me everything later?"

She swallowed hard and reached for his hand. She had to stop pushing people away. Had to stop being afraid every time someone reached for her. "Even if everyone keeps telling me I couldn't have met him? That I'm psychotic and need to see a shrink."

"We should get along just fine then. Everyone thinks I am too."

"Trent-" John began.

Trent shook his head. "I don't want to argue about it. I haven't got a clue how to explain anything, but I believe she and Cameron were locked up together."

"That's only because you can't stand to think he was there alone."

"They were together," Trent stated.

John ran his fingers through his hair. "I'm

surrounded by lunatics." His gaze fell on Shelby. "Come on, crazy girl. Let's feed you before you pass out."

"I'm not hungry. I want to watch Trent look for the house."

"You are hungry. You just don't know it yet." John held out a hand and waited for her to take it.

Shelby clung to Trent's hand a moment longer before she let him go and walked past John, ignoring his hand. "I shouldn't have told you that. Now you're always going to think I don't know when to eat."

John fell into step beside her, carrying a candle. "You'll figure it out again. Now, what do you want for breakfast?"

John made eggs and toast, took a plateful to Trent then joined Shelby at the table. By the time they'd eaten, tidied and washed up, Trent came running into the kitchen.

He waved maps he'd printed out. "I've found some places it could be." He spread the maps on the table. "It depends which bridge you spent the day under. There's three of them within reasonable distance of each other and each leads off to a different creek. There's one more similar bridge, but it's a few hours away from them so I'm guessing that's not it. It'd be better if we had more exact measures of time, but we can find the house. As soon as we know which bridge it'll pinpoint the area we need to search."

Shivering, Shelby wrapped her arms around herself, and stood staring at the maps in the flickering candlelight. The last place she wanted to see was Larry's home.

"Don't start the conversation without me." John strode for the doorway, pulling his keys from his pocket. "I'll be right back."

"Where are you going?" Trent asked.

"One minute," John threw over his shoulder.

Trent stared at Shelby a moment. "When you were with him, how was he?"

She didn't need to ask who Trent meant. Cameron was constantly on her mind too. "I don't know. We were always in the dark. The windows were boarded up and the light bulbs had been taken out."

"What did he sound like?"

Shelby smiled slightly. "Depends what he was talking about. Every time he spoke your name his voice changed. The only word I can use to describe it is love."

Trent dropped heavily into a kitchen chair. "I keep thinking it must be a mistake. Cameron's strong. How could anyone overpower him and kidnap him?"

When she saw Trent's tears, Shelby felt her own begin. "He didn't. He tricked us. Used drugs."

John burst into the kitchen, holding a black hoodie out to Shelby. He looked between them and swore. "I can't leave you two alone for a second. Focus on the maps for now or we'll never figure this out."

Shelby took the hoodie and hugged it to her chest. "I don't think I can do this."

Trent pushed the paper across the table towards her. "Have a look. Do any of these aerial views look familiar?"

Looking at the pictures she shook her head. "I think I have to be there."

"Shelby."

She turned to look at John.

"I know you think you can't be in the sunlight-"

"I can't."

John held up a hand. "Wait a minute. Hear me out." He fell quiet. When she nodded, he continued. "You won't be alone. We'll be with you." He held up his hand again. "Uh-uh. Hear me out."

She pressed her lips tightly together and glared at him.

"I know it won't be easy, but they're expecting you to wait until night. They think you won't be able to do anything and they'll take care of it. You'll never get to go back there."

"What makes you think I want to go there?"

"I don't. But I know I would. I know if I had to leave someone behind I'd have to be the one to get them out."

She continued to meet John's gaze. "You don't think he's there."

"It doesn't matter what I think. What do you think?"

She closed her eyes as she replayed the last moments she was in Larry's home. She swayed, her eyes flying open as a hand grasped her upper arm. She stared into John's green eyes. Absolutely still. Forcing herself not to pull away. Reminding herself John was safe, that she didn't have to pretend he wouldn't hurt her. He really wouldn't. "I don't know if I can."

"We can't make you do this."

"I can borrow a four-wheel-drive with dark tinted windows," Trent said.

"How dark?"

Trent waved his hand around the kitchen. "It won't be as dark as this."

Her stomach muscles tightened and she shivered.

John let go of her and took the hoodie. "What was the point in getting this for you if you're going to stand there shivering?" He held it out so she could slip her arms into the sleeves.

"Thank you." She didn't tell him it was going to take more than a hoodie to stop her shivering. She faced Trent. "Can I see it? Try it?"

Trent nodded. "Yes. If you can't manage it, we'll wait for dark."

She watched him leave the room and turned to John. "Larry might be there."

"What does he normally do on a Saturday?"

The word Saturday echoed in her head. This time last week she was meant to be catching a bus. She covered her face with her hands. "I can't do this."

"Shh, I'll tell Trent not to bother." He started to move away.

Chapter Thirty

"Wait." Shelby reached out and grasped John's arm. Her heart raced. She tried to tell him it was okay. She could do it. Instead she dropped her gaze to the ground, her shoulders slumping. "I'm a coward," she whispered.

"Not that I've noticed."

"You weren't there. I told him what he wanted to hear. Cameron fought him while I pretended to be his daughter."

"Sounds like a smart move. You're here, safe. Aren't you?"

Trent entered the kitchen saving her from answering. "The four-wheel-drive will be here in less than half an hour. Do you want a shower or anything? I don't have a change of clothes for you though."

She shook her head. "No."

John reached out and pulled her hood up. "I've got sunglasses in the car. They're not very dark."

"I've got some mirrored sunglasses," Trent said. His lips slowly curved into a smile. "They're lime green. I'm not sure they'll go with the Goth look you seem to be aiming for."

Their efforts for her made her vision blur and she pressed a hand to her mouth.

"You don't have to wear them," Trent's smile faded quicker than it had arrived. "It was only a suggestion."

"I'm sorry. I want to wear them. I just-" she wiped at her eyes, not sure what to say.

"I'll go find them." Trent hurried from the room.

John laughed softly. "Now he might cut me some slack when I want to run from the room when he starts to cry."

"Don't you ever want to cry?"

John shook his head, his eyes narrowing. "No. I want to kill Larry."

She stepped back at the look in his eyes.

"Hey." He reached out to her, his expression softening. "Only Larry. No one else, okay?"

"You're serious?" Was this why he wanted to go with her? No, it couldn't be. No one would even think of taking on an armed lunatic.

"If I had the chance I'd beat the crap out of him. And I don't know if I'd be able to stop." His hand tightened on her arm. "Cameron didn't deserve what he did to him. No one does, but especially not Cameron." He paused. "And you didn't deserve what he did to you either."

"He didn't do much."

"No? Then why are you terrified of the light?" His jaw clenched. "See. I can't even mention the word without fear coming into your eyes. No wonder the thought of killing him is regularly on my mind."

"I found the sunnies." Trent held them up as he entered the kitchen. "And I got a text a few minutes ago to say my friends are nearly here."

Shelby tensed.

John rubbed her arm where he had held it. "It's okay. We're not going to force you to do this if you can't."

Shelby shivered, closing her eyes to savour the sensation. For once it wasn't from fear. When John's hand left her arm, she opened her eyes. "Maybe… maybe I might be able to hide under a blanket." A net. She pushed the thought away. She had to get past all this craziness. Somehow.

A horn beeped. "That'll be my friends." Trent headed for the front door.

"I don't want you to feel trapped, crazy girl."

"You haven't seen crazy until you've seen me in the light."

"Would it help if I hid under the blanket with you?"

Shelby couldn't help the laughter that erupted from her.

"What?" John eyed her cautiously.

She was still smiling. "No wonder you have to rely on your cousin to set you up if that's the kind of comment you make to girls. It sounded like the winner of the worst pickup line."

John grinned. "I'm sure I could come up with a lot worse."

"I hope you can. I'm going to need all the distractions possible when I'm in the car."

"Four-wheel-drive."

She rolled her eyes. "Vehicle. I can say that, can't I? No matter what it is."

"Yeah." He paused. "Do you want to wait here or come with me while I get a blanket?"

"Come with you."

John nodded, took her hand and headed for the linen cupboard. He chose two thick blankets. He'd barely closed the cupboard when Trent found them.

He held up a set of keys. "I've put the four-wheel-drive in the garage. The interior light's off, and the garage light."

John turned to Shelby. "Are you ready?" When she nodded, he continued. "I'll grab my bag and then I'm ready. Go with Trent to the garage."

"I have to get the maps," Trent said.

"I'll get them," John offered. When Trent nodded, John headed for the kitchen.

Shelby watched him go. She wanted to run after him and tell him to be careful. Even reminding herself he was only going to be a couple of rooms away made no difference. Nowhere was safe. Not anymore.

"Are you coming?" Trent asked.

She dragged her gaze to Trent. "Yeah."

"Come on then." He led her back to the front door, opening a door to the left of it. The external garage door was rimmed in light that struggled to enter, casting a dappled gloom over the area.

Shelby got into the back seat of the vehicle. So far, so good. But they were still in a dim garage and she wasn't covered by a blanket. She tensed when Trent climbed into the front seat. She could do this. Cameron needed her and no one else was willing to help. She had to do this. When the door beside her opened, she flinched back.

"Hey, crazy girl. It's only me." John dropped his bag and a cricket bat onto the floor. "Shift over." He waited until Shelby moved to the middle of the seat before he got in and closed the door.

"Let me know when I can open the garage door," Trent said.

"It might be a while." Shelby looked out the rear of the vehicle. It was fairly dark. She didn't want that to change.

"That's okay. Whenever you're ready. I haven't any place to be," Trent said.

"Don't you work?" Shelby asked. "IT, isn't it?"

"I've taken time off."

She turned to John. "What about your job?"

"My next shift isn't until Monday after school."

"School." She groaned. "They're going to expect me to finish year twelve."

"I bet they can give you stuff to do at home." John unfolded one of the blankets. "Are you ready for this?" He leaned forward and whispered near her ear. "I lost my teddy. Can I snuggle under the blankets with you instead?"

She giggled, amusement and fear blending. She tried to focus on the amusement. "Is that the best you can do? I've heard worse."

"Give me time to warm up." He pulled the blanket

over them. "Which I'm going to do pretty quickly under here." John buckled up. "You ready for Trent to raise the door?"

"I guess." There was that little girl lost sound back in her voice. She buckled up and tried again, trying to ignore the feeling of being trapped by the blanket. "Yes." That sounded much better.

"Okay, Trent. Raise the door and we'll see how this works."

Shelby froze as the space around them lightened.

John took her hand. "Breathe."

"I'm trying to."

"Do you think Trent can back out of the garage and you can see what it's like?"

"Maybe."

John raised his voice. "Okay, Trent. Let's sit in the driveway for a bit."

The car started and Shelby gasped as the light level increased. "I can't do this." Her hands clasped together against her chest, white knuckled and trembling.

"Close your eyes for a minute."

"Why?"

"I'm going to put the other blanket over us and this one might shift a bit."

"Okay." She closed her eyes and covered them with

her hands. Then waited, trying to remember to breathe.

"You can look now."

She dropped her hands and opened her eyes.

"How's that?"

"Ahh… okay. I guess." It had to be, Cameron needed her.

"We can go?"

She hesitated then nodded. "Okay." She tried to sound confident, but the word was a hesitant whisper.

John raised his voice again. "We can go, Trent."

The vehicle started to move. "Do you mind if I put on some music? I usually listen to music on a long drive," Trent said.

"Long? How long?" Shelby demanded of John.

John sighed. "Put your music on, Trent."

"How long," Shelby persisted.

"It's been a long time since I played doctor, you want to remind me how to play?"

She glared at John in their shadowy blanket cave. "Don't try and distract me. How long?"

"You were the one who told me to distract you."

Her hands curled into fists. "If you don't tell me how long, I'm going to be the one beating the crap out of someone."

He lowered his voice. "Is that a promise?"

"John." She ground his name out through gritted teeth.

"A few hours."

"What!"

"Shh, it'll be quicker than you think."

"Do you want me to turn around," Trent called out.

"No," John said at the same time as Shelby said, "Yes."

"What am I doing?" Trent asked.

Chapter Thirty-One

"Driving." John lowered his voice. "Give it half an hour. If you can't cope we turn back or find somewhere to hole up until night."

Shelby pressed her fists against her chest. "I don't think I can do this."

John took her hands, threading his fingers through hers so she had to relax them. "I know you're a lot stronger than you think. And before the sun goes down you're going to figure that out too."

"Then you better be real good at distractions."

"Oh I am. A lot better at some than others."

She smiled, staring at him a moment. "What would you do if I decided to take you seriously?"

John chuckled. "Thank you for needing the blankets because I'm not an exhibitionist."

"Are you ever serious?"

He was quiet a moment before he replied. "More than people think."

She stared at him, wondering how she should take his comment. Before she could ask, he spoke again.

"Are you free tonight… or will it cost me?"

She giggled. "Now that one was awful."

"I told you I just needed to warm up." He paused. "Speaking of warm, you're looking rather hot. Want a hand getting out of some of those clothes so you can cool down?"

She grinned. "Tell me you'd never say that to a girl."

"I thought I just did."

"Okay. Would you say it seriously?"

"I don't know how serious I'd be. I'd be shit faced if I was trying lines like that. And no one can be completely serious if they're that drunk."

"Have you ever tried that line before?"

"I just did." He sighed theatrically. "Guess I can cross it off my list. It doesn't work."

She decided it might be best to change the subject before she was the one looking for seriousness. It took her a moment to think of something to say. "What are you doing for your birthday?"

"Nothing."

"You're turning eighteen. Don't your parents want to throw you a big party or something?"

There was a long pause before John finally answered. "Yeah."

"So why won't you let them?"

"I thought I was meant to be keeping you distracted."

"This is distracting me. Now stop avoiding the question."

"Because I've got nothing to celebrate."

She drew back at the anger in his voice. "Cameron won't want that."

"I know. Of course I know. But I can't help it."

Shelby had no idea what to say. And really, how could she say anything when she couldn't face the light? Not being able to face a birthday party was minor in comparison. She looked away from him, focusing on the music instead. John remained silent beside her.

One of her favourite songs came on and she closed her eyes as she remembered the last time she'd listened to it. An eternity ago on the last day of her old life. When the next song came on, she kept her eyes closed. It was all so normal, driving along, listening to music, something she'd done so many times. But it wasn't. She could barely remember what normal was. Each song that played only reminded her how far from normal her life had travelled.

Trent's voice interrupted her thoughts, causing her eyes to open. "Do you want me to keep driving?"

John pulled out his phone and checked the time. "We're over a quarter of the way. What do you say, crazy girl?"

She raised her voice so Trent could hear her over his music. "Keep driving." She lowered her voice. Just because she'd forgotten normal didn't mean John should. "About your birthday-"

"That conversation's over."

"If Cameron told you to have a party, would you?"

"Don't. Just don't. He's not going to be there."

"Then why are you going there with me?"

"Because Larry might be."

She grabbed fistfuls of his shirt. "Don't be stupid. You'll get hurt. A cricket bat can't compete with a gun."

"Don't cry, crazy girl." He brushed his fingers across her cheeks.

"You'll get hurt."

His hands went to her shoulders and he slowly slid them around to her back, lightly pulling her towards him until her head rested on his chest. "I already am."

She closed her eyes as his heartbeat sounded in

her ear. How long had it been since she'd last felt safe? She wasn't sure what that felt like anymore, but for now at least she wasn't terrified out of her mind. "I won't let him hurt you." She felt his arms momentarily tighten around her. "There's already been too many hurt by all this."

They fell silent. Shelby kept her eyes closed and drifted into a half sleep, warmed by John's arms and the blanket around them. For once she felt almost safe. It probably wouldn't last so she needed to enjoy it while she could. If they ever found Larry's home, safe was going to be the last thing she felt.

She was dragged from sleep by Trent swearing.

"What's wrong?" She started to pull away from John, but when his arms tightened, she relaxed against him, reminding herself that for now, she was safe.

"The first bridge has a heap of cops around it. I hope it's not the one you need," Trent said. "I'll head to the next one."

"What's the time," Shelby asked John.

He moved slightly then held up his phone. "Nearly nine."

"Less than fifteen minutes and we'll be at the next one," Trent said.

Shelby froze, a trapped feeling beginning.

"Breathe, crazy girl."

"I can't. I have to get out of here." She reached out to claw at the blankets.

John grabbed her hands. "Stop. You're safe. Shelby. Look at me." He pulled her hands against his chest with a single hand and turned her head with the other. "I'm not going to let anything happen to you. We're going to find the house. Together. The three of us."

She shuddered. "Three."

"Yeah." He kept his voice soft.

Her breath came faster, images from the photo albums flickering through her mind. "Larry, Robert and Melissa. Three."

John swore. "You and me then. The two of us if that's what it takes."

She met his gaze. It took her several minutes before she could speak. "What if we find the house?"

"Isn't that what you want?"

"What if Larry's there? I can't go back in that room. And what about you and Trent? What if he hurts you? Locks you up or… or…"

"He's not going to kill me. I still need to take my ute for her first drive."

"You haven't driven her yet?"

"Nah. I was waiting for Cameron to be found.

And then…" he trailed off momentarily. "Then there didn't seem any point. We were going to get a roadworthy and register her then take her on a long drive. Just the thr… ah… Cameron, Trent and me."

She stared at him, trying to slow her breathing as she struggled to find something to say. Comforting words. But none came to mind.

"We're at the bridge," Trent said.

The drive became bumpy and then the vehicle came to a stop. The engine was turned off, bringing silence. Shelby continued to stare at John in the blanket cave.

"Are you ready?"

"Want the sunnies?" Trent asked.

Shelby stared at John. "Give me another bad pickup line."

He was quiet a moment before he grinned. "I'm a hurdle. Wanna jump me?"

"Yes."

John laughed. "You're terrible on the ego, crazy girl."

"I'm serious."

"No you're not. You're just desperate not to go out in the light. I'll tell you what, you say yes when it's dark and we're somewhere safe with no other distractions and I'll say hell yeah."

She looked away from him, tugging her hands back to herself. "I'm an idiot."

"No you're not."

"A coward." Her heart skipped a beat when she heard the front door open. "Trent?"

"I'm just stretching my legs. I've left the sunnies on the passenger seat if you want them."

"Okay." John answered when Shelby remained silent.

She heard the door close and wished she could bring herself to leave the vehicle.

"Come over here." John tugged her back to his side.

She rested her head against his shoulder. "Why?"

"If we're going to sit here all day we might as well be comfortable." He paused. "Being comfortable will make it easier to think of something to tell the cops when they eventually arrive to search this area."

"Damn it." She pulled away from him.

There was a tap on the back door. "It's only me." Trent opened the door and shoved his phone under the blankets. "Check these pics. See if this is the bridge."

Shelby took the phone and flicked through the pictures. "I need to have a look in person." She pushed the phone out under the edge of the blankets.

"It's up to you," John said when Shelby remained silent.

She closed her eyes, leaning forward to wrap her arms around herself. "I'm such a coward."

John slid an arm around her waist. "Shh. You're not."

She rounded on him. "Then what am I?"

"Crazy." He grinned. "I thought we'd already figured that out."

She couldn't resist smiling back at him. She looked away and sighed. "Where are those bloody sunglasses?"

"I'll get them," Trent said.

Chapter Thirty-Two

Shelby listened as the front door was opened then the sunglasses were pushed under the blanket. She slid them on, pushing the blanket out of the way. She froze at the sudden brightness.

John reached out and pulled her hood up. "Everything's okay, crazy girl." He took one of her hands. "Let's get out there, have a look and then you can rejoin me in our love nest."

She smiled weakly, but slid out of the vehicle. Her heart raced and she struggled not to jump back inside and slam the door. When John put an arm around her, she pressed herself to his side.

"It's over here." Trent gestured in the direction they needed to go.

Shelby trembled as they walked out of the trees' shadows and stopped on the bridge. She stared around. "Which direction did we come from?" There was a waver in her voice.

Trent pointed.

Shelby turned to face that direction then looked off to her left. She crouched on the road, near the edge of the bridge. Dizziness hit her. The only clear image she had in her mind of the bridge was the view from underneath. "I have to get under it."

"Under where?" John asked.

"I think she means under the bridge. In the water." Trent said.

"Try going to the edge of the creek," John suggested. He helped her to her feet. "Come on."

When they reached the edge of the creek Shelby shook her head. "I have to go under there." She nodded towards the bridge.

John bent and plunged his hand in the water. "It's too cold. You've got nothing else to wear."

"Turn around. I'll wear my underwear."

"Wait there." John pushed her towards Trent. "And stay out of the water."

Shelby watched him race back to the vehicle.

"Can I help?"

Shelby met Trent's gaze and shook her head. "Unless you can make me forget the past week." Images of the week came back to her. Sights, sounds, lack of light. Especially sounds. The sound of Cameron talking to her. Her trembling lessened. "No. I don't want to forget. That'd mean not knowing Cameron."

Trent smiled sadly. "I know exactly what you mean. This pain," he pressed his hand against his heart, "I'd never give it up if it meant never having known him."

John reached their side, a blanket thrown over his shoulder, a black t-shirt in his hand. "Wear this. We can hold the blanket up so you can change."

"And I'll coil your hair up so it stays dry," Trent offered. "It's so thick and long it'd take ages to dry."

Shelby took the shirt, the material soft against her hand. "Okay." She looked up at the bridge when a car crossed, the driver slowing to look out at them.

"Maybe we better move back in the trees a bit," John suggested.

Shelby nodded and clutched at the hand he offered. It didn't take her long to change into the t-shirt, folding her clothes into a neat pile, tucking her underwear between her jeans and shirt. John took the garments when she tugged the blanket down and Trent coiled her hair up on top of her head, threading it through itself.

"Now don't get too energetic or it'll fall down." Trent tucked a last strand up.

"Okay." She again clung to John's hand and walked with him to the edge of the creek. A deep breath and she let go of him, moving into the water. She gasped at the cold and her trembling increased. The water rose up her body as she headed for the middle of the creek, veering towards the bridge. Then she was under it and looking out at the view. She looked in every direction, trying to frame the trees with the edge of the bridge like they'd been the day she'd sheltered under one. Her gaze met those of Trent's and John's as they watched her. She slowly shook her head.

"Come out then. You must be freezing." John held a hand out to her.

Shelby slowly made her way to the bank and grasped his warm hand, she wanted to wrap him around her, steal all his warmth for herself.

"Hurry up and get out of that wet shirt," Trent said as they moved to the tree line.

John laughed. "Shouldn't that be my line?"

Trent smiled sadly. "I could always push you in and then it'd be my line."

Shelby stepped behind the blanket they held up. "What if it was the first bridge? The one the police were checking." She stripped off the clinging shirt and handed it over the blanket to Trent's waiting hand. Taking the clothes John held out, she struggled to pull them on over wet limbs.

"If it's not the next one, then we go back to the first," John said.

"I don't know if I can do this again." She pulled up the hood and tugged the blanket away.

John stepped close and draped the blanket around them. "You're so cold. We can turn the heater on as soon as we're in the vehicle."

She couldn't stop shivering but didn't know if it was from the cold water, being trapped by the blanket, or the light. "Did you hear me? I don't think I can do this again."

John helped her in the vehicle. "I heard, I just don't believe you."

"So now I'm a liar."

He sat beside her, arranging the blankets. "Nope. Just learning what you're capable of."

The front door opened and closed. "Is everyone buckled," Trent asked.

As soon as they were, Shelby answered. "Yeah." A second later she thought of a question. "How far to the next bridge?"

"Ten minutes at the most," Trent said.

"This is the longest day of my life," Shelby muttered.

John pulled her against his side, putting an arm around her. "You still feel cold, crazy girl." He wrapped his hand around one of hers. "Are you shaking from being cold?"

"No."

"Not much longer and we'll find you a coffin you can use until sunset."

She elbowed him in the ribs.

John laughed. "Was that an earthquake or did you just rock my world?"

She tried to hold onto her glare, but it evaporated into a smile. "You're an idiot."

"My cousin tells me that all the time. I guess she's got to get something right occasionally." He pulled her back against him. "I'm sorry you had to go in the creek."

She didn't answer, just leaned against his side soaking in his warmth. Closing her eyes she tried to stop shivering. It was an impossible task and she was still shivering when Trent pulled up at the next bridge. Within minutes she came to the conclusion she'd have to go in the water again.

"I'll get the shirt you wore earlier," Trent said in answer to Shelby.

"And the blanket," Shelby said.

Trent smiled. "I'm not the one who'd deliberately forget it." He sent a glance towards John before he strode to the four-wheel-drive.

She stared at the water, her hands clasped tightly together. "What if this isn't the right one? I can't go half naked in the creek with all the cops at the first bridge."

"They won't stay there forever."

"I can't sit around in the car all day. I'm a mess." She held out her shaking hand. "Look."

John took hold of her hand, holding it steady. Tremors continued to run through her. "Let's worry about that after we check this bridge."

Trent joined them. "I rung the shirt out as best as I could."

"Thanks." She took the black t-shirt and headed for the tree line, changing into the cold, clingy garment once the blanket was held up. Trent then recoiled her hair and she walked to the water's edge. Sunlight sparkled off the water and she shrank back, wishing the sunglasses were a darker tint.

John put his hands on her shoulders. "It's okay."

Her breath came in gasps as she pulled away from him to wade through the creek. The sunlight sparkling off the water drove her at a faster pace to the safety of the bridge. Relief coursed through her, competing with the fear and she leaned against the concrete walls of the bridge. There was barely enough space for her head between the top of the bridge and the water. She looked out the way she'd come and gasped. Memories rushed in on her and she shook harder. Closing her eyes, she pressed herself against the bridge, sobs making her breath come in shorter gasps.

"Shelby?"

She couldn't answer John. She barely managed to stop from screaming.

"Shelby."

The fear in John's voice echoed the fear she felt.

He swore. "If you don't come out in a couple of seconds I'm coming in after you."

She tried. All she managed to do was force her eyes open. The shadows under the bridge and the sunglasses were all that kept the light from getting her. She shrank back further. Then her attention was caught by John stripping down to his boxers and wading into the water.

"This is too friggin cold. My balls are going to crawl so far up I'll need surgery to retrieve them."

Her sobs were threaded with laughter and then

John was beside her, his arms around her. "I'm s… so s… sorry."

"Shh, crazy girl." He stroked her back as he pressed her cheek against his. "You know if I smelled that bad you thought I needed a wash you could have told me before we left Trent's. There's nothing wrong with hot water."

"You d… don't smell bad."

"Was that a compliment?"

"No. Telling you that you smell good would b… be a compliment."

"So… you complimenting me, crazy girl?"

"I don't know."

"Close your eyes." John paused. "Tell me when you have."

"Why?"

"Because I can't see in the dark like you."

"Why close my eyes." She desperately wished she could stop shaking.

"Trust me. Just close your eyes."

Not everyone was like Larry. Surely some people could be trusted. But more importantly, Cameron had trusted John. She closed her eyes. "Okay." She felt him tighten his arms around her then push her feet out from under her. She stiffened.

"Relax. I'll have you back under the blanket in minutes."

She tried to relax. When he swung her up in his arms, with one arm behind her back, the other under her legs, she let out a shriek.

"Not much longer."

Then she was in the back seat of the vehicle and the door was being closed.

"You can open your eyes now," John said.

Chapter Thirty-Three

Shelby cautiously opened her eyes. Trent and John stood outside the vehicle, their backs to her. Beside her were her clothes and the blanket. She hurriedly stripped off the dripping shirt before the seat could get any wetter and struggled into her clothes. "I'm dressed." She pulled the blanket over herself, hiding in its darkness. Her breathing quickened as she tried to make the cave like space that two people under a blanket created.

The door opened. "Give me a minute to get dressed and I'll join you," John said.

She couldn't reply. She could only focus on breathing and trying to press the blanket away from her. Then John was crawling beneath the blankets with her, putting his arms around her. His chest was still bare and cool from his dip.

"Shh, crazy girl. Everything's okay now. We've only got one more to look at."

"No we don't."

"Okay. If you want to leave it for now, that's fine."

"That was it." She felt him tense then pull away enough to be able to look at her. She met his green eyes and watched as a smile slowly formed. "This is the creek."

His smile became a grin. "I knew you could do it."

The front door opened. "Are we ready to check out the next bridge?"

They said no at the same time and John laughed.

"No need," John said. "This is the right one."

"Thank god for that." Trent started the car. "I don't think I could go through that again. I suppose it's time to check the properties near this creek." He sounded reluctant.

The drive was silent. Shelby slowly warmed as John's heat sank into her skin. Her shaking slowed and she sniffed, reaching a hand up to wipe at her eyes.

"You feel any better, crazy girl?"

She pressed her hand against his chest. "Your skin is so warm. It feels like forever since I was that warm. It's like my body's forgotten how to warm up."

John grinned. "You want me to teach you how to heat things up?"

She slapped his bare chest and smiled slightly. "You're going to run out of lines eventually."

"Never." His grin faded and he turned his head towards the front of the car. "Did we just leave the road, Trent?"

"Yeah."

"How can you tell?" Shelby asked.

"The tyres are making a different sound. Probably a concrete driveway."

The vehicle stopped and a moment later Trent was handing his phone under the blanket. "Is this the house?"

She looked at the picture on the phone, framed by the windscreen. The house was lowset, a few tufts of grass in the dust bowl that was the front yard. She handed the phone back. "No. It was highset."

The vehicle moved off again and John pulled her close. "You can do this."

Her stomach lurched at the thought of finding Larry's home. She could do this. She had to do this because Cameron was counting on her. Maybe she was stronger than she thought. Look at how she was getting over thinking that everyone who reached out for her was going to attack. "Distract me."

He lowered his head and spoke near her ear. "How do you feel about going me halves in a bastard?"

She pushed him away with a burst of surprised laughter. "Holy crap. I said distract me, not give me heart failure. That has to be your worst pickup line yet."

"Do I take it that's a no?" He looked sorrowful.

"It's a hell no."

He grinned. "Thank god for that. I'm too young to have kids."

"Idiot." It sounded more compliment than insult, even to her.

The vehicle slowed to a stop again and Shelby's fear returned. She gripped John's hand when he took hold of hers. "I don't know if it's worse hiding under here or pulling away the blanket, so I can see where we are, and putting up with the light."

"It's your choice." John took the phone Trent handed back to him and held it out to her.

She held John's gaze a moment while she searched for the courage to look at the picture. When she finally looked, the screen was black. She recoiled.

John looked down at the screen and brought the picture back up. "Here you go."

She stared at the picture. It was highset, but she

couldn't see any bars on the windows. She shook her head.

John handed the phone to Trent then turned back to her. "When you pulled away like that I thought you'd found it. What is it about a blank screen?"

"It's how he caught us." She recounted the facts, her gaze on their hands.

His hands tightened on hers. "He needs to be staked out on a meat ants nest."

"I guess that's one way to poison off the nest."

John laughed, a short sharp sound. "That's much better." He touched the side of her face near her smile.

The smile faded when the vehicle pulled up again and Trent gave his phone back to them. She shook her head and handed it through to him. "How many more houses are there?"

"Fourteen." Trent drove off again.

"I can't do this fourteen times." Her fingers twisted together.

John pulled on his shirt then reached out to tug her hands apart. When she looked up at him, he grinned. "Your lips look lonely. Do they want to meet mine?"

She couldn't stop a smile forming. "How do you think of these?"

"I can't take credit for all of them. You'd be amazed

at the comments guys come up with when they've had a few drinks."

"Probably not. I have a fifteen-year-old brother."

"I'm surprised you haven't heard him and his mates talking about important issues like what pickup lines to use."

"I really try and avoid them when they're at our house. One of–" The vehicle stopped and she abruptly ended her conversation, waiting for the phone. Her eyes closed when she looked at the picture of the front of the house. "I think this is it."

John slid out from under the blankets. "There's no car here. The place looks deserted."

"I'll drive out the back and check," Trent said.

Shelby fought with the warring urges of wanting to see what was happening and not wanting to face the light. Making sure the hood was drawn up and putting the sunglasses back on, she eased the blankets up. Her breath froze in her throat as they pulled up out the back. The small window at the rear of the house still had the plywood half pried away. "This is Larry's home." The words were a whimper.

"Hey, crazy girl." John grasped her hands. "Hang in there."

"I'll park here and have a look around," Trent said.

"I'll make sure he's not home before we try and get in the house."

"I'll call the cops." John pulled out his phone. "It'll probably take them over half an hour to get here."

"Don't go." Shelby reached out to Trent.

"It's okay. I won't go far." He got out of the vehicle.

Shelby stared after him, wanting to call him back. She clasped and unclasped her hands while John talked on the phone. Then she couldn't stand it another minute and threw open the door and raced after Trent. She ignored John as he called her name.

Trent stood on the verandah at the front door. He glanced towards her. "We could try and pry this door open."

Shelby stood there hugging herself. Fear kept her throat closed and she could only stare at Trent. At least he was unharmed.

John joined them on the verandah. "What are you doing?"

"Trying to find a way in," Trent said.

Shelby remained silent.

John held onto one of the bars on the window. "The idiot who put these up screwed them on from the outside. Has your mate got any tools in the vehicle?"

Trent shrugged.

"I'll have a look." John started to move away.

"No." The word burst from Shelby. "Stay together. Please."

"One minute, okay? If I don't find anything in a minute I'll come back." John didn't wait for an answer before he ran to the vehicle.

Chapter Thirty-Four

Shelby stared in the direction he'd gone, wanting to follow so she could keep him in sight. Her body ached from how tense it was. Every breath felt an agony and she wanted to huddle against the wall to be as far from the light as possible. But she couldn't. She was frozen to the spot and the only movement she could make was to shake and tremble as she blinked and tried to make her voice work again.

John came around the corner at a run, holding up a screwdriver, the cricket bat in his other hand. "Looks like I'm going to be the first to use it. What's the point of owning tools if you never use them." He looked at Shelby and swore. Sliding an arm around her waist, he drew her closer to the house. "It's not as bright here." He paused. "Or would you rather wait in the vehicle?"

"No." She shook her head. Now if only she could make her legs obey.

John stared at her a moment longer before he turned to the bars and used the screwdriver to remove them from the window they stood near. He then used the cricket bat to break the glass.

"We're breaking into his house." Shelby stared at the broken bits of glass John was knocking out of the frame.

John grinned. "Yep. It's not like you aren't welcome here. He enjoyed having you stay so much that he tried to make sure you'd never leave."

Shelby shuddered. "It seems wrong."

"So is kidnapping." John paused. "I'll go first."

Trent pulled a small torch from his pocket and handed it to John. "Be careful."

Once he was inside, John helped first Shelby and then Trent through the broken window before he switched on the lounge room light. A low wattage bulb filled the room with dull light.

Shelby slid the sunglasses into her pocket as she looked around, drawn to the photo albums still on the coffee table. Staring up at her was Melissa, being swung around by Larry.

John swore from beside her. "She could be your twin. How uncanny is that?"

Trent turned the album and stared at the picture. "No wonder he took you." He turned several pages and stopped with a sharp indrawn breath. "This could almost be Cameron." He tapped the picture of Robert.

"They say everyone has a look alike." John shrugged. "But I didn't expect them to be so alike."

"There are differences." Trent ran his finger over the picture, then quickly moved his hand out of the way when Shelby closed the album.

"We need to go upstairs." She led the way to the bottom of the stairs but was drawn to the kitchen where the light bulb had been left on. She stared at the chest freezer. Why had he freaked when she'd tried to open it? She crossed the space and put her hand on the door.

"Don't open that."

Shelby spun to see Cameron across the kitchen, a shimmery figure. She covered the gasp that escaped with her hand.

John swore. Trent cried out.

"Cameron?" She stepped towards him, her hand outstretched. When she reached his side, her hand slid through him. Her eyes closed and she groaned, swaying on her feet. Warm arms encircled her and she buried her head against John's chest. "No." The word was a long drawn out moan.

"I'm sorry," Cameron said. "I couldn't tell you. You were already thinking you were going insane. And why would you come back for someone already dead?"

She turned her head to see him. "Why did you want me to come back?" She was surprised by the accusing tone of her voice.

Cameron gestured towards the chest freezer. "To find the rest of me."

Trent cried out again, a wounded sound that filled the room.

"You should have told me. I'd have come back." Her words were soft. "How could you think I wouldn't?"

"Cameron?" Trent took a couple of faltering steps forward.

Cameron turned to him. "Now I'm dead, you no longer call me gorgeous?"

Trent choked back a sob. "How am I meant to live without you, gorgeous?"

"I'm sorry I wasted so much time. If I hadn't been such an idiot when I first met you we could have had weeks longer together," Cameron said.

"I'd give anything to be able to hold you again."

Trent reached out to Cameron. His hand went through him. "Why? Why you?"

"I don't know." Cameron's voice was soft.

"If I'd driven you home-"

Cameron shook his head. "No. Don't even think that. If it wasn't that moment it would have been another. He was watching and waiting for a chance to kidnap me. Nothing could have stopped him."

There was a crack as the front door was thrown open and it crashed into the wall. Larry roared, "Who's here." He stopped in the kitchen doorway, his gun pointed at them.

Shelby started to shake and John pushed her behind him. She saw the gun move towards John and fear drove her forward. She shook John's hand off her arm when he tried to drag her back. "Daddy."

Confusion crossed Larry's face. "Mellie?" His gun started to lower.

"Forget about them, Daddy. Let's go. You and me. Before the police arrive."

"You called the cops?" The gun rose again.

"Not me." She shook her head.

"One of them?" He pointed the gun first at Trent, then John.

Shelby took another step forward. She couldn't let

him kill anyone else. "Come on, Daddy. They'll take me away if we stay."

"Don't do this, crazy girl."

Shelby took another step forward, her gaze holding Larry's. "Don't you love me, Daddy? You said we'd be together forever."

"Don't you dare go with him, Shelby." Cameron crossed the room to stand beside Larry.

She momentarily met Cameron's gaze. "This is the right thing to do."

Larry nodded. "Yes. I've got to keep you safe. You're right." He held out his hand. "Come on, Mellie."

"Tell him Robert's standing at his shoulder. Tell him, Shelby. For some reason he can't see me, or hear me. You have to tell him for me."

Shelby shook her head.

"Do it, crazy girl or I'll do it for you."

Her mouth dried at the thought of Larry's attention turning to John. "I can see Robert, Daddy. At your shoulder."

Larry turned. "Where? Where is he?" He waved the gun around as he searched the shadows.

"Right beside you." Shelby pointed. "He said he lied. That he didn't want you to know." She repeated Cameron's words.

"Know what?"

"When he barrelled you with the mattress. He made up the name Cameron, but it was Robert. He didn't want to live with you. He wanted to go home to Mum."

Larry slowly shook his head. "No."

"He's raising his hand to point at you. He said you killed him. You killed your own son." Her voice trembled.

"No." Larry stumbled backwards. "Never. I could never hurt Robert. I'd sooner hurt myself."

"He said you killed him. You hurt him and killed him and he's going to take you with him."

"Where is he?" Larry looked around wildly.

"He said it doesn't matter where he is. The cops are minutes away. They'll shoot you and Robert's going to take you with him. You can't have both of us. It's Robert or me. And Robert said he's the oldest so he has first claim."

"I'd never hurt him."

"Don't you remember all the blood? You even had to rip up the carpet to get rid of it. And when you shot him, he fought you. But it was too late. He watched you hack apart his body, muttering that they'd find the DNA and put you back in jail."

"Robert." An anguished wail tore from Larry. "I

didn't mean to. You wouldn't stay. I just wanted you to stay."

"Robert says that when the cops shoot you then you'll be with him forever. Can you hear that noise? That's probably them now."

There wasn't any noise but Larry ran, sobbing and screaming that he didn't mean it.

Chapter Thirty-Five

Shelby stared at the empty doorway and felt her legs give way. John was there, grabbing her before she hit the ground, his lips pressing against hers, his hands pulling her close.

"I felt useless." He continued to hold her close. "I was terrified I'd lose you."

Shelby's hands slid across his chest, sliding around his neck. "I was so scared he'd kill you." She could hear the soft sounds of Cameron and Trent talking, Trent's words broken by sobs.

John pressed his lips against her forehead, his breathing fast. "I'm sorry. I shouldn't have done that."

"Done what?"

"Kiss you."

"You didn't want to kiss me?"

John's lips curved into a smile. "Oh yeah, I wanted to. I wanted to the moment I saw you standing near my ute. Looking wide eyed, fragile and determined. Very determined."

"Then why shouldn't you have kissed me?"

"Because you're..." he frowned.

"Crazy?"

John grinned momentarily. "You might be, but that's not the reason. Because you're upset, terrified. I shouldn't have taken advantage."

"I would have pushed you away if I wasn't interested."

"Really?" His grin returned.

"What? No pickup line?"

He chuckled softly. "You've made my mind go blank."

"John. Shelby." When they turned to face him, Cameron continued, Trent at his side. "I have to go."

"Forever?" Shelby asked.

"I don't know."

Pain clutched at her heart, quickly followed by anger. "What if I want to see you again? You made me care for you when you knew it was going to hurt when I found out you were dead."

"I'm sorry. It wasn't just that I wanted you to come back, I wanted to share what happened in my last months with you." Cameron sent a sad smile to Trent before he turned back to Shelby. "They were some of the best days of my life. I wanted you to have those memories."

Trent made a strangled sound. "How will memories keep me warm at night?"

Cameron turned to Trent. "I'd give anything to spare you this pain."

"I wouldn't give up my memories to avoid this pain. I love you, gorgeous. I always will."

"I love you too." Cameron reached out and ran a ghostly hand down Trent's cheek.

Trent closed his eyes on another sob.

John stepped forward and clasped Trent's shoulder, one arm still around Shelby. "Shelby said you had a name for my ute."

"No Name."

John frowned. "I kept telling you that. You're the one who insisted she needed a name."

"The name is No Name." Cameron grinned.

John chuckled. "Ya crazy bastard."

Cameron laughed. "I love you too, man." He momentarily turned, a sound catching his attention. "I have to go. Promise me none of you will be in the kitchen when the cops open the freezer."

"Okay." John answered for them.

"Tell my parents to cremate me. I don't like the idea of being worm food. And what would they do if they buried me? Stitch me back together?" Cameron shuddered. "I'd look like Frankenstein's monster." He smiled sadly. "Take care of each other." He started to fade.

"Cameron." Trent reached out but no one was there.

Then things happened quickly. The police arrived. Searches were made and John dragged them out of the kitchen before the chest freezer could be opened. Shelby insisted on seeing the room she'd been locked in and they went with her, Trent's torch showing them the way. She clasped John and Trent's hands as she forced herself to climb the stairs, the torchlight reminding her of her time with Larry, yet different with them at her side. Almost comforting in the fact she was the one choosing to enter the room, rather than being forced.

By nighttime, they were sitting out the front of Shelby's house, her handbag Larry had taken from her on her lap. She fiddled with her phone, unable to turn it on since the battery was flat. She kept it facedown so she didn't have to look at the blank screen.

"Now you've got your phone back, can I have your number?" John asked.

Shelby nodded and recited it while he typed it into his phone. "You'll have to text me so I can add your number after I've charged my phone." She started to remove his hoodie she still wore.

John reached out a hand to stop her. "You need it more than I do at the moment."

She grasped the door handle then let go to turn back and hold onto John instead. "I'm terrified to let you out of my sight." She glanced towards Trent in the front seat. "Both of you. Terrified if I let you go something will happen to you."

"I'd like to promise you nothing will, but we all know bad shit happens." John tangled his fingers in hers. "You can crash at my place if you want. My parents won't mind, but they're nosy and will ask you a million questions."

"You can stay at my place. Both of you," Trent offered.

She was torn. She looked from one to the other then at her house. She finally shook her head. "No. I have to do this." She smiled weakly. "It can't be as bad as walking in the light." She pressed a finger against John's chest. "You owe me a coffin."

"I'll see what I can do, crazy girl."

She leaned forward and brushed her lips across John's before she hopped out of the vehicle. After a hurried goodbye to Trent, she raced for her front door before she changed her mind. The door opened as she approached it and her steps slowed as she saw Katherine. "Mum." She slid on Trent's lime green, mirrored sunglasses to block out the light shining from behind her mother.

Katherine stepped back and let her in, staring outside at the vehicle heading down the street before she closed the door and faced Shelby. "Is this going to be a regular thing?"

"What?"

"Taking off with strangers. Making us worry about what had happened to you. Haven't you learned anything from this?"

"Yeah. Life's short and you could die tomorrow." She turned and walked away, glad she still had the sunglasses with the amount of lights on in the house. She wasn't going to let her mother ruin what she'd accomplished.

Chapter Thirty-Six

Shelby paced her room. It had been nearly a week since Cameron had said goodbye and she hadn't left the house once. The shrink visited her in her room, schoolwork was brought to her and even the police had visited her at home and told her how stupid she'd been. They had of course used other words, but it was all the same. The couple of times she'd talked about going out, Katherine had panicked, particularly since she only wanted to go out at night.

The only other things she'd done was restlessly paced the house and searched online for what had happened to Robert and Melissa. They had died in a car accident. Robert seventeen, Melissa only sixteen. Larry had been correct. It hadn't been that bad an accident. If someone had found them sooner, they would have all survived and Larry wouldn't have spent eight years in jail for involuntary manslaughter.

Staring out her window, she forced thoughts of the past from her mind.

It was Friday afternoon and she was holed up in her room, watching her life slip away from her. That wasn't happening. Turning away from the window, she grabbed her phone off the bedside drawers and sent a text to John.

I'm not a genie, but I bet I can make your wish come true.

She waited for an answer, smiling when her phone rang. "Hey."

"I'm listening."

"Are you now?"

John chuckled. "Absolutely. So when's my wish coming true and how do you know what it is?"

"I want to spend the weekend with you. At your place, Trent's, anywhere. I don't care where it is. Please just rescue me from here." Her mother hadn't even let her step out the front door and although John had spoken to her every day on the phone, he hadn't been allowed to visit.

"Does that anywhere include sitting at the department of transport with me? I got a roadworthy done on No Name and she passed."

"Yes. But only if you hurry up."

"I'll be there in twenty. But you better be waiting or we won't get her registered today."

"Should I start feeling jealous of No Name?"

"Nope, because I want to make sure she's registered so I can take you with me on her first real drive."

"I'll be ready in ten. Sounds like you'll be the one holding us up."

"I'm on my way this minute."

Shelby looked at the clothes spread across her bed. "What clothes should I pack?"

John chuckled. "You're making it too easy for me. How about as little as possible?"

She laughed. "Seriously. I have no idea what we're doing this weekend, so what should I pack?"

"A bikini. But if you do forget it, I've got a t-shirt you can borrow."

"Okay, I'll see you soon." She was still smiling when she disconnected the phone and threw some clothes in her backpack. She pulled on John's hoodie and slid on the sunglasses. She'd been practising standing at windows the past week and was getting a little better. But she still couldn't stop the fear that filled her every time she was in bright light.

Hoping she'd packed enough she went looking for Katherine and found her in the kitchen. "I'm going out."

"No you're not."

"I wasn't asking." She started to turn away.

"Don't you dare step out of the house. I'm not going through that again. He's still out there somewhere. Do you hear me?"

"Yeah, I'd have to be deaf not to hear you. I'm going out. You can't lock me away for the rest of my life."

"I'm trying to keep you safe."

"So was Larry." The soft words brought with them silence. Shelby watched her mother pale, a stricken look coming into her eyes. "I'll have my phone with me and I'll be back Sunday night." She was halfway to the front door when Katherine caught up with her.

"You can't do this to me."

"Maybe you should be the one speaking to the shrink, not me. I'll suggest that to her when she comes Monday."

"You'll do no such thing," Katherine warned.

"Then stop behaving like Larry. I've been having sleepovers with friends since I was five, you can't change everything because of what happened. I want my life back." She continued to the front door, feeling both sick and victorious at the look Larry's name caused on Katherine's face. She opened the front door and waited, unable to go outside until she had to. When John did arrive, driving No Name, she raced through the sunlight, her head down as she threw herself inside the ute. "You need dark tint on your windows."

"I'd offer to take your mind off the light, but we can't be late."

Shelby rolled her eyes. "I knew I should feel jealous of her."

John chuckled and reached out to rest a hand on her leg as he pulled onto the street. "I missed you."

She kept her head tilted forward, the hood casting shadows across her face. She rested her hand on his. "Mum isn't much better than Larry. He kept me in one room. She's keeping me in one house."

"How did you get her to let you go for an entire weekend?"

"I didn't."

John laughed. "Should I worry about your dad coming after me with a shotgun?"

She tensed, an image of Larry and his gun coming to mind.

"Hey crazy girl, what's wrong?"

She let out a shuddery breath. "Sorry. And you don't have to worry about my dad, he's gone back home." He obviously had more important things to worry about than a crazy daughter.

"That doesn't tell me what's wrong."

She drew in a shaky breath. "Some words take me back there."

He swore. "I'm sorry. It was the gun comment, wasn't it?"

"Yeah. But I don't want everyone to watch every word they say around me. How will I ever beat this if you all treat me like glass? I want my life back." Her voice dropped. "I'm just not sure how I'm going to manage it." She focused on her breathing, not wanting to pass out from lack of oxygen.

John double parked near the Department of Transport's door. "I'll meet you in there as soon as I find a park."

With a nod she slid out of the ute and raced for the door. It wasn't any better inside. Lights. People. Noise. She felt bombarded on every side. She took a couple of hesitant steps forward. Someone pushed past her and she shrank away, her breath coming faster, her heartbeat equally fast. Her gaze darted around, looking for somewhere safe. There was nowhere. Then she spotted the sign for the restroom.

"Shelby?" John joined her.

"I need to u… use the b… bathroom." She fled, locking herself in one of the cubicles. Sitting on the closed toilet, she leaned forward, struggling for breath.

Her phone beeped an incoming message. It took her a few moments before her hands were steady enough to pull her phone from her pocket and read it. She tensed as she steeled herself against the dark screen.

Do you want me to come in there?

No!!!! She stared at the cubicle door, half expecting John to come in anyway.

Another text came through. *What can I do?*

She had no idea how to answer. There wasn't anything he could do. After a moment she thought of a reply. *Distract me. What are we doing next?*

We could find a dark cave to hide out in until sunset.

What happened to the coffin you keep telling me you'll get me?

I couldn't find one big enough for two.

A reluctant smile formed and her shaking reduced. She eyed the door. Her first day out of the house in ages and she'd locked herself in a toilet cubicle. How messed up was that?

Want me to come and get you?

Give me a bit of time and I'll be out.

Okay.

She stared at her phone until the screen went blank.

Her stomach lurched. She forced herself to keep watching it. Then pushed the button to make the screen brighten. Her breath caught in her throat, then started again. It was getting easier. She rested her head in her hands and focused on remaining calm. She could do this. There was no way she was going to spend the rest of her life shut away in a house. Any house. Her phone beeped, jarring her from her thoughts.

You ready to go? All done.

She checked the time, surprised at how much time had passed. She forced her unsteady legs to take her out of the restroom. John stood outside the door. She fell into his arms, closing her eyes against the light.

Chapter Thirty-Seven

"Come on. Let's get out of here." John kept Shelby close as he took her back to the ute.

She buckled up with shaky hands while John got in the driver's seat. "Do you want to drop me at mum's house?"

"Do you want to go home?"

She couldn't help flinching at the word home. She shook her head. "No, but you must be getting sick of this."

John grinned. "Sick of a pretty girl snuggling up to me all the time?"

She reached out and rested her hand on his thigh. "Thank you."

"There's nothing to thank me for." He paused. "Where do you want to go? How about my room? No one's home right now and I've got a really big… bed."

She laughed at his antics. "Okay, but all I'm agreeing to is your room, not your bed."

"And I thought you were going to make my wishes come true."

"You better recheck your text. It was wish. That's singular, not plural."

John glanced at her, a smile in place. "It was worth a try."

Closing her eyes, she rested her head against his shoulder. "I like bench seats."

"I'm getting fonder of them by the minute." He paused. "My bed is even more comfortable."

Laughter escaped before she became serious. "If Larry hadn't kidnapped me, I never would have met you." She felt John tense, then relax.

"Nah, I bet we'd have met eventually."

"This way we met sooner rather than later." She hesitated. "My shrink's making me look at all the positives that have come from Larry."

"Yeah? What did you come up with?"

"You, Trent and Cameron." Silence filled the cab. "I might have met you and Trent some other way, but not Cameron. Never Cameron."

John's hand covered hers. "I'm glad you met him. He was worth knowing."

"Yeah."

They fell silent for the rest of the drive and John hurried her inside to his room, pulling the curtains across the window and closing the door.

"Is that dark enough?"

She nodded, wrapping her arms around herself as she looked around the room. Her gaze fell on the queen-size bed and she smiled. John chuckled and she looked over at him. "What can you expect? Where else would I look when it takes up most of the space?"

"When you asked me to distract you earlier, texting wasn't the first thing that came to mind." He crossed the room to stand in front of her. "Want me to show you what I think is the perfect distraction?"

"Maybe."

"Think I can turn that into a yes?" His lips met hers and time spun out. Somehow they ended up on John's bed.

A phone ringing interrupted them and swearing, John looked at his screen. "What?" He listened, dropping onto his back with a sigh. "I'll talk to her." Another pause. "She's here with me... yeah... no, just wait... I know I have... but don't pressure her... okay... give me a few... bye."

Shelby watched him, trying to figure out what was going on by his side of the conversation. When he put his phone on the bedside drawers, she asked, "Who was that?"

"Bryce." He rolled to his side so he could face her.

"What did he want?"

"To talk to you."

"Why?" Shelby sat up.

"We've been talking to him, Trent and I. He wants to talk to you."

"About Cameron." It wasn't a question. There was nothing else he could want to talk to her about. Not after their last conversation.

"Yeah." John sat up and took her hands. "He's willing to listen. He wants to believe, wants to think Cameron had a chance to say goodbye."

"He wants me to tell him about…" She faltered as her throat tightened. "I don't know if I can. I haven't even been able to tell my shrink everything. Not that I can tell her about Cameron without being labelled a lunatic." That was the hardest part. Pretending to her family that she'd never met Cameron.

His hands tightened on hers. "No one's going to force you. Trent and I can be there." He grinned. "We can even organise a dark room if that helps, crazy girl."

She tried to return his grin, but even a smile was beyond her. "I don't know."

He let go of one hand and cupped the side of her neck, drawing her closer. "How about we pick up where we left off while you think about it."

"There's no way I can think while you're distracting me."

"You probably just need some practice at it." He was still grinning when his lips met hers.

It was Shelby's phone that interrupted them next. John rolled away with a groan. "Why didn't we turn them off?" He sat up when Shelby stared at the screen of her phone, letting it ring. "You going to answer that?"

"It's Courtney."

"And?"

She took a deep breath and answered. "Hi."

"What took you so long?"

"I was busy." She hit John when he sniggered.

"Who's with you?"

Shelby remained silent.

"It's that guy, isn't it?"

She tried to think of something to say. Nothing seemed right.

"Every single day I've begged to come and see you. Why? Why can't I visit? Do you think everything is my fault because I started the Saturday movies?"

"No." The word exploded from her. "Courtney… I just… I need more time."

"We've known each other ages. You barely know him. I never thought you'd be the type of person who ditched her best friend because she had a boyfriend."

"I'm not… I haven't… it's just…" she trailed off, closing her eyes so she didn't have to see the questions on John's face. "Just give me more time. Please."

Courtney was silent a moment. "Did you ever think I might need to see if you're okay? That I keep asking myself why I came up with that stupid Saturday movie idea."

"It wasn't your fault." She remembered Cameron's words to Trent. "He was watching me. If it hadn't been then, he'd have found me another time."

"I still need to see you."

"Soon. It'll be soon. I promise."

"I was so worried. I couldn't sleep."

"I know." Shelby felt herself growing impatient. Courtney had told her this every time she'd rung. Then she felt bad. "I'll call you."

"You never do."

"When do I get a chance? You ring me every day."

"So if I don't call you Saturday you'll ring me."

She tried to say yes. But all she could think of was Courtney and Saturday. A shudder ran through her.

When John tugged her against him, she opened her eyes and leaned on him.

"That's what I thought." There was anger in Courtney's voice. "If you ever forgive me, you know my number."

Shelby started to protest, but it was too late, Courtney had already hung up. She closed her eyes again, dropping the phone to the bed. "She's never going to talk to me again."

"Sure she will, she's your best friend. Just organise a time to see her next week."

Shelby tensed.

"Okay, what am I missing here?"

"I haven't seen her since… since the day before I missed seeing the movie with her."

"Why?" He pulled away and met her gaze.

Shelby looked away. "Because…"

"That sounded like it was part of a larger sentence. The rest of the words wouldn't happen to include none of your business, would they?"

"No."

"Has your mum been keeping everyone away? I thought it was just me and Trent."

"She keeps asking when Courtney's going to visit."

"Draw me a map here."

"I can't see her. What if… what if she thinks…

what if she doesn't want to be friends? That I'm too crazy to deal with."

"Then you delete her number from your phone. Quit beating yourself up over it. Wouldn't you rather know? It's a bit like being left in the dark."

Shelby turned back to him, almost wishing for more light so she could see his expression better. "What would I do without you?"

"I'll be the one asking something like that when you get your shit together and move on to someone who doesn't remind you of Larry."

She shook her head. "No. You never remind me of him. You're more like a dark room."

John laughed. "From anyone else I'd take that as an insult." He reached out to brush his hand across her cheek and then to behind her head. "How about we pick up where we left off?"

"Would you be annoyed if I asked you to ring Bryce instead?"

"What about Courtney?"

"No. Bryce first. He already thinks I'm crazy."

"Remind me what I'll be missing, crazy girl. Then I'll ring Bryce." He was grinning as he tugged her towards him.

Shelby willingly fell into his arms, making sure he

did know what he'd be missing. When she pulled away minutes later she laughed at his groan of protest.

"Are you sure I can't talk you into forgetting the call?"

"Probably, but let's get it over with."

"Okay, I'll make the call. When do you want to see him?"

"As soon as possible." She hesitated. "Do you think I could try and talk to him in a dark room." She reached out for his hand. "And I want you there. Trent probably should be too."

"Okay, whatever makes it easier for you."

Chapter Thirty-Eight

It didn't take John long to ring first Bryce and then Trent. He arranged to meet at Bryce's home in about an hour. When Shelby found out that John's parents would arrive home as they were leaving, she asked to go earlier. She wasn't up to meeting them yet.

When she went to open the ute door, a mark on the guard caught her eye and she knelt to see it better in the fading light. On the guard, between the tyre and the door, in cursive writing was 'No Name'. She smiled as she ran her fingers lightly over the black lettering.

"You're mauling my ute, aren't you?" John asked from the other side of the vehicle.

"Yep. Sanding the paint off your car with my fingers."

"Ute. And stop doing it. Why has everyone got to maul her?" He slid into the ute and waited until

Shelby joined him. "If you want to maul something, try mauling me."

Shelby grinned. "Can I coat you in an excessive amount of clear first?"

"It wasn't excessive. It was five coats, so stop mauling her." He reached out and tugged her hand over to his thigh. "Should I buy you a matchbox car?"

She shook her head. "When I get my own car I'll be able to maul it as much as I want."

"Do you want to borrow my sedan?" He started the ute and headed for the street.

"Only your sedan? What if I wanted to borrow No Name?"

"You're trying to give me heart failure, aren't you?"

"Does that mean I can't borrow her?"

"How about I let you drive her instead?"

"Seriously?"

"Yep. Right after I drink a bottle of Jack." John grinned.

"Is that so you can forget the whole traumatic episode?"

"Yep, now about my sedan. Did you want to borrow it?"

"Nah. Then you'd have to take No Name everywhere and I'd be worried she might get scratched or something. You'd probably hold it against me for life."

"I wouldn't do that." John sent her a glance, grinning. "I'd be too busy going into a decline."

She rolled her eyes. "Now that I'd believe." She rested her head against his shoulder. "Am I going to be invited to the wedding?"

"What wedding?"

"The one Cameron said you and No Name are having."

John chuckled. "Sure. You can be my best man."

"And you think I'm crazy. Best man. Notice the man on the end?"

"So? We can be different. After all, you're crazy."

"Maybe it's contagious."

"Sounds good to me."

She couldn't prevent a smile as she fell silent, her head still against his shoulder, her hand on his thigh. She wasn't looking forward to talking to Bryce, but it was probably long overdue. Even her shrink kept telling her talking about things helped. This might not be exactly what the shrink meant, but Bryce, Trent and John needed to hear everything. Telling her shrink everything would be a really bad idea. Continuing to say she believed Cameron had been with her would probably have her medicated and seeing a shrink for life.

When they reached Bryce's house, Trent's car was already there. Shelby took a deep breath before she slid out of the driver's door after John, grateful for the darkness and John threading his fingers through hers. They walked towards the front door and Shelby noticed there were no lights on in the house. She had a moment of panic about what she'd say and then they were at the door, Bryce letting them in and leading them to his lounge room. Several candles were set around the room to cast a soft glow.

Simon came towards her, arms outstretched and she shrank back, freezing as she tried to fight the impulse to run. She focused instead on the brightly coloured shirt he wore with his black trousers.

"Darlin, I've been waiting an age to meet you." He patted her cheek, dropping a kiss on the other. "Any friend of Cameron's is doubly welcome in our home." At a sound from Bryce, Simon sent him a glare. "I know our boy would've found a way to say goodbye to Trent. They're soul mates."

"If they're soul mates, then why the fuck did he have to die?" There was anger in Bryce's demand.

"Do I look like the creator of the universe to you?" Simon turned back to Shelby. "Can I get you anything? Did I light too many candles? Is this room comfortable enough?"

Trent came into the room and from the look on his face he'd heard the conversation between Bryce and Simon. He paused inside the doorway, meeting no one's gaze.

Shelby looked away from Trent. John's comforting warmth against her back was all that kept her from running. "Uhm… I don't know."

"You don't have to do this. If you've changed your mind we can leave," John said from behind her.

A breath shuddered through her as she remembered sitting in the dark talking to Cameron. The bare floor, sometimes tiles, but always dark. "Not carpet. Wooden floor or tiles."

"Simon's workroom, or the guest bathroom," Bryce said.

"Workroom?"

"It smells of Simon's paint and stuff."

There'd been no strong smells in the dark. Would it be better to make sure things were different, or the same? "The bathroom… I think."

John brushed his lips against her ear to whisper, "You can always change your mind if it doesn't suit." He stepped to the side and held out a hand. "Ready?"

She stared at his hand a moment. Taking a deep

breath, she reached for it before she changed her mind. She walked beside him to the bathroom and sat on the floor against the vanity. When John would have joined her, she shook her head. "Not right next to me."

He sat an arm's width away. "I'm here if you need me."

She nodded and, with a glance towards Trent sitting on the edge of the bathtub, turned to Bryce and Simon who sat near the door. Bryce's arm was around Simon's shoulders and Simon held a candle. "Close the door and put out the light." As soon as it was dark, she inhaled deeply. It felt so familiar. No lights. Cold floor. "It was like this every day. I had no idea what time it was, or how long until Larry appeared at the door. There was only the dark and Cameron's voice."

"Are you sure you're up to doing this?" Bryce asked.

She smiled. Her anxiety lifted some at the almost familiar voice. "You sound a lot like him. Your voice is a little deeper, but it's the same tone."

"How can you doubt Cameron waited for Trent?" Simon asked.

"Quiet," Bryce ordered when a sound was torn from Trent.

Her smile temporarily became a grin as she heard Simon's offended sniff. "It was different from this. I was alone. I begged Cameron so many times to let me sit with him. I didn't know he was a ghost. All I knew was he didn't want me there beside him. Didn't seem to need the comfort I was desperate for. But I guess I should start at the beginning. When I walked to the bus shelter and sat down, waiting for the bus to arrive so I could join Courtney at the cinema."

By the time Shelby reached the end of her story, her throat was dry. She'd been so caught up in talking it wasn't until she stopped that she realised someone was sobbing. Then she heard Bryce's comforting murmurs and realised it had to be Simon. In front of her she heard Trent's ragged breath and reached across the space to his knee.

When he placed his hand on hers she tugged him forward and felt him shift to sit on the floor near her, his hand clutching hers.

"Shelby?"

She turned her head towards John's voice. "Yeah?"

"Can I sit next to you?"

She almost lost it at those words. "Yeah." Her voice was unsteady.

"I know there's barely any space between us, but

I feel like I'm reaching across a chasm." His hand brushed her shoulder.

She took his hand, tugging him closer. "You learn your space and then it doesn't feel so big." She felt safe with Trent clasping one hand, John the other.

John's lips brushed across her face until he found her lips, dropping a light kiss on them. "You're amazing, crazy girl."

"John." There was shock in Simon's tone.

Shelby laughed. "It's okay, Simon. It makes me think of when you call someone something they're not instead of what they are. It makes me feel less crazy."

"Can we have light again?" Trent asked.

"Yeah, we don't all have cat's eyes like you, crazy girl."

"You can light a candle." Shelby squinted when a flame flared and was touched to the candlewick.

"I don't know how I'm going to convince my sister to have Cameron cremated," Bryce said.

"Do you believe us now?" John asked.

"Of course he does," Simon said.

"Do you?" John continued to stare at Bryce.

"Yes and no. Everything the three of you have said sounds true and matches, but as much as I believe it, my head keeps telling me it's impossible." Bryce shook his head. "I completely believe you at the same time I'm telling myself I'm an idiot for swallowing such a tale."

John chuckled. He turned to Shelby with a smile. "Crazy is contagious."

Bryce rose to his feet. "These tiles are too cold to sit on all night." He held out a hand to Simon who grasped it to be pulled to his feet. Bryce checked his watch. "I should give Emily a call." He turned to Simon. "Coming?"

Simon nodded and left the candle on the edge of the bathtub before he followed Bryce. "You stay as long as you want, darlin's," he called over his shoulder.

"What do you want to do now, crazy girl?"

"I don't know." She looked from John to Trent. She owed Courtney the same opportunity. Maybe she couldn't tell her anything yet, but she could see her and let her know she was okay.

She met John's gaze. "How do you feel about taking me to see Courtney?"

"If you're up to it," John said.

"I'm not sure. Maybe."

John grinned. "I guess there goes my plan to park somewhere dark and quiet and talk you into christening No Name with me."

Her tension eased at John's familiar teasing. "I don't know. No Name might feel jealous."

Trent laughed, an unused, almost surprised quality to it. "Cameron regularly said she was jealous of the time you spent with any of us. He often asked if she minded if you spent the day with us."

John nodded. "Yeah."

Trent rose to his feet, slowly letting go of Shelby's hand. "You two can stay at my place if you want. The place is still on low lighting."

"Thanks." John rose and held out his hand to Shelby. When she continued to sit there, he said, "You don't have to see Courtney. Everything doesn't have to be done in one day."

She took his hand and let him pull her to her feet. "I know, but it's something I keep putting off. I think if I leave it too long I might never be able to do it. She's my best friend. You're right, if she doesn't act like one then it's better to find out now."

"Do you want me to come with you?" Trent asked.

Shelby shook her head. "No. If I could, I'd do it on my own. I'm getting sick of being so dependant on everyone. It's worse than being a little kid again."

"You don't have to do things on your own," Trent said.

"I know that, but I also know I need to be able to.

Right now the only thing I can do on my own is hide in my room."

John grinned. "If you ever need help with that, give me a yell."

Chapter Thirty-Nine

Before Shelby could reply, her phone rang. It took her a moment to decide if she really wanted to answer her mum's call. "Yeah?"

"The police rang with some good news."

"What?" The word was heavily laden with caution.

"They've got surveillance camera footage showing Larry a couple of hours away in New South Wales at a petrol station and another one about an hour further south than that."

"He's heading south?"

"Along the coastal road. It's only a matter of time before they pick him up"

"He's not in Brisbane?"

"No."

"I don't believe it." She tried to ignore the questions in both John's and Trent's eyes.

"Do you want me to have the police send you copies of the images?"

"No, that's not what I meant. I just… it's just that… I'm glad." A lightness filled her and a smile began. "Thanks for ringing, Mum."

"You're safe? Where you are."

"Yeah. Sorry. I just needed to get away, before I suffocated."

"I don't want anything to happen to you."

"Me neither."

"Call me in the morning, Shelby?"

"Okay. Night."

"Night."

When Shelby put away her phone, she could only grin at John and Trent.

"If you don't hurry up and tell us what that was all about, I'm going to have to torture it out of you." John's grin matched hers.

When Shelby finished telling them, Trent threw his arms around her. "They'll catch him soon and then you won't have to worry about him."

"Where's my hug? No Name isn't the only one who can get jealous."

Shelby let go with one arm and pulled John into the hug. "I can't believe it. Every car I hear, I'm at the window making sure it's not him. Every noise,

I think he's coming for me. I just can't believe he's headed south."

John pulled away from her with a frown. "Will you stop saying that? You're making me think it's not true."

"Of course it's true," Trent said. "He's obsessive, not an idiot."

"Exactly, he's obsessive," John said.

Shelby stared at John. "You're right. Do you think it's not him on the cameras."

"No, it'll be him, but I think he's leading them away from you so they stop looking for him around here. Give him time and he'll be back."

Shelby nodded slowly at John's words. "You're right. He's not an idiot."

"Just a complete head case," Trent muttered.

John reached for her hand, squeezing it lightly. "But you should be safe for a couple of days. It'll take time for him to lead them away." He paused. "Do you still want to see Courtney?"

She nodded. "I'll text her and see if I can come over." She tugged her hand back and sent a message.

The reply came back immediately. *YES!!!!*

Shelby smiled. *It'll have to be outside. In the dark.*

I don't care. Please come.

Okay.

YES!!!! YES!!!! YES!!!!

Shelby's smile became a grin and she showed the message to John. "I think she might want me to visit."

"I don't know. Her answer was a bit ambiguous." His serious expression lasted only a few seconds before a grin replaced it. "You want to go now?"

Shelby nodded. "Should we say goodbye first?"

"I'll take care of that." Trent hugged her. "You go see your friend before you change your mind." He tightened his arms around her. "Thank you for telling us."

She could only nod as she drew away, her throat tightening.

Trent turned to John. "If you want to crash at my place, just turn up. Any time."

"Thanks." John clapped him on the shoulder before he dropped an arm around Shelby's waist and headed for the front door. "You tell me if you change your mind, crazy girl."

"I can do this."

"I know you can. I'm just not sure if you know you can."

She waited for him to unlock the car. "It's more that I know I have to."

John nodded. "Fair enough, whatever it takes. I guess you better tell me where she lives."

The drive to Courtney's house was quiet. Shelby spent the entire trip trying to convince herself she could do it. When John parked in front of the house, she stared at the lights shining from it, cutting paths in the dark. Her phone beeped and she checked the message.

Is that you parked out the front?

Yeah.

I'm on my way.

Shelby hurried out of the vehicle, not wanting to be cowering in there when Courtney came outside. John joined her on the footpath, his arm going around her waist again.

"You can do this." His words were quiet but firm.

She started to nod when the front door was flung open. Courtney dashed outside and the door slammed shut behind her as she ran towards Shelby with a squeal.

Shelby panicked. With a yelp she scurried behind John.

John held up a hand to stop Courtney. "Back off. What are you trying to do?"

"Get out of my way." Courtney stood hands on hips, anger in her voice.

Trembling, Shelby placed a hand on John's back and peered around him. "I'm sorry. You surprised me, that's all." She took another step from behind John's back while still keeping a hand on him as if he was her anchor point.

"I've been waiting forever to see you." Courtney reached out to her. "Stop hiding behind him and let me see you. He might be hot, but I'd rather look at you than him."

Shelby took another step away from John, reaching out to take Courtney's hand. Within seconds Courtney was hugging her fiercely and Shelby struggled not to run screaming.

John put a hand between them. "Let her breathe." He tugged Shelby back to his side.

Courtney's hands went to her hips again. "Stop telling me what to do. We've been friends forever, you barely know her."

Shelby wanted to tell Courtney she was the one who barely knew her, but it was all she could do to breathe. She knew her breath was coming too fast and if she wasn't careful she'd hyperventilate and pass out. But she couldn't help it. She wasn't ready for this. She should've known better.

"Shelby?" Courtney sounded uncertain.

John's hands cupped her cheeks. "Hang in there, crazy girl. Everything's okay."

She continued to shiver, unable to talk.

"I shouldn't have let you sit on the cold tiles. You're freezing." John lightly rubbed her cheeks before he picked up her hands and rubbed them briskly.

"Shelby? You're freaking me out. What's wrong? I thought you said you're okay." Courtney reached out towards her then pulled back as if she'd been stung.

"How about I put the heater on in the ute and you can sit in there." When she didn't answer, John guided her back to No Name and started the ute, turning on the heater. "Sit here and you'll warm up." He helped her sit in the driver's seat, still facing him, her feet on the doorsill. "Is that any better?"

She looked past John to Courtney who hovered behind him. "I'm sorry." Her words were soft and had a tremble in them.

"What's wrong? Did I do something wrong?" Courtney rung her hands.

Shelby shook her head.

John said, "Yes."

"What did I do?" Courtney demanded.

"You didn't take things slow," John said.

"But that's the way we always-"

John interrupted Courtney. "Things aren't the same as always. Give it time." He continued to hold Shelby's hands in one of his, turned sideways so he could see Courtney too.

"I'm an idiot. No wonder you didn't want to visit me, Shelby."

"You're not. I'm the one who's useless." She forced the words out, not able to bear Courtney's tone. "I shouldn't have left my room."

"Of course you should. You're doing okay now. You've nearly stopped shivering. How about you slide over on the seat and Courtney can hop in from the other side and I'll get in and shut the door. You'll warm up much quicker."

"I don't know." She tried to stop shivering. It was impossible.

John smiled slightly. "Maybe you should stay where you are and Courtney and I'll hop in from the other side. I'm in the middle though and I'm taking heaps of pics so everyone at school can see I'm not lying when I tell them I had two hot chicks in my ute this weekend."

A reluctant smile formed and Shelby swung her legs around and slid across the seat. "It's okay, you don't have to do that." She relaxed against John the moment he was beside her. The trembling lessened.

Courtney hopped in on the other side of Shelby, keeping as much space between them as possible. The dash lights were bright enough to show her expression was wary.

Shelby couldn't meet her friend's gaze. "I didn't want you to see me like this. I'm such an idiot."

"Of course you're not. I'm the idiot for not knowing I'm too much. I'm always too much. How many times has my mum told me I'm over the top? That I don't think before I act. You'll probably hate me forever now."

"That's what I thought." Shelby spoke softly.

"Isn't there any way you'll forgive me?" Courtney reached out for her hand, but stopped centimetres away.

Shelby shook her head. "That's not what I meant. I thought you'd hate me forever."

Courtney laughed, tears tracking down her cheeks. "We're both idiots."

Shelby grasped Courtney's hand. "Yeah."

"This is worse than watching a chick flick," John muttered.

Chapter Forty

Shelby wiped at her eyes as she turned a smile on John. "Thank you. For the millionth time."

"Thank you? Is that it? What happened to actions speak louder than words?" A grin destroyed his serious expression.

She reached for him with her still damp hand and threaded her fingers through his. With another smile, she faced Courtney, her back against John's warmth. "Tell me some normal stuff, like what's been happening at school."

"School isn't normal. It's abnormal." Courtney grinned, but after a pause she complied and filled Shelby in on everything that had happened while she'd been gone. She mentioned a couple of break-ups, a kid suspended for setting off the fire alarm and two of their friends currently not talking to each other.

A yawn made Shelby realise she was tired and after checking her phone she found it was nearly eleven. "We should probably go."

"Can I visit you tomorrow?" Courtney asked.

"I don't know what I'm doing tomorrow. What about Monday after school? You can come over and tell me everything that happens."

Courtney snorted. "It won't be much, I can tell you that now. But I'll be there."

After lengthy goodbyes, they drove off, waving to Courtney who stood at her front door. Shelby rested her head against John's shoulder.

"Where do you want to stay tonight, crazy girl?"

"Trent's. I'm not up to getting the third degree from your parents."

John laughed softly. "They should already be in bed." He shrugged. "But that's okay. We can head to Trent's place. Can you send him a text to let him know we're coming over?"

Shelby nodded and sent off a text, smiling when Trent messaged back, *One bed or two?* She kept her gaze on her phone. "Two beds?"

"Whatever you want. But I wouldn't argue if you said one."

Shelby smiled as she sent a reply message. "What if I was a bed hog? Would you complain then?"

"If there's not much space left that means I get to snuggle closer."

"Two beds."

"Ah well, I can dream. Actually, I can dream really good dreams. Want to hear them?"

She shook her head when she saw his grin. He chuckled and reached out to rest his hand on her thigh. The rest of the drive was made in silence.

Trent met them at the front door, a candle in his hand, eyes red rimmed. He placed the candle on a cabinet within arm's length of the door.

John reached out to him. "Aww man, I wish I could fix this."

"Life has no colour without him," Trent said.

Shelby pressed her clasped hands against her chest. "This is all my fault. I shouldn't have told you everything tonight."

Trent pulled away from John to hug Shelby, holding her lightly. "I needed to hear what happened. It meant everything that you told me. Don't you dare think this is your fault."

Shelby had frozen when Trent first hugged her, but managed not to pull away. "I wish Larry had never been let out of prison. They should have locked him away for life."

"Life isn't very long in prison sentences," John said.

"It should be."

"He'll be back there soon enough," Trent promised.

"I hope so."

Trent stepped back. "You look tired and I'm keeping you at the front door talking. I've got the bedrooms ready for both of you." Trent picked up the candle as he walked past it.

Once Trent had shown them to their rooms and Shelby used the bathroom, she returned to her room to find John sprawled on her bed, his hands behind his head, a lit candle on the bedside drawers near him.

"Did you get lost?"

"Nah." John grinned. "Making sure you're not lonely." He rose to his feet and crossed the room to stand in front of her. "Do you want some company, crazy girl?"

She smiled. "Goodnight, John."

He reached out and slid his hands across her hips to rest them at the small of her back. "Are you sure you don't want me to convince you?"

"Mostly sure."

"If you need me in the night you can tap on the wall." He paused. "But I still don't know Morse code."

Her expression became serious. "Thank you. For everything."

"No." He shook his head. "Thank you."

"What for?"

"Reminding me there's more than sadness in the world." His lips brushed across hers.

"Goodnight." She reached up on tiptoes and pressed her lips against his. When she finally drew back, she stared at him for a moment. "Sweet dreams." She pulled away to walk towards her bed.

John chuckled. "I certainly will."

She smiled as she sat on the edge of the bed and leaned forward to blow out the candle. She watched as John stood there a moment longer, a shadowy figure by the door. Then he left and she was alone, sitting on a too soft bed.

She tried to sleep in the bed since it was the normal thing to do. Her shrink had told her she needed to gain some normality in her life. Sleeping in a bed wasn't going to be it. Pulling a sheet and pillow from the bed she settled on the floor between the bed and the doorway. She immediately felt more comfortable. Normality could wait, she wasn't ready for it. Sleep came much easier this time.

Shelby woke, heart racing and body tense as she tried to figure out what had dragged her from her restless sleep. The darkness surrounded her as she opened her eyes and stretched. She considered going down the hall to John, but there was no point in both of them being awake because she no longer knew how to sleep properly. She frowned as she tried to think what dream must have woken her. She could have sworn her sleep had been dreamless.

A noise came from the window and she froze, her breath stopping. She forced herself to sit up and look around, trying to tell herself it was yet another normal night time sound and to stop being stupid and go back to sleep. It didn't help. It never did. She silently rose to her feet, just as the curtain swept back from the window and a large figure climbed into the room along with a quick splash of streetlight.

Shelby dropped to the floor, pressing a hand against her mouth to keep a scream from escaping. Her body started to tremble and she listened to the slow, soft steps cross the room to the bed. She had to get out of the room. Keeping against the floor, she inched her way to the open door. Then she was in the hallway, sitting with her back pressed against the wall. Her breath came fast and she wanted to scream, but she couldn't. More soft sounds came from her room, as if someone searched. The noises brought her to her feet, hurrying to John's room.

She reached out to wake him, shaking his shoulder,

and he pulled her on the bed with him, sighing contentedly.

"Crazy girl. What took you so long?" He nuzzled the side of her neck.

"He's in my room." Her voice shook.

"What?" John pulled back to look down at her. "Shel-"

She reached up and covered his mouth. "Shh." She pulled him closer so she could whisper in his ear. "We have to get Trent and get out of here."

"I'll call the police."

"No. He might hear you."

"I'll text Bryce. He can call them."

Shelby froze. "Did you hear that? He's in the hallway. Coming this way."

John rolled with her, pulling her over the side of the bed closest to the window. He took his phone from the bedside cabinet.

She watched him send the text to Bryce. *Larry in Trent's house. Call cops.*

A text came back. *Get out. Now!*

"He's right. We have to leave." John lifted his head above the bed then rose to his feet, going to the window.

Shelby joined him, gasping when she saw the

screen had been cut and the window was open. "He was in here too."

John swore. "I didn't even know." He paused. "You get out the window. I'll get Trent. He headed in the opposite direction to Trent's room."

Shelby pulled the curtain closed. "No. I can see better in the dark than you."

"I'm not letting that bastard near you."

"I'm the only one he won't hurt."

"Accidents happen. I'm not letting you near him."

Shelby smiled slightly and reached up to cup his face with her hand. Her trembling stopped and she rose to press her lips against his before she started to pull away. "I can do this, the dark is my world. Wait here for me."

"Crazy girl-" he broke off and captured her hand as it started to leave his cheek, holding it against his chest as he leaned forward to press his lips to hers. "Don't you dare let anything happen to you." He followed her to the doorway, waiting against the wall near the light switch.

Shelby paused in the hallway, her gaze searching up and down. There was no movement. They were safe for now. She silently headed for Trent's room. His door was closed. She turned the handle, biting back a curse when she found it was locked. Her fingers ran over the knob and she found the slot that would unlock it. But she had nothing she could use to turn it. She inched her way back to John.

He reached out for her. "What's wrong?"

"Trent's locked his door. Have you got a coin or something I can use to unlock it?"

"Yeah." He pulled away and crossed to the bedside cabinet where his wallet sat.

Chapter Forty-One

Shelby clasped her hands together, watching John as she strained to hear any sounds. She took the coin he handed her and paused before she hurried down the hallway. There was no time for moving slow. How much longer did they have before Larry realised she wasn't in the rest of the house and returned to the bedrooms to look for her again?

The coin unlocked the door and she dropped it on the carpet, slipping into the room and leaving the door open a crack. She reached for Trent, covering his mouth as she whispered. "Wake up. Larry's in the house."

Trent pulled her hand from his mouth. "Where?" He slid from the bed.

Shelby pulled him towards his door. "I don't know. He went down the hallway away from the bedrooms." She hesitated. "Wait here." Before Trent could argue she was across his room and checking his window. The screen had been cut. Then she was back at Trent's side and peering down the hallway. It was empty. "Come on. John's room." She took his hand and they moved down the hallway.

"Stop." They were halfway when the order came from the end of the hallway. A torch was turned on and pointed at them.

Shelby froze in the light, wanting to hide behind Trent.

"Mellie." There was relief in Larry's tone. "Come here, honey."

"You can't take her," Trent said.

Larry pointed his gun at Trent. "Don't tell me what to do. Now let her go."

Fear for Trent rushed through her and she pulled away from him. "No. Don't hurt him. Please." She walked shakily forward. What was taking the cops so long?

"I knew if I watched you like last time I'd find you. I thought you'd be at your house where you've been all week. I came here to get Robert first. Where is he?"

Shelby continued to slowly walk towards Larry. She didn't want to remind him Robert was dead. "He's not here. He's staying with a friend." If only she'd agreed to stay at John's place Larry probably wouldn't have found her tonight. But what about Trent and her family, would he have hurt them if he hadn't found her? Another couple of steps and she'd be walking past John.

"You can show me how to get there next. Then we have to leave town. The false trail I set for the cops won't keep them busy forever."

"No fucking way." John pulled her into the room, pressing her against the wall when she struggled. He lowered his voice. "He can't have you."

Larry roared.

"Trent's out there." She tried to pull away from John.

"Don't you move," Larry ordered.

Shelby demanded, "Let me go, John."

John dragged her towards the window. He reached up and pushed at the curtain rod. It clattered to the floor. "Leave. Now."

Shelby shook her head. "I'm not leaving Trent out there with him."

John moved away from her and picked up the cricket bat lying under his bed. "You get out. I'll get Trent."

"Keep your hands where I can see them," Larry barked. "And move slowly towards me."

Shelby looked towards the doorway. Larry stood there, gun pointed down the hall.

"John."

They both turned to see Bryce and Simon at the window. John shook his head. "Don't come in." He reached out for Shelby. "Take her away from here. Please."

Shelby pulled away from John. "I'm not leaving Trent here," she hissed.

There was a banging at the front door. "Open up. Police."

A gun sounded and Trent cried out. Larry stood frozen in the doorway. There was a crash at the front door. Shelby grabbed the cricket bat from John and dashed across the bed, swinging it at Larry's arm. He bellowed, the gun flying.

John was beside her, grabbing the bat from her, swinging again and again. Bryce tackled John. They crashed into the wall and Bryce tore the bat from his grip. Larry ran in the direction of the front door. Noises and demands that Larry stop came from the front of the house.

Shelby looked around, trying to make sense of everything. Then she saw Trent lying on the carpet, slumped against the hallway wall, blood spreading across his chest. She ran to his side, grabbing his blood-smeared hand. Behind her she heard Simon screaming for an ambulance then John was beside her.

"Damn it, Trent. Don't you dare leave me too." John grabbed his other hand. "Damn it." He pressed his hand against the wound.

"I've called an ambulance." Bryce knelt beside them, Simon sobbing as he moved to stand closer.

Trent looked past them all and smiled. "Gorgeous."

They turned to see Cameron standing there, grinning. "You coming? I've missed you." He held out his hand.

"No, don't you dare go," John ordered Trent.

Trent ignored John, his gaze fixed on Cameron. "You have no idea how much I've missed you." He reached up and took Cameron's hand, leaving his body behind. His other hand cupped Cameron's cheek. "Gorgeous." The single word was filled with emotion.

"Cameron." Bryce rose shakily to his feet, his words a broken cry.

Cameron held onto Trent and turned to grin at his uncle. "I'd ask you to tell Mum and Dad that I love them, but they'd probably want to have you committed."

Bryce swore, taking a single step towards his nephew. "You never should've died."

Cameron's grin faded. He turned his gaze to Simon. "Take care of him, Simon. He's always there for everyone else, make sure he has someone there for him too."

Simon nodded, sniffing.

Cameron winked at Simon, "You never know, I might see you in another lifetime." His gaze moved to Bryce. "You were the one I always looked up to. My hero. You never failed me. Ever."

Simon reached out to Bryce.

Shelby continued to kneel at Trent's side, unable to speak past the lump in her throat. She wanted to beg both of them to stay. John reached for her hand that still clasped Trent's.

Sounds in the house caused Cameron to glance over his shoulder. With a smile, he turned to Trent and reached up to caress his face before taking his hand and walking down the corridor with him. The two of them faded before ambulance officers strode into view.

"You're too late," Bryce said.

They were sent out of the way, all ending up in John's room. Shelby and John clung to each other, ignoring the blood on themselves and their clothes.

"I told you," Simon said to Bryce. "There is rebirth. I've always said your Christian beliefs are stupid."

"He winked at you, Simon. Cameron was always up for a joke," Bryce said.

"They're soul mates. Now they can be born again together."

"Rebirth is crap made up by people who can't face the thought of the nothingness of death."

"You can say what you want." Simon glared at him. "I know they'll be born again. Born to families that can accept them for who they are."

"You don't know that. It's what you want to believe."

John whispered to Shelby. "Now might be a good time to leave. Before Simon starts with the dramatics."

She pulled away from John and stepped between the two of them. "What does it matter? Heaven. Rebirth. Whatever. All I know is they're together. That's all that matters. And who knows what's true. Everyone thinks I'm crazy because I believe in ghosts."

"I didn't get to say goodbye to him," Bryce said softly.

"He got to say goodbye to you," Shelby said.

"I'm sorry. For everything I said when you tried to tell us the truth," Bryce said.

Shelby smiled wryly. "I probably would've been as sceptical too."

"Excuse me. I'm Constable Williams."

They turned to see a police officer in the doorway. John moved to Shelby's side to place a protective arm around her.

"We apprehended Larry and–"

Shelby stepped forward, pulling away from John. "I need to see him."

"There's no–" Constable Williams began.

Shelby interrupted, "I need to see him. I need to know he's been caught."

Constable Williams nodded before he led the way. John held Shelby's hand, the blood on their hands wet and sticky. They walked to the police car, Bryce and Simon beside them, the grass damp beneath her bare feet.

Larry looked up at them through the window. His eyes lit up when he saw her.

"I want to talk to him." Shelby continued to stare at Larry, bruises beginning to show where the cricket bat had hit him. Blood smeared on him from where it had broken the skin. She felt grim satisfaction when she saw the size of the bruise on his arm from her.

Constable Williams hesitated, then opened the door, his attention on Larry.

"Mellie." He reached out to her with handcuffs around his wrists.

"Remain in the vehicle," Constable Williams ordered.

Shelby shook her head. "I'm Shelby. Shelby West. I have parents. I have a brother and his name is Kyle."

"No. I know you. You're my daughter. Melissa."

"I wish your daughter was still alive, but she's not. I'm sorry, but I can't be her. You've given me some of her memories, but that doesn't make me her. I can't ever be her."

"You're Mellie. My Mellie."

"I am Shelby." Her voice was firm and she felt John tighten his grip on her hand, the blood now tacky and starting to dry and tighten her skin. "I know exactly who I am." She turned and walked away, ignoring Larry's calls for his daughter.

Chapter Forty-Two

Shelby sat on the hard wooden crematorium pew beside John. It was almost evening and this was the second cremation Shelby had been to in as many days. There were very few people still inside with them.

"Are you ready to go?" John squeezed her hand.

She shook her head, fiddling with the lime green, mirrored sunglasses that sat in her lap. "Soon." A movement caught her attention through a window and she was instantly on her feet. She heard John gasp.

The pair of them dashed outside, heading around the side of the building. Cameron was there with Trent. Shelby came to a halt in front of them, a smile warring with tears.

"Cameron." Her hands trembled as she fought the urge to slide the sunglasses on, but she wanted to make sure she didn't miss a second of Cameron and Trent's visit. "I thought I'd never see you again."

"This is the last time. We wanted to make sure everything was done right," Cameron said.

John grinned. "You always need to tell us how to do things."

"Wasn't I right about No Name?"

John chuckled. "Okay, I'll give you that one." He sobered. "I miss you, Cameron."

"Yeah, I know. We miss you too." He paused a moment. "I need you to do something for me."

"Anything." John and Shelby spoke the word together.

Trent laughed. "You're right, Gorgeous. They're perfect for each other."

John cleared his throat. "What do you want us to do?"

It was Trent who spoke. "Put a pinch of my ashes with Cameron's and a pinch of his with mine. We want our earthly remains together too."

"How are we going to manage that?" John asked.

"Uncle Bryce will help."

John nodded.

"Thank you." Cameron smiled. "I've always been able to rely on you." His smile became a grin. "Even if it's only to take the blame for something so I don't get in trouble."

John chuckled, rubbing the scar on his shoulder. "That's what mates do."

"Cameron, Simon thinks you and Trent will be reborn into families who'll accept you and you'll find each other and fall in love again," Shelby said.

Cameron shrugged with a smile. "Who knows? The possibilities are endless."

"You didn't always think that," Shelby said.

Cameron turned to Trent, his smile widening as he touched Trent's face. "Now I do."

Trent grinned. "They always were endless, Gorgeous. We just didn't realise it."

Shelby smiled and sniffed, trying to hold back the tears that threatened to fall. "If you ever come back, find a way to let us know, okay?"

Cameron chuckled. "Then you need to do something for me."

"What?"

"It's time to let the light be your friend again. Remember when you made the dark your friend? You need to finish reclaiming your life. I don't want you to let Larry win."

It was what she wanted too. "Okay."

"Take care of each other." Cameron looked from one to the other.

"Goodbye," Trent said. "It's been a privilege to know you. Both of you."

"Goodbye." Shelby's eyes blurred and she blinked, stepping forward as Cameron and Trent turned and walked away, fading into the distance once John had said goodbye. "No."

John slid his arms around her. "That felt final."

She nodded. "I don't know how he expects me to make friends with the light when I can't even face catching a bus in the dark. I can't get within arm's length of a bus shelter."

"Did you want to borrow No Name?"

Shelby shook her head, pulling back slightly to stare at him.

He grinned momentarily. "Don't look at me like I've lost my mind."

"I think you have, or I have. You did offer to lend me your ute, right?"

"Yeah."

She reached up to press her hand against his forehead. "Maybe you're coming down with a fever."

He pulled her hand away from his forehead and dropped a kiss on it. "Crazy girl."

"I'd be terrified someone would run into me."

"Then we'll get you your own car. You know, the sweetest Q came into the wreckers the other day." He kept hold of her hand as they started to walk back to the front of the crematorium.

"Q? Like yours? I don't think I'm the ute kind of person."

John shook his head. "Nah, a sedan. Same year as mine though. Almost fate."

"You better not be thinking matching colours, that'd be too lame."

"I was thinking purple. Dark enough to nearly be a shadow."

"That'd be cool." She paused. "Does that mean I get to name him?"

"Him? Cars are girls, not boys."

"You can have a girl car if you want, mine's a boy."

John rolled his eyes. "Fine, but you're not naming him."

"Yours has a name."

"That's different."

"Nope. Mine needs a name too."

"You'll probably pick something stupid."

"No I won't." She frowned, then had the urge to grin. "What about Barney?"

"You're not naming a car after a character from a little kid's show."

"He's purple."

"No."

"How about Jake?"

John shook his head. "What have I got myself into?"

Shelby grinned momentarily. "You were the one who offered."

"I knew craziness was contagious." He stopped to face her, his hands going to the small of her back to draw her close. "Good thing I love crazy."

Shelby stared up at him. "Prove it."

"Anytime." His head lowered and his lips met hers.

"You pair aren't at it again, are you?"

Shelby laughed as Bryce came around the corner and interrupted them, Simon at his side.

"His timing sucks, as usual," John muttered before he turned to face them. "I need to talk to you, Bryce." He paused. "But it could've waited at least a few more minutes."

Bryce grinned. "Glad to see I was able to save you the effort of finding me."

"I spoke to Cameron."

Bryce's grin faded instantly. "What did he say?"

John recounted the conversation.

Simon sighed, pressing a hand against his heart.

"That's the loveliest thing I've ever heard. We've got to put that in our will, darlin."

"We can mix all our ashes together if that's what you want Simon. No one's going to complain." Bryce turned back to John. "Get me Trent's ashes and I'll take care of it for you."

"Me?" John frowned.

Bryce withdrew an envelope from his jacket and held it out to John. "Trent's will. He left everything to you. There's a letter." He cleared his throat. "I'll leave you to read it."

Shelby watched as Bryce and Simon walked away. "Do you want me to give you time to read it?"

John shook his head. "No. Read it with me." They opened the envelope and, after a quick glance at the will, stared at the scrawling words on the letter.

'Dear John, other than Cameron, you've been the most important person in my life. More for what you were to Cameron than me. But you accepted me because of Cameron, accepting I was worth having around because he said I was. I have never known anyone who gave loyalty and trust so completely, never questioning the person once you had given it. I want you to look after my photos. The ones I took once Cameron was in my life. They're a record of our love and all the precious moments we shared. I don't want them thrown away and our love forgotten. Take them out and look at them occasionally. Maybe on the day Cameron promised to tell everyone except his parents about us. I thought I was an idiot for accepting so little, now I know I was an idiot for not realising how much he was offering me. I don't care what you do with the rest of my crap, only the photos. I hope one day you know a love like ours. It might have only lasted months, but a single moment with Cameron would have been better than a lifetime of mediocrity. All my best, Trent.

Shelby wiped at the tears that ran down her face and turned to John. She reached out to brush her hand against his damp cheeks.

John stared down at her. "Why didn't he tell me?"

"I don't know."

He crushed her to him. "I can't believe they're gone. Both of them."

Shelby held him tightly, like her mother had when she was younger. Tight enough he'd know it was impossible to fall apart. "At least they're together." She frowned. "But I wish they were both still alive."

"Yeah, me too." He rested his forehead against hers. "Come on, let's get out of here."

They walked towards No Name, Shelby waving to Simon and Bryce across the car park talking to their friends. "You know if I have to make friends with the light you should have a party."

John unlocked the ute. "No."

Shelby slid across the bench seat. "Yes."

"We're not discussing this."

"It's only three days away. We have to discuss it."

"The only thing I'm interested in discussing about my birthday is the fact it's on a Sunday. How am I meant to upgrade my license on a Sunday? I've got to waste an entire day. Which means it'll be an extra day before I get my opens." He started the ute and backed out of the car park.

"Sunday is good. It means no work and no school. You can have a party instead."

"No party."

"What about cake?"

"Cake's good."

"And candles?"

"If I have to."

"A couple of people."

"You and me. That's a couple."

Shelby grinned. "Okay, we'll have a private party."

John glanced down at her. "I'm guessing your definition of a private party and mine may differ a little."

She laughed and snuggled against his side. "I'll bring the cake. And the candles."

"What time do you want me to pick you up?"

"Early. I want to spend the whole day with you. Someone has to remind you that there are still things in life worth celebrating."

John pulled up in front of her house and stared down at her. "I already know there are things in life worth celebrating." He smiled and drew her close.

Shelby wrapped her arms around him, not wanting to move. "I'm glad. Cameron would be too."

He pulled back far enough to be able to meet her gaze and grin. "Now about that bastard we were going halves in."

She burst out laughing, hitting his arm with the back of her hand. "You're going to ruin the mood with comments like that."

He slowly shook his head, tracing her smile with his thumb. "No, not ruin the mood. Make you smile. It makes me sad when you're sad."

She felt her eyes water.

"Don't cry, crazy girl."

"They're happy tears."

John frowned. "How the hell am I meant to tell the difference?"

She laughed, throwing her arms around his neck.

"If you're confused ask me. Now about that mood you reckon you weren't ruining."

John glanced behind her to the window. "It won't be me ruining it."

"What-" Shelby's words were cut off by John's kiss. Then there was knocking on the ute door and Kyle asking her if she was coming inside. She decided to follow John's example and gave Kyle her middle finger for an answer before she put her arm back around John and returned his kiss.

Free Ebook

Subscribe to Avril's newsletter to receive a free ebook. This ebook is exclusive to those on her mailing list. To find out more about this offer visit: http://www.avrilsabine.com/free-ebook/

*

We value your privacy and will not sell, rent, exchange or loan your email address to third parties. Your information is confidential and you are under no obligation to remain on the mailing list and can unsubscribe at any time.

Acknowledgements

Thank you to all my beta readers and editors. What would I do without you?

To The Reader

If you enjoyed this book, why not consider leaving a review to help other readers discover it too? Reader engagement is one of the few ways that lets an author know readers want more books in a particular series or genre. So leave a review and tell friends, not only about this book but also about other ones you've enjoyed, so you can continue to enjoy books by your favourite authors for years to come.

Dreams are meant to be lived,

Avril.

About The Author

Avril is an Australian author who lives with her family on acreage in South East Queensland. She writes mostly young adult speculative fiction, but has been known to dabble in other genres. You can find more information about her at her website www.avrilsabine.com where you can also subscribe to her newsletter to be kept informed about new releases, current projects, blog posts and exclusive news.

Titles By Avril Sabine

Stories about strong characters and characters who discover their strengths.

SERIES

Assassins Of The Dead- Young Adult Fantasy/ Paranormal

Book 1: Dark Blade

Book 2: Dragon Touched

Book 3: Society Against Vampires

Book 4: King's Request

Dragon Blood- Young Adult Urban Fantasy (with elements of romance)

(5 book series)

Book 1: Pliethin

Book 2: Wyvern

Book 3: Surety

Book 4: Knight

Book 5: Mage

Dragon Mage- Young Adult Urban Fantasy (with elements of romance)

(Series two of Dragon Blood series)

Book 1: Promise

Dragon Blood Chronicles- Young Adult Urban Fantasy (with elements of romance)

(Companion stand alone series to Dragon Blood)

Book 1: Oath

Book 2: Betrayed

Guardians Of The Round Table- Young Adult Fantasy LitRPG

(Co-written with Storm and Rhys Petersen)

Book 1: Dexterity Fail

Book 2: Goblin Boots

Book 3: Singed Feathers

Book 4: Frog Mage

Book 5: Crystal Mine

Book 6: Cursed Harp

Rosie's Rangers- Young Adult Western Steampunk

(6 book series)

Book 1: Justice

Book 2: Vengeance

Book 3: Treachery

Book 4: Accused

Book 5: Wanted

Book 6: Corruption

Mark Of Kings- Children's Fantasy

(Upper middle grade/preteen)

(4 book series)

Book 1: The Arena

Book 2: The Island

Book 3: The Assassin

Book 4: The King

STAND ALONE SERIES

*Demon Hunters- Young Adult Urban Fantasy/
Horror (with elements of romance)*

Book 1: Blood Sacrifice

Book 2: Retribution

Book 3: Tainted

Book 4: Premonition

Book 5: Cursed

Book 6: Feud

Book 7: Extrication

Plea Of The Damned- Young Adult Urban Fantasy/Paranormal

(6 book series)

Book 1: Forgive Me Lucy

Book 2: Forgive Me Aiden

Book 3: Forgive Me Jena

Book 4: Forgive Me Kobe

Book 5: Forgive Me Marti

Book 6: Forgive Me Dawson

Realms Of The Fae- Young Adult Urban Fantasy (with elements of romance)

The Sword (short story in Like A Girl Anthology)

Heart Of Stone

Book 1: A Debt Owed

Book 2: Marked By The Hunt

Book 3: The Magic Collector

Book 4: An Unexpected Betrayal

Book 5: Imprisoned By Iron

Fairytales Retold (Short Stories)

Snow-White And Rose-Red

The Twelve Brothers

The Light Princess

Beauty And The Beast

Sleeping Beauty

Aschenputtel

The Golden Bird

The Frog Prince

The Death Of Koshchei The Deathless

Myths And Legends Retold (Short Stories)

Ion, Son Of Apollo

Sir Gawain And The Maid With The Narrow Sleeves

Princess Ilse, The Giant's Daughter

YOUNG ADULT NOVELS

Young Adult Fantasy (with elements of romance)

Elf Sight

Earth Bound

Young Adult Urban Fantasy

Stone Warrior (with elements of romance)

The Jungle Inside

Young Adult Contemporary (with elements of romance)

Through Your Eyes

The Ugly Stepsister

Perfect Little Princess

Young Adult Contemporary/Paranormal

Whispers In The Dark (with elements of romance and same sex relationships)

Over Too Soon (with elements of romance)

Young Adult Sci-Fi

Experiment X-One-Six (Urban Sci-Fi/Superheroes)

An Endless Dawn (Post Apocalyptic Sci-Fi)

CHILDREN'S BOOKS

Dragon Lord (Preteen/early teens) (Fantasy)

The Irish Wizard (Upper middle grade) (Urban Fantasy)

SHORT STORIES

Urban Fantasy

Eternally Late

Dealings With Joe

Glimpses (short story in That Moment When Anthology)

Contemporary

The Brat Next Door

Fantasy LitRPG

(Set in the same world as Guardians Of The Round Table Series)

Tales Of Inadon 1: The Disc (Co-written with Storm and Rhys Petersen) (short story in Game On! Anthology)

Post Apocalyptic Sci-Fi

Compulsive Directive

NONFICTION

A Year Of Weekly Writing Exercises (Creative Writing)

Cooking For Families With Allergies (Cooking) (Co-written with Storm Petersen)

Tell Me A Story, Grandma (Memoir)

For the most up to date details on available titles visit:

www.avrilsabine.com/books/bibliography

Disclaimer

This is a work of fiction. Names, characters, businesses, places, events and incidents are either the products of the author's imagination or used in a fictitious manner. Any resemblance to actual persons, living or dead, or actual events is purely coincidental. The opinions expressed or beliefs held are those of the characters and should not be assumed to be the opinions or beliefs of the author.

www.ingramcontent.com/pod-product-compliance
Lightning Source LLC
Chambersburg PA
CBHW030959190726

48285CB00004BB/1377